LOVE IN ONE EDITION

Peter Cunningham

LOVE IN ONE EDITION

THE HARVILL PRESS
LONDON

First published in 2001 by
The Harvill Press
2 Aztec Row
Berners Road
London N1 0PW

www.harvill.com

1 3 5 7 9 8 6 4 2

© Peter Cunningham, 2001

Peter Cunningham asserts the moral right to
be identified as the author of this work

A CIP catalogue record for this book
is available from the British Library

ISBN 1 86046 827 6 (hbk)
ISBN 1 86046 828 4 (pbk)

Designed and typeset in Sabon at
Libanus Press, Marlborough, Wiltshire

Printed and bound in Great Britain by Butler & Tanner Ltd
at Selwood Printing, Burgess Hill

Carol

COVER NOTE

Sweet evening mists hang in the valley over Monument. Tender light, a wash of pale hope, is slipping behind the western ridges of the Deilt mountains, and the first, cool breath of night is rolling into the foothills. Rain on the swathes of fir below me has freed their resinousness and allowed it to float all the way up here to Glane.

I am well and have been for some time. How great a blessing is health only the very ill can say. I have come up from the very depths of malady and disorder on a number of occasions, I know what it is to fall right down into the numbness beyond recollecting, where time loses its hardness, where even the soft kiss of love is unfelt.

Just below my position, in a pool surrounded by ancient oaks, lies the spring of the river Lyle. Its waters, by tradition, have healing properties and in the rock niches and tree clefts you can still find rags and other tokens of faith wedged there by the pilgrims who once came all the way up here from Monument.

Day's birth and death are my pet times in Glane. Evening light, as now through the trees to the east, picks out one by one like sea shells the white boulders and their inset stile in the shape of a "V" at the base of the hill. The mists gather and my town rises to me from its river valley. Sometimes I can hear it, not distinct sounds, of course, but a beat that is part of my blood. I imagine the ships at berth on Long Quay, their cargoes loaded and making ready for the early tide. I imagine the tiers of the town in their climb from the river, smoke oozing from chimneys, the smells of cooking, the settling down that has begun all the way from Buttermilk to Balaklava. Then I open my eyes and watch the sun's final plunge into the valley.

3

PART ONE

One

Monument shone. From every plane and surface rebounded autumn's golden sun. In bobbing sunglasses, in the windscreens of cars, in the shell of the river Lyle the sun's warm, burnished face was reproduced. And summer's heat still breathed from the earth and from the little outskirting hills, where it danced in heady columns. In the flowerbeds of traffic roundabouts and in the striped awnings above shop windows, it was still summer. Summer persisted in the minds of the girls whose bare legs kept the town's juices moving. Summer's warmth endured for the old stagers, propped at strategic corners, still in jackets only, even if some had donned a precautionary cardigan beneath. A warm, sunny autumn place this, then, I could once more confirm, a town of not quite fifty thousand souls tucked beneath friendly mountains at the head of the estuary of a wide, abundant and navigable river in the infant years of the new millennium.

I cycled in along Captain Penny's Road, passing the defunct but still unsold "Home for Indigent Persons" – the name was scrolled over its front door – and then, at the junction of Captain Penny's Road and the top of Cuconaught Street, Monument's Courthouse, a Greek Revival building of the nineteenth century. Cuconaught Street leads down eventually into O'Gara Street, where the first glimpse of water is possible, and as I breasted the next hill I paused, as suddenly the river and the masts of ships appeared at my feet. (Even though traffic was light, being Sunday, I had decided that this roundabout approach to Long Quay was less likely to be anticipated than the more direct route using the new bypass.)

I loved this tiered town, whose ambiance of trade and tides was embodied in the half-hoops of its Mediterranean doorways and in the faces of its citizens. Monument, a town on Ireland's underside, is in thrall to its river, its business is ships. I had grown up here and so knew every step and wharf, and had acquired, before I went away the first time, a nodding acquaintanceship with people whose names I did not know; now on this, my unscheduled return, I noticed gaps in the skyline, and realised too that many of the old stagers would have disappeared since my last visit. I was saddened, all at once. Those missing buildings and old men represented links to the past for me and I have always felt that I am part of a continuum, a mysterious vanity. I cycled past the premises of Love & Son on Small Quay and then, with unwarranted omnipotence, wheeled up Military Parade. Turning into the lumberyard behind Love's, I dismounted and brought the bike to the very back and left it behind a stack of milled four-by-twos. Then I walked out onto Long Quay and stood for some moments absorbing the sheer power of the Lyle. Its long, deep muscles rolled and flexed as if it were making ready for its inland journey, forty miles of which remained from the point where I stood. Great ships turned here without qualm, riding the broth. This was where I had come from Demijohn Street, then my home, when trouble had occurred, or when on summers' nights I awoke to feelings of intense loneliness, the kind that prayer could not assuage, when something more fundamental than my heart ached for inexplicable connections, as if voices called me; on such occasions I had come to this spot and found balm in the constancy of the river.

I met no-one as I passed the cathedral, then cut up Dudley's Hill. In the old days, when at lunchtimes we had walked down here on our way to the river, people had always said hello. I could still see our names on their lips. The entry off the top of Dudley's Hill, a lane of forty yards with high walls of concrete either side, was so narrow that if two people came face to face one had to step sideways. At the end, a high, iron gate was wedged open at right angles. I had come here to birthday parties; and now the sense of wonderment that I recalled was renewed as I reached Pig and Litter. An oasis carved from the hill itself, gardens behind a railing to the left of the path, a terrace of houses to the right – properly, Vaseur Terrace – the delight of Pig and Litter was further heightened that morning by an absence of wind, by a warm sun and by the explosion of colour and drenching scents that awaited at the end of its uterine entry-way. The grass had been cut within the last hour, for the air was still redolent. Along the snug, brick wall, purple and cream clematis and climbing roses drank in the heat. The heavy door to No. 3 wore its uniform of red and white striped linen to preserve its paint from sunlight that day, its brasses alone obtainable. I sat, comforting wall at my back, and formed as I did each day the same thoughts, beginning always with Jasmine's words.

The time has come to reach some big decisions, Kaiser. My reasons for them are set out in this letter. After this, I want you and me to go forward, unafraid, our heads high and our eyes only on the future.

You are, as are we all, made up of so many stories. Villains and heroes and broken hearts inhabit all our stories, but they are our stories and they make us the people we are, whether we like them or not. There is nothing any of us can do about the past. Only the future holds any meaning.

. . . And so I have made my first decision: that everything I have discovered will change nothing and thus I'm going to kick it back where I found it – into the past. That's right, I'm erasing it all and moving forward. Nothing is to be gained from what I found. It has no bearing on your future

happiness. I'm coming home and I'm going into the library and I'm dumping the whole lot. Why did I embark on it in the first place? Many reasons, and I'll tell you of them soon. But in the meantime I'm getting rid of "Kaiser's Gazette".

I beheld the house. From its first floor, I knew, the aspect down to Candle Lane and the *Monument Gazette* was unblemished.

And now to my second decision. I do love you and only you, Kaiser – as I hope you have known long before now . . .

2

My story began last month, on September 4th – my third morning at work at the *Monument Gazette*. I was collecting files from the front office and I looked up as a man came in through the door. The sunlight caught his face and it made me gasp. I thought for a moment I had seen a man whose face was lit from within. But then I caught his startled look as he saw me and I smiled at him.

"That's Kaiser," the girl on reception told me. "He's got bad hearing, you have to shout or he doesn't hear you." She then shouted at him. "Kaiser! This is Jasmine! She's our new librarian!"

I felt for him, then. I felt it was demeaning for him to be shouted at like that.

That was how this began. So simple – or is human attraction ever simple? He is older than me by a few years, which makes him about thirty. He was dressed that day in blue overalls and his brown hair was wavy and thick and it curled down over his neck. Quite tall, well built. Kaiser.

I had known, of course, that he existed – Monument is a small place and Kaiser has something of a reputation. But I had never met him before and now I was fascinated by my own reaction. Who is he? He grew up, I know, in the orphanage in Demijohn Street and went on to an industrial school where he got into some sort of trouble – that I do know, because he then did time. He came back several years ago to Monument and was given work as a maintenance man at the *Gazette*. Sometimes he can be seen doing odd jobs around the town. But where does "Kaiser" come from? In my previous role as assistant in the Monument Library, I have done research into local families and Kaiser is not a name I have come across – although Monument, being a port town, throws up more than its fair share of unusual names. So once or twice over the past few weeks, as Kaiser was leaving the *Gazette*, I have managed to bump into him and ask him a few questions about himself.

He tells me he never knew his parents, that he has made assumptions about his background, based on what he was always told – by the brothers in the orphanage in Demijohn Street, by the teachers in Binn's Street School, in fact, by almost everyone with whom, as a child, he came in touch. His father, he believes, was Oswald Kaiser, a fine-featured, natural horseman from somewhere in Ulster, unmarried, who, aged forty-one, not having any great career opportunities in his native province, answered an advertisement in the *Belfast Telegraph* for a position in stables near Monument. His mother was Vanessa Grainger and the Graingers came to Ireland around 1920.

But what about the evidence? Vee Grainger, as Kaiser knows, is buried beside her mother in the grounds of the Protestant cathedral. And his father? There is a Kaiser Street in Monument, a narrow link between Pollack and Mead Streets; when one walks from MacCartie Square towards the Balaklava side of town, one crosses Kaiser Street almost without knowing one has done so.

Archivists are not storytellers, I accept, and much of what I've begun to put down here on the library's new computer is the result of educated guesswork. I began my search for Kaiser in the archives of the now extinct Grainger family, Bohall House, a family I already know quite a bit about. Call this research, if you like. Or maybe I should be honest and call it love.

* * *

1957

February. Oswald would have not known what to expect. Brought
up to regard the Free State beyond the border as a wild, uncertain
place of rampant idolatry, at the same time he would have been
ready to find the extraordinary if not the magical. Sign-posts with
their strange letters stand alongside roads in need of repair as his
bus weaves, climbs up to and over mountain passes and plunges
into valleys where the men wear brown dustcoats and the public
houses never close. In his inside pocket, we can imagine, two
character references, one from the rector, the other from the
doctor, both addressed to Mrs Selwyn Grainger, Bohall House,
Monument. At last a town in dim light on a river. The inverse of
his homeland. The scene had been rehearsed over the years.
Alighting on Long Quay, he is bid climb into the open back of
a Morris van by a groom with a crooked grin, who drives him,
freezing, to Bohall House.

A gigantic, ugly Greek Revival monstrosity, it had been built as
the replacement for a rat-infested barracks (itself the successor to
a castle) by the descendants of Elizabethan land pirates; they lived
in their Greek Revival house for ninety years, then fled with the
merry gunfire of Irish independence crackling in their ears. Along
came Selwyn Grainger from Leeds, heir to a sweated-labour fortune,
keen to put distance between himself and his origins; so although
born a Catholic, he turned Protestant since Catholic Anglo-Irish
is oxymoronic and Anglo-Irish was what Selwyn wished to be. He
learned to ride a horse, to shout and to become known for his
eccentricities. Selwyn married and fathered three children and ate
each of their placentas as kitchen women swayed in terror and
recited the "Hail, Holy Queen". He began a programme of storing
his own blood in Stilton pots and died of anaemia two years before
Oswald's arrival, on Christmas Eve, 1956.

Oswald is assigned to Burke, the head groom who collected him

13

from Monument, a shifty-eyed chancer for whom petty theft is a way of life. All new hands lodge in a stable loft and eat their meals in Bohall House's basement kitchen, to which access is gained by means of a tunnel and in which the family's governess, Mrs Deevy, holds power. Mrs Deevy lives at Bohall with her fifteen-year-old daughter, Heather, and has reared Vee Grainger with iron discipline. Mrs Deevy is a severe, embittered woman, who looks down her nose at everyone. Upstairs, Mrs Grainger, the widow, a small, Welsh woman (about whom only one persistent rumour survives), does her best to keep the farm of 400 acres going, and the tradition of hunting, although since her two sons have by then left home, only herself and Vee, who is seventeen when Oswald meets her, still ride to hounds. Small, vivacious, imperious and beautiful, no horse has ever got the better of Vee, according to Burke. Riding out along the mountain paths, Oswald sees the muscles in her thighs rippling beneath the thin fabric of her britches. No doubt she ignores him.

Bohall House has long been a gathering point for Monument's landed gentry, especially in the summer when the lanes around Bohall are thick with woodbine and montbretia. After Sunday service in the Church of Ireland in Sibrille, these Protestants of declining fortunes withdraw the couple of miles to Bohall House for drinks and occasionally coffee. They bring bottles of gin and home-made biscuits in wicker baskets, since Mrs Grainger can hardly be expected to provide, and sit in the big, front room and behave for an hour or so in that courtly, unconcerned manner of people for whom reality is an irritation. Nothing specific ever arises except that it involves England, a place where those with money send their children to school and have their clothes made still, and maintain their membership of clubs, and whose politics, social gossip, taxation policies, wars, mores, geography, history, bitter, royalty and cricket are every Sunday morning the subjects of fond analysis. On the new-found politics of the country in which most of these families have lived for several hundred years, they never touch. Nor is it permissible to visit the fact that more than 95 per cent of the population worship in a different faith from that held by the brave little group in Bohall House's big front room. Yet they love their country, Ireland, for its fields and streams, its strands and rocks and wild, barren mountains. After summer worship they exchange enthusiastic yarns about fishing, and in the winter, if the week before the Bohall foxhounds had a ten-mile point, each leap and fall is meticulously recounted, and where Irishmen or women were involved too in those chases their feats are retold, often by General Santry from Main in what the group cheerfully supposes is a good take-off of an Irish accent.

(In his day General Santry had to travel the best part of eighteen miles to worship in Bohall, a journey hard to justify in times of scarce petrol, particularly since he had to pass his own church outside the front gates of Main, in which there was regular Sunday observance. Mrs Grainger, then a widow, had a way with her, and some sources reported the general describing her as "my little pit pony". This gave rise to the one, persistent rumour.)

Oswald is just one of half a dozen men in the stable yard and farm; they come and go the whole time and not everyone in the house is, on any given day, able to name all of them. So at the start, it is reasonable to assume, Vee Grainger treats him with a mixture of condescension and teasing – her second nature. Then when she realises he rides as well as she does, her curiosity is aroused by this man of funny accent whose features make him look younger than he is. I can see the scene clearly, Kaiser: one morning in September, hacking back together to Bohall after cubbing, their knees touch and Oswald leans across the gap and kisses her.

The rest is easy. Next day when she sees him she looks the other way. Oswald knows that he has intrigued her; yet, as often now as he tries to get her on her own, in the tack room, or when she is disposed to groom, or out exercising on the leeward side of a mountain when Burke is still out of sight, if Oswald speaks her name Vee looks at him with eyes of ice. He has in his lifetime fallen in love several times, but love has always eluded him in the end, why he cannot say. Perhaps this is one of the reasons he came south.

Now Oswald is unable to get Vee from his mind for long enough to eat or sleep with any comfort. Out of sight of her, the image of her in his mind grows rather than decreases until he has in his head a whole catalogue. Her ears preoccupy him for long hours, their tidiness, even though he cannot be sure if he has seen them both at the same time. As for the brightness of her eyes, it was never more apparent than at the moment of her slighting him, as he was being wiped from the slate of her memory; and yet, just for the eruptions that took place within those spheres, he would go down the same road again. He often drifts off to sleep during that winter clad only in the warmth of her long hair, its texture on his chest, scenting the difference between the days she has and has not washed it – unwashed being musky and evoking more mysteries and questions as to the parts of her he can only imagine as opposed to the fresh innocence after shampooing, a more stereotypical but nonetheless alluring sensation. With the flats of his thumbs he strokes out the long ferns of her eyelids. He keeps her lips for nights in his loft room when he wants to cry himself to sleep.

It is all a fantasy. He will never be accepted by someone like Vee Grainger, he, the poor man from the North. Yet every time he sees her he knows that he cannot exist without her. The impossibility chokes him. He thinks of nothing else, sees her beautiful face every-where he looks, envies hotly the man who will one day win her hand, someone who does not yet even know of her existence but who nonetheless, in the great scheme of life's uneven distribution, is out there, unbeknown, waiting. Oswald becomes slovenly in work, irritable with the horses, earns Burke's reprimands. One day a horse crushes his toe, causing Oswald to scream and kick the horse with his free foot just as Burke comes into the stable. He calls Oswald a filthy name. Oswald hands in his notice.

And the following day without warning, in the feed room where there stood a big steel bin of crushed oats, she comes up behind and holds him around his waist and says, "You cannot go."

In a moment of unique revelation Oswald understands the problem: reticence. Instead of his worshipping Vee from afar, aggression is called for, not easy, since he is not an aggressive man; yet now the tide of his want sweeps his caution and, turning, he catches her up and carries her by way of a wooden ladder to his quarters.

And now comes his happiest time, the remaining four months in Bohall. Having withdrawn his notice, the days and nights become dedicated to no other purpose than the loving of Vanessa. They make love in every out-house in Bohall. Their urgent love is enacted in saddleries, dairies, hay byres, garages, woodsheds, lambing pens and occupied stables. She can never get enough of him and tells him she adores older men. At first amazed by the symmetry of her young body, he now loves her for her urgency, her speed, her recklessness, advantages on the hunting field turned into assets beyond price. With the same sense of personal disregard which allows her to pole out over a stone-faced, briar-topped bank whose unseen landing side hides lethal dangers, Vee begins to bring him into Bohall House itself, in broad daylight, even as Mrs Grainger is entertaining to tea in the music room downstairs. The danger is a drug for both of them. Starting from the relative safety of her brothers' empty rooms, the quarters for guests, warming cup-boards – the irony! – and linen cupboards, they progress, as if ever seeking out the extra ounce of madness, to the

17

room in which Vee herself sleeps. As with the chase, speed is all. So much can be accomplished so quickly. She can have him out of riding britches and in her hands, engorged, in under half a minute. In a china press beside the kitchen they stand naked, enwrapped, as outside the door Mrs Deevy dictates the week's menus to the cook.

Who knows what is going on? Burke, to be sure. He winks, surely, and says nothing. Who else? The kitchen servants, the yard hands. Everyone, in other words, except Vee's mother, which is the standard position in these circumstances. But what about Mrs Deevy and her daughter, Heather – do they know? One imagines it impossible that by this stage they do not. Heather spends much time around the yard and the horses. Granted there may be men there, temporary hands, with whom she might not be familiar. The same goes for Mrs Deevy. The governess does not pay the wages, after all. But Oswald is not temporary. He eats in the kitchens and Mrs Deevy and Heather are fully aware of everyone who eats in the kitchens and so a love affair of this intensity could scarcely escape their notice. One imagines that if Mrs Deevy did know, given her effective role as Vee's adoptive mother, that she would quickly effect the removal of the new groom from Bohall. Yet this does not happen. Perhaps events are moving too fast for everyone. Perhaps . . . Who knows?

At any rate, the story resumes. Late April. Vee enters the room below the loft whose bridles and martingales Oswald has soap-chamoised a thousand times and he sees at once from her face that something is amiss.

"It can't be."

But it is, she tells him, a doctor has confirmed it. Three months gone. Soon she will begin to show.

Now any choice she might have had in their affair is ended. She needs Oswald. Oswald, terrified at first by the situation, tells Vee he will never leave her. She fears more than anything informing her mother, or her mother finding out. They cannot think what next to do. They find an ally in Burke.

The groom, a natural for intrigue and no longer constrained by his position, reveals a hitherto unsuspected background in English racing stables and a profound knowledge of the greater world. The three of them ride out into the hills, where Burke is free with his advice concerning the termination of pregnancies, a solution which, although denied to those of his own religion, is available to Vee. England, the groom proclaims. He had a brother there, another jockey, who lives in Yorkshire. Over there it's like getting teeth pulled, he says. They can stay with the brother on arrival whilst they get sorted out, Burke will write a note. Oswald has never been to England. On the last, blowy day of April, looking back down over land in flood to Bohall, it seems to Oswald and to Vee that they are blessed in their misfortune to have at least one friend, albeit a thief.

Fact: Vee had money left her by her father, one hundred pounds plus interest, in her own name in the Munster & Leinster Bank in Monument. Fact: on May 8th she withdrew the principal. On May 10th they elope. They never meet the jockey. In the toilet of the ferry the representative of a group based in Nottingham which is dedicated to the emancipation of womanhood comes upon Vee fainted. On arrival she takes the couple with her to a doctor outside Liverpool, who pronounces Vee's pregnancy as five months and rules termination out of the question. The group, now three, return to the Mersey, where the Ireland-bound ferry awaits. But at the last minute Vee refuses to board and thus their first night in England is spent sharing a room in a boarding house with the lady from Nottingham.

Kaiser's story is that his father now secures a job with a racehorse trainer not far from Southport, a man of bushy, ginger sideboards whose day-job is selling cars and whose horses are galloped along the fringes of the lapping tide. The trainer's sister rents a bedroom to the couple. Vee spends most of every day in bed.

Imagine Oswald: he begins awakening in the grip of dreams in which his lovely wife has been snatched from him by the sea. He will, as he has done before, he knows, die without her, and turns to her in bed and clings to her back. His anxieties involve her haemorrhaging to death as she has their child, or of being taken by the bad flu, or of succumbing altogether to the increasing bleakness of her outlook. He sees the look she gives him, empty even of recognition sometimes, the girl who said "You cannot go" a memory. He wants to put his hands on her body and feel the heartbeat of his child, but she seems to take this wish as an opportunity to remind her of her plight and goes to sleep at nights in the centre of the bed, so that he has to doze off in the chair or on the floor for fear of waking her. She laments the leaving of Bohall, ignoring the fact that she has not bothered to write to her mother. One day she looks at his big hands and calls him lout.

Fact: Vee was rushed to Southport Hospital on September 1st where, after a labour of sixteen hours, a child, a boy, was born. Vee had to be given blood. Within five days she is back in the digs, where a bigger room has been provided. After a week the trainer's sister calls the doctor who confirms that the baby is suffering from malnutrition. Women from Southport bring cockles which Vee consumes with gusto. And on the Sunday Vanessa Grainger arrives downstairs, dressed in riding clothes.

"I need a job," she announces.

The trainer's eyes go round and he puffs out his ruddy cheeks.

"I'll be blowed," he says as he gives Vee a leg up on a five-year-old gelding that needs a bit of holding and watches as horse and rider glide out across the sands.

*

Time must go by quickly in the little yard, where there is always much work on hand. For the next three years, or thereabouts, Vee rides out by day and looks after her skinny child who is never without a cold. Oswald too enjoys the flat coastline and the sand dunes on which the horses are worked, the occasional outings to race meetings, travelling in the truck, stroking the ears of the horses with affection, calming them ahead of their races, whispering, "Shush, there's the good girl, shush the baby."

When he is not working, he brings his tiny son on certain expeditions and speaks to him about the things he knows. The earth, the trees, animals. The boy often seems distant and unresponsive. Oswald wraps him inside his coat on cold days. The child cries.

Fact: Vee was killed in a simple accident, her horse falling on a bend of the road as the string walked home after morning exercise, the blow to the side of her head resulting in immediate death.

Poor Oswald. Perhaps if he was able to see beyond the all-prevailing depression in which Vee's death enwraps him, he might be able to seek the help he needs. But he does nothing. One imagines that as the trainer's sister takes charge of the child, moroseness possesses him. One mild December evening, the horses groomed and rugged and bedded for the night, he walks out on Southport beach at low tide, the last that is seen of him.

Might he still be alive? Just about. He might well have gone back to the North and found another woman. He could even be in Liverpool still. More likely though, with night falling, he is cut off by the in-creeping tide, not a dramatic affair, just stealthy and treacherous, bad enough by day if you've gone far out, but in failing light you can be marooned and not even know it has happened. His last moments: the lights of Southport in the distance, water to his chest – can he swim? One doubts it – the line of the beach where he has so many mornings perched on the withers of a filly, out of reach. And as night comes at last and the currents pick up, he surely thinks with fond regret about his little son there somewhere amid the distant, yellow lights. And in the final moments, said to be sweet, I can see him smiling at the image he has conjured of the man his son will one day become.

Three

A FEW YEARS BEFORE ...

The way I prefer to remember Jasmine is the way I first saw her in the front office of the *Gazette*. Her arms were full of old archive volumes, but when I came in she turned around and looked at me. I saw a face so pale it must have sprung from limestone. So pale and perfect. Hair of copper, tied at the base of her neck. She looked at me like a child might look at someone for the first time; and then two things happened. She smiled and her eyes came on. I can still feel the fillip in my blood.

"That's Kaiser," I saw one of the other women say. "He can't hear you very well, you have to shout. Kaiser! This is Jasmine! Our new librarian!"

I smiled at her.

She said, "Hello, Kaiser."

By the way she spoke my name I could see that she had a rich voice with deep, satiny sides.

"Jasmine?"

She smiled. "From jasmine. You know – the plant?"

I shook my head.

"My mother's in the flower business," she said and walked out by me, leaving the scent from her hair to eddy around my head.

The basic gear in the *Gazette*'s machine shed had not much changed since my first day there. Four black and white, Pacer 36s – the only items salvaged from the 1972 fire. A new colour Lino press that had cost a fortune. Across the floor, for the fancy colour jobs, the Heidelberg Speedmaster. A Brehmer folding machine, a trim stitcher, a laminator, a Sulby binder, a Hang drilling machine and a Stahl three-knife trimmer. Most of the older men who worked here had seen their original and highly prized skills become redundant and although they could still spell backwards, or accurately hand-fold a layout of thirty-two pages in correct numerical sequence in under three seconds, by the time I left such skills were called for only at parties.

My journey home took me diagonally across Monument: down Milner's Street, through Moneysack, across Pollack Street, over Kaiser Street and into MacCartie Square, then, via either Conduit or Ladies Walk, to the senior home in Demijohn Street. I began to see Jasmine everywhere. No matter what route I took home from work – if, for example, I cut up Palastine and over Skin Alley into Binn's Street – I would bump into Jasmine. She lived in a flat off James Place. On her half day she helped her mother in the flower shop in MacCartie Square. Within range of the pistillary balms of her mother's rioting blooms, I would stand drinking in the sight of Jasmine stooping to pick out from a pot a dozen pink carnations.

"Kaiser? Do you have a minute?"

It was a Friday in April. As I was leaving the *Gazette* she tugged my sleeve. We walked across Candle Lane and sat on the low wall on the other side.

"I'm doing some research into local history, names of people, backgrounds. Can you tell me something about yourself?"

"Why?"

"We were just discussing you the other day – me and my mum. I'm interested in you."

I told her who my parents were, about Vee Grainger of Bohall House, my mother, who was buried in the Church of Ireland cathedral, and about how my father, Oswald Kaiser had come to work in Bohall House and had eloped with my mother to England.

Jasmine looked at me with a long, thoughtful expression.

"That's very interesting, Kaiser," she said at last.

Jasmine began to sit with me during breaks. At my table in the canteen she asked me questions about my childhood and I told her how, as a child in Monument, I had developed a diversion to the daily grind of Demijohn Street and to the long, shapeless summers. I had cycled out in all directions, I told Jasmine, and collected evidence of the bushmen who had lived seven or eight thousand years ago on the cliffs in places like Sibrille or in the mountains near Glane. They had worked out the solstices then, and lived in small communities, often on the easily defended promontories of steep cliffs. Jasmine was absorbed. Intelligence shone from her. Before Jasmine there had never been a librarian at the *Gazette*. Before Jasmine the only attempt to preserve the past had been in filing away each week's edition between hard, tall covers and then, once a year, binding them into volumes. Jasmine came from the Monument Library where she had been assistant, and whose records and reference indexes she had computerised. At the *Gazette* she was transferring every edition since 1881 onto hard disk, then making an index, cross-referenced and linked to that in the library she had just left.

Having once done a computer course when the other obligatory choices were car maintenance and tailoring, I was somewhat familiar with the *Gazette*'s computer system, and a tradition had arisen whereby my foreman, Philly Dixon, would on request release me from my duties in the shed when either the journalists or sub-editors had a technical problem. A gentle, Monument-like ambience was the rule on their floor. Each journalist worked from his or her own Apple-Mac. They used a software programme called "3B2" which connected them to an Agfa "Avantra", a machine that produced page-sized film. Ads were canvassed by telephone, pages laid out on screen. Reporters who had covered a sitting of the circuit court swapped yarns with colleagues who had attended the sod-turning ceremony for a new factory extension. A fast-breaking story would hardly have raised an eyebrow up there; for although the *Gazette* was printed on a Tuesday, due to long-established distribution practices it never appeared in the shops until Thursday around noon.

One Saturday morning in mid-November when I was buffing up the outer doors to the Monument Library to have them nice in good time for Christmas, I discerned Jasmine's presence in the atmosphere behind me. In Demijohn Street we had learned the value of denying spontaneous actions, of never allowing the whirring of our hearts to be seen even for an instant on the surface of our faces; and so although she was standing behind me, I continued to paint, knowing full well that she would put my lack of reaction down to my hardness of hearing. Her cheek was so close I could feel the velvet emissions of her skin. Then she came around.

"Hi, Kaiser."

"Jasmine."

"Feel like a coffee?"

I was in love. I'd heard about this, the speed with which it happens, but like everything in life it had to be encountered before it could be believed. We went inside and down the marble steps. We sat on stools at a high, uncomfortable tripod table. The coffee came in styrofoam mugs and the plastic spoons, if put astirring for more than a few revolutions, melted. Some people describe such encounters in terms of being able to remember nothing, but in my case no detail escaped immortality. To the spacious lawns of my mind was appointed every single particular of our rendezvous in a great whirl of gathering, beginning with such items as stools and tables, ashtrays and flower pots, machines for vending chocolate and cool drinks, the red and white one-foot-square floor tiles, the face of the lady behind the counter whose Saturday mornings were being spoiled by the library's opening hours, and the only other customer in the coffee shop, an old man, half-blind, whose name I could never remember but who lived alone in a flat on O'Gara Street; to these supporting details the outline of my love came into view: the texture of her copper hair, the shape of her face, the slimness of her shoulders, her collected waist, the way her hips filled that part of the blue jeans I had never seen her in before, her red shoes and her toes, or those I could see, whose nails blushed with ruby varnish. Every part of her I beheld provoked my deep longing and admiration.

"I was telling my mum about what you told me," Jasmine said. "She remembers Bohall House."

It was as if her jeans meant that her legs had never before been visible to me; for although I had previously regarded her legs to the extent that I might have been considered an expert, here I was relishing them all over again: especially the thighs, firm and tidy, displayed to advantage as she perched, as she had to, the sole virtue of the seating arrangements.

"She asked me to ask you if your father or mother had brought away any memento of Bohall with them – you know, some little item that would have reminded them of the Grainger home – and, if they had, whether you had been given it?"

I had come to Demijohn Street with nothing but the clothes on my back, I told her, and Jasmine reached across and, for a moment, laid her hand on mine. She was wearing a cream shirt with vertical blue stripes, the cuffs rolled up a few folds, her forearms short and tanned and with copper coloured hairs exuding a kind of limitless competence. Any more than I needed prompting in the matter of her legs did I need reminding about her pert chest, upon which every man in the *Gazette* had remarked; but again, in the

27

loose shirt, it acquired another life, or lives, nothing less than the shirt's unbuttoning being my ambition. What colour were her eyes, I wondered? Grey or blue, or even green, it was hard to say, a matter of light, or mood, not that she was anything but happy that day – but even happiness, like a peaceful river, is a thing of degrees, look into it closely and all the kinds of different happinesses are in constant flux; she lived through her eyes in every moment we sat there that day, laughing or wondering or daring me to love her.

4

The more I see of Kaiser, the less I understand; the less I understand, the stronger his attraction. How can this be? Everyone I
meet, especially my mother, tells me to be wary. This is a man of
proven volatility, they say. I asked my mother to elaborate, but she
went funny across the eyes, the way she does when she's trying
to hide something, and said there was nothing to elaborate on. Yet
what lies at his core? I have to find out.

Between him and the world, he tells me, lie veils of the lightest
weave. Clamps compress his temples and make outward images
shudder and grow small. On such days he floats above the span of
hours, forgets his appetite, sleeps at noon and awakens when the
stars stand out in the heavens. He smells horses and hay from
the inner leaves of his memories. He still retains the aftertaste of
black and white sweets. In his mind, the picture of an old man
upside-down and the devil with fire in his eyes.

His life has always been, it seems, linked one way or another
with the *Monument Gazette*. That august paper, which began life
in 1878, was founded by a man called James Pender. Twenty-two
years later, when he died, his son, George, known as Boss, took
over. No official photographs remain of Boss – strange that, for
a man who led such a public life. Apparently his portrait once
hung in the *Gazette*'s hall, but has now joined that of his parents
upstairs. Legend, more than fact, surrounds this son and heir of
the founder of the *Monument Gazette* and much of what I'm about
to relate is based on the hearsay of old stagers around the town

whose anecdotes and tales of past times have always been a source of interest to me. I have taken them and, where needed, added my own reasonable interpretation. I doubt if the result is too wide of the mark.

*　*　*

1907

It is said that in July of that year, he had come up to Coleraine to buy a Boston Wire Stitcher from a printer whose three sons aged fourteen, eleven and eight had all died in one month from influenza; it is said that when Boss Pender had done the deal with this distracted man, he was walking, cane in hand, down the main street of Coleraine when he heard a commotion. A horse had bolted and with its carriage swaying in extremes to either side behind it was scattering the market-day crowd. Boss Pender, six foot three inches – tall as a church steeple, broad as the nave, they said in Monument – could see the white, rolling eye, the foaming muzzle. Stepping out, he raised his stick. It appeared to onlookers that the charging horse collided with the standing man. But in fact it stopped dead, a yard short, flanks a-quiver, steam in geysers rushing from each arched nostril. The Proprietor of the *Monument Gazette*, to Coleraine people as unknown as the Lyle, grasped the head as others ran to the carriage and helped out the trembling figure of a porcelain-skinned young woman.

This story is told by many people. Lydia Albutt was the name of the young woman. Her family were crayfish men living in Gua on the north Antrim coast. Boss Pender took her home after her ordeal and over the next four months wrote to her every other day.

Lydia, it seems, when she made her mind up – that is, if it had not been made up that very first day in Coleraine – came south almost immediately. In later years she often spoke about her journey, dead of winter, snow lying like a shroud over the country, she'd never before been more than twenty-five miles from the sea. Worshipped the man she was coming to marry, would never alter that viewpoint, forever saw him at the head of her horse, his fearless gaze, her deliverer. She was changing everything for him; her coastline, her name, her religion. They were married on January 4th, 1908 in the cathedral in Monument. Only the Hunters, her sister and her sister's husband, came down, and they stood in sleet outside the church for the duration.

*   *   *

1922

Fifteen years go by, Lydia bears three sons for Boss Pender: Tom, the eldest by nine years, and then twins, James and John. James has got his mother's colouring: people describe his hair and complexion as gold, butter, wheaten straw. White. John is the opposite. So rare, everyone says to find hair so black. Raven. Coal. Soot. These are all words people use to describe his hair. Straight and oily, when he brushes it to an inky pat it shines. Black. Their mother forbids the nicknames "Black" and "White" in the house or within her earshot, tries to insist on John and James. One of Lydia's defeats, you can see it in the set of her shoulders, hear it in the way she draws her breaths. Black glows for Boss and Boss becomes radiant for him. Two sides of a coin, they are called, he and his father. Sit together when Boss goes out as far as Sibrille and up to Deilt and Baiscne about his business; on Sundays sit together at the gleaming table in the first floor dining room in Pig and Litter, where luncheon is served. White gets measles, wets his bed, sears his hand on a candle to get his father's attention.

"You're like those damn crayfish men from your mother's side," Boss Pender growls at White. "Skinny-arsed teetotallers. Perishers."

Not that drink means much to the Penders, Boss drinks port wine on Sundays only, writes his editorials denouncing shebeens, supports Father Matthew's crusade. On summer evenings Boss takes Black with him out to Glane in the foothills of the Deilt mountains, a special place extending over thousands of acres. Boss's father planted tens of thousands of trees in Glane and Boss himself has planted even more. When the sun picks out the Deilt mountains, from Monument you can see the new trees as if someone has painted the mountains black. But something even more important can be found up there. At the heart of Glane is an oak wood, as old as Ireland, and in the centre of the oak wood lies a pool whose waters are said to have the power to heal.

Dangerous times in Ireland; Monument escaped the worst of it, but even so. Young John, along with White, his twin, and their older brother, Tom, lives with his parents in three houses along a terrace known as Pig and Litter. That wasn't really its name, a yellow tin sign saying Vaseur Terrace stood high on the wall of No. 1, and that was the name their mother preferred and stamped on their notepaper. Black never understood the nickname for their terrace until one day down beside the river on Long Quay an old stager had pointed his walking stick and shown him how, beneath the bluff of Balaklava, the houses looked like bonhams feeding at the belly of a sow.

For a time Boss Pender calls Black "Black and Blue" because his thin arms and legs are always bruised from the other two, White and Tom, White particularly, his twin, who is now six inches taller than him and a foot wider. His father tells his mother to bring him up to see the new doctor, and Dr Armstrong gives her a bottle for the boy, but it changes nothing. Later a man, Mr O'Kelly, comes to the house in Pig and Litter to give the boys their lessons. They call him Mr O'Jelly because of his chins. Mr O'Jelly sits them down every morning for two hours in the dining room, and teaches them mental arithmetic, and how to write so that each letter touches the top and bottom lines, and to read aloud items from their father's paper. Tom too is taught, but more advanced lessons. Once a week Mr O'Jelly jumps to his feet and stands with his hands behind his back as Boss Pender steps into the dining room, his dark eyes matching the table and other appointments, and surveys his sons.

"Well, Master?"

"The lads are doing the finest – really, really they are, sir."

"*All* of them?" asks Boss Pender, seizing on the wafer of doubt in the teacher's reply.

"Well ..." and here the teacher's transient loyalty to his three young pupils is tempered by his awe of his employer, "Black here is a good boy, but he needs to give it more of his mind. Otherwise . . ."

"Hmm." Boss Pender bites his lip for a moment, then strides from the room.

The boy doesn't thrive. His mother, anxious and terrified of her husband, takes it all as a failing of hers, whether of her blood, or her cooking, or the way she manages her household, whatever, she frets at a high rate and Black seems to worsen in direct ratio. Boss Pender has his son examined by doctors in Dublin. Boy, how they could charge! He is a wealthy man who expects results. All the way home in the train he grumbles about value for money. One said it might be draughts, another that he needed more air, mentioning the Pyrenees. In Monument there is a Franciscan priest who in a box keeps a scapular that was once kissed, it is believed, by the lips of St Robert Bellarmine. Children suffering from the gripe benefit if they kiss the leather thongs. Boss Pender brings his son, sees his pale lips touch the holy relic, leaves a large donation.

"I sometimes think it's in his head," Mr O'Jelly confides.

So it is, but not something you can see, or press with your fingers, or even that Black himself can begin to describe, just a noise to begin with, loud rushings, his fingers on the bedsheet sound like scurrying mice. Then his eyes. All he sees goes small, though it remains perfectly visible. His hand a postage stamp, his twin brother the head of a pin. Mr O'Jelly's voice comes in rolling waves, like the wheels of a dray cart. The milk always tastes off.

Boss Pender walks his land out at Glane in clothes tailored for him in Scotland: green tweed with a pale yellow stripe, plus fours and jacket. Matching cap. In Glane he can walk all day and never once cross his own path or leave his own land. He loves the scent the Glane trees give in the hour after rain. In Glane Boss Pender sees the full dimensions of his life's ambition. Away from Candle Lane, from the thundering presses, from home and from the ever-anxious face of his wife he can consider in one broad sweep the growth of his own power. Like other men fixated with greatness and infallibility in matters temporal, Boss Pender believes in the pre-ordained nature of his achievements and feels the weight of obligation to pass on what he received from his father, James. It will not be Tom. Should be, the eldest, but Tom has no quickness to him. Fatal that, especially in a fast-changing world. Excitement is the word. Boss Pender gets up every morning excited by the potential of the coming day. Nothing about business excites Tom even though Boss has tried, has brought Tom around with him to meetings, still does, tries to inspire him with the atmosphere of money and success. No use. He gives the lad a task and an hour later finds him with his pad and crayons.

Then, White. Again, *should*. But just as people dislike a certain vegetable and cannot say why, Boss Pender's aversion to his son, White, is immutable; and although he tries – and he does try – to alter this view, to come to terms with what he sees, he fails. The child is a projection of something loathsome in Boss himself and

34

to accept White Boss would have had to confront this. He will never do so.

Which leaves Black. If the child were a machine and had shown the same weakness, Boss without hesitation would replace him. Also, a bad machine would irritate Boss, but with his sickly, vacant son he shows nothing but patience. Brings out a new side to the Boss, people say with a grudging smile. Compassion. Nothing to do with it, Boss growls to himself. His success in life, just like his father's, is in picking. Insight. Some people can do it with newborn horses. Even if Tom and White were contenders, Boss would pick Black as the one to carry on.

Glane is so many different places: not just the pool and ancient oak wood, the heart of the estate, but also the great plateau of grass on which cattle have grazed for centuries, a place of almost a hundred acres, beyond value, and then the dark, planted slopes, many of the trees put in over twenty years before at his own command and already tall enough to be called woods. Beyond the trees lie the bare foothills of fern, gorse and heather, miles of them in every direction, bisected by streams that contain the sounds of musical instruments, where his own hornies graze, leaping from rock to rock ahead of him – a kingdom! Boss had piers put up on the lower road and drew out with his own hand the gate to hang between them; and on the top edge of the plateau he had a cottage of stone built for the woodmen, and for the shepherds during their twice-yearly collection of the mountain flocks.

Boss Pender is driven everywhere by Hart, a County Louth man who got the job as driver because not only can he drive Boss's car, a Vauxhall with a 30-horsepower engine, the talk of Monument and which cost Boss £1,000, but he can also attend to the mechanism. When Boss wants to be in Glane, Hart leaves him by the road gate and watches his employer head uphill in big, devouring strides.

The pool, the centre of Glane, is not a place Boss Pender is much drawn to. He knows that local people hold it in high regard, chiefly for the treatment of illness in cattle; yet he seldom goes there. Nothing to do at it and he is a doer. Too confined. And, strange, too quiet. Yes, he comes out from Monument to escape the clamour of the *Gazette* and the town, or rather to exchange them for the sounds of Glane; but the pool is too quiet. Movement catches his eye one day from where he stands on the plateau, early autumn but still warm, middle of the day, in Candle Lane they've just sent down this week's edition and rather than go home Boss has come to Glane. He often comes across men at different tasks within his kingdom, they all keep a respectful distance, but sometimes he stops to inquire about the progress of the thinning or the incidence of twin lambs born – insight again. Men never lie to him. Six months later he can stagger them with his grasp of statistics. Now he thinks he recognises the stooped though broad back, prematurely old, as many of these people are, but this one radiates a natural ability around timber. Boss feels his feet drawn downhill, he climbs the white boulders – ancient clearings; in local legend, petrified bulls – and walks down the short path to the circle of water. Most men would jump to their feet, but this one remains seated, nods good day. The calmness in his face strikes Boss. He asks the man about timber, the forester gives his reply. Boss asks about the level of the pool, by how much it can vary since the Lyle itself rises here; the reply comes: by never more than a foot and a half, which is the secret of its stillness. Then, without any expectation that he was going to do so, Boss Pender says:

"My son is not well."

Within the woodman's eyes, two grey pools, Boss can see himself, topped by his tweed cap.

"Ah."

"He won't eat. He's small and thin. He's easily distracted."

"You can sometimes get that in boys. With some of them it's an inner sickness, with more of them it's the burthen of their age. Either way, some grows out of it, but some never does. Hardest of all on a father, the waiting to see which way."

"The doctors know nothing."

"Some of them does," the woodman says, causing Boss Pender to blink; he is not used to challenges to his opinion. The man chuckles. "Dr Church was a mighty man to cure the gripe, God be merciful to him. But with the hard cases I'd agree with you in the main. Then it's like a gaol cell with a hundred different keys to let you out. You have to find the key."

Boss Pender asks, "What key? What keys?"

"Sometimes it's the doctor, like poor Dr Church, simple enough, he has the key, you're out of gaol. Other times it's a woman with a good bottle, or it can be the priest another time, or a strong dream. Some have come and found their key right here, where you're standing. It's rare enough in each case and, like I said, not everyone gets out."

For someone whose mind conforms overwhelmingly to the scientific this sort of arbitrary philosophy appeals little to Boss Pender; yet his success in life is due also to a certain imagination and it is this that holds him. The forester has got up, produced and put on a cloth cap.

"Where is this key here?" Boss Pender demands. "What is it?"

"There're those around here who says that when the full moon goes under Jupiter a healing wish at this pool is never refused."

"Pagan stuff!"

"Aye, right enough. I've never needed any of it myself, thanks be to the Lord God, the old trees keeps me healthy, I'm like a tree myself, they'll have to cut me off at the ankles to get rid of me."

*

37

Oh, in Ireland, those were times of great uncertainty. Great convulsions. A lot of the best young men had died from wounds, everything was scarce unless you had money or knew someone, people travelled only in emergencies.

Boss Pender is not a man to put any store by gibberish, but at the same time he has worked long enough at the helm of a provincial newspaper – twenty-five years at this point, if you take it that since the age of fifteen he was by his father's side – to know that daily life resonates with the unaccountable. Dead men sit up at their wakes. Calves are found in a field of bullocks. Out near Sibrille an entire family of poor cottagers, a man, his wife and their children, disappeared. He is a most handsome man, Boss Pender. Big boned, six foot three in his stockings. But he has few friends. People say that no-one really knows Boss Pender, or, put otherwise, that there is another Boss Pender, known by no-one. Not that anyone is prepared to be more specific, but such rumours make folks wary.

Black gets worse. Boss brings his son to a healer in the midlands – the seventh son of a seventh son, a gaunt man who himself looks at death's door and whose power resides in his fingertips, and to a – very rare – woman doctor in Dublin whose specialty is backward children, and to, in total, six other practitioners who are variously recommended by Boss Pender's business associates, employees and social acquaintances, or by hackney drivers or by people encountered on trains. Most of them give the opinion that the child will, over time, improve. They are all wrong. Black grows thinner. His twin brother is now nearly twice his size. Black's skin is translucent, like the wings of a fly. Every time his mother sees him her mouth puckers.

There is a harsh winter. Young Black spends most of it wrapped in rugs in the big, warm, upstairs sitting room of Pig and Litter, drinking egg yolks beaten with essence of vanilla into warm milk, or trying to eat blood puddings – meant to boost the iron – or sleeping with wads of brown paper on his chest, a sure way to kindle energy, someone, no-one can remember who, insisted. With December, wet and cold, the boy sinks further. "Receding," Dr Armstrong admits. People go hushed about the house. Death beats its wings above Pig and Litter.

No-one could look at Boss Pender and realise from his expression the extent of his gathering sorrow, the deep dread to which he now awakens, the effort he needs to keep going and the bleakness with which he regards the future. Some signs: the blandness of the editorials show them to have been penned by the hand of a sub-editor; Boss is, unheard of, late for meetings; some nights he drinks. So powerful, so impotent. He finds it hard to bring himself to look at the fading child, as if it is already over.

And then one January night, as the paper is in the course of being printed, a telephone call to the *Gazette* from Mrs Pender, itself an event so unusual that it makes Boss go pale.

"Come home."

Ah. He slumps forward, his forehead on the desk. Women know. They know the coming and the going. He staggers downstairs and out to where Hart stands by, silent and acquiescent. Boss, winded, rests his elbows on the roof of the car. Agony. The moon picks out his tortured face without mercy. In the car for the short drive up Dudley's Hill his head is back, his neck sinews staring. Hart walks in behind him along the narrow entry. Hart sees how his employer's feet drag.

"Hart."

"Sir?"

"What . . . what is that . . . ?"

Hart has been around for years, on call whenever Boss needs him, never speaks unless addressed, reads books while he waits, looks like a schoolteacher and when he does utter, does so in the accent of the border counties. Boss Pender has paused on the step below his own hall door and is gazing at the moon. God help us, Hart thinks, to see such a powerful man levelled.

Then, "That . . . bright star . . ."

A fierce star burns to the left of the almost full moon.

"Jupiter," answers Hart.

"And . . . is it . . . rising?"

"Aye, he's rising the whole time tonight," replies Hart. "He'll be on top of her before long."

Boss turns, open-mouthed.

"Wait here!"

Pushing inwards by way of the heavy street door he runs upstairs, past a pair of red-eyed housemaids who, interpreting the worst from his actions, begin wailing anew, into the sweltering living room with its overlaying fetor of resigned fate, where around the cot set by the fire are gathered his wife and Father Whittle, the priest, and a local woman who is normally a midwife.

"Stand back!"

The group scatters, wild eyed. Boss Pender scoops up his child in the bedclothes and runs out.

Outside, Hart has not moved. He now hurries ahead of Boss Pender back up the entry and opens the door of the Vauxhall. Boss climbs up into the back, child across his knees. Hart primes the tank, presses down the starting knob and they turn on the spot, roar downhill. In the upstairs room in Pig and Litter Father Whittle sinks to his knees, takes out his rosary and leads with the Sorrowful Mysteries.

For men in whom unquestioning compliance was not so ingrained, the escapade might have led to hesitation or even to queries about the wisdom or humanity of the venture; not so with Hart. As that night and future events prove, he has met in Boss

40

Pender the man to whom he will give his life, he is the extension of Boss's design and now he drives through sudden blots of snow, up into the mountain foothills with his boss and a dying child, to Glane. Boss keeps peering out the window, but the night sky, up to minutes ago so clear, is lost. The car's great headlamps probe with ghoulish interest. Through the gossamer snow amber eyes slide into newly wreathed bushes. At the gate Hart leaps out, drags back the heavy iron, they rock through.

"Leave it open," Boss cries, and they climb.

He curses himself for forgetting the woodman's story until now. Now it is all he has. Terrifying. The boy of his life, ebbing in his arms, whose approaching death represents such a terrible failure, now depends for his very endurance on something so vague and unproven as to make this wild expedition censurable – and yet, as Hart urges the car up the steep, flinty, snow-covered path, Boss is convinced of his own rightness.

A smooth rock remains, part of the track. They drive it, then Hart pulls up. Boss gets out, the boy in his arms. He'd not put on his topcoat leaving Pig and Litter and now Hart tries to fix it on his shoulders. They climb, master with his son and servant, their heads dusted white. On level ground, they pause. Boss, unbreathing, places his ear to the open mouth.

"He's still here!" he cries and runs on.

Through a "V" of white boulders, a shepherds' design, into the great meadow, which in summer grazes up to a hundred head of beef cattle, they dash. Their feet sink, especially Boss's, laden as he is. The force of the snow, head on, and the blindness, and the sense of demented hopelessness would finish a man of lesser will than Boss Pender, but he keeps on, not even knowing if he is headed for the oak wood and the pool. The most remarkable thing – so far – about this life and death event is that young Black knows what is happening. Not the meaning of it, of course, but he is aware of whose arms he is in, that he is no longer in the stifling front room of mournful faces but outside in a mountain snowstorm. Never so warm as then, never so happy, young Black Pender. He will never die, he knows, so long as the love he feels for the man carrying him remains. Love burns him. He feels his lungs gulp down the wet globs of night air, but still he burns. In the room he has been aware only of outlines; now he sees each snowflake in its most intricate detail like a veil across his father's face.

The snow ceases. They have run uphill too far, for below them the wood stands out against the strangely deep blue sky, the moon, the vastness of stars. Boss needs Hart to take the boy as he climbs over the boulders, then retakes the bundle and hurries on and down, making occasional checks of the moon and of the pilot star. Hart hangs back. He has seen the look on the child's face and he knows that anything further he does will be an intrusion.

What takes place over the next thirty minutes is never clear. Hart observes from a distance. Black is aware only of his father. And Boss – he has no idea of what should be done now that they have arrived at the pool where the moon and its star are depicted in perfection on a surface so still and smooth it defies the notion it is water. So Boss sits on the ledge where the woodman sat and he holds his boy. Now and then he dips his fingertips into the water and although conscious of the dichotomy between the pagan and the Christian, blesses himself and Black, and brings his moistened fingers to the boy's lips, and his own, and at one stage kneels down and cups a double handful to his own mouth, although he stops short of wetting the boy's head, a baptismal gesture. Once when he looks up, Boss sees Jupiter standing on top of the moon; a few minutes later it has begun to slip around. It becomes cold. The boy is sleeping: good, even breaths. Perhaps the earlier fuss was overstated, you never knew with doctors. Hart helps them back over the stones. The drive down into Monument is like descending to a seabed. In Pig and Litter, Boss has them draw open all the drapes, a shocking notion. But for the sleeping child, no longer feverish, his face at peace, they all would think Boss Pender has taken leave of his senses.

The boy grows and prospers. He likes the outdoors, all weathers. Few remember the crisis. He becomes the only person in whom his father confides. The love between son and father is so intense it would buckle iron, they say in Monument.

PART TWO

Five

I dipped my hand into my trousers' pocket and felt with satisfaction the sharp edge of the disk. In Leire, where three hours still remained to roll-call, they would have assumed I was down the land as usual, digging out onion beds, or picking windfalls, or scuffling through the last of the potatoes. I decided to linger a little longer in the garden of Pig and Litter, to feel the sun on my face, to leave aside for another bit the task which I had appointed myself that day in Monument.

Jasmine's mother was Mrs Rice and she was small in build, like Jasmine, and had busy, tireless fingers. Flowers spilled from her shop and along the pavement. I stood deep in marigolds and watched her as, a long-ashed cigarette in her mouth, she plucked and snipped and nipped and pinched an order of roses and carnations and chrysanthemums into the lengths and shapes that pleased her, and then laid them together on a bench, where she poked and tweaked anew and wadded sprigs of fern into the equation, before uniting all the aligned stems with a rubber band and setting the bouquet into a sheet of cellophane. Ribbon from a wall-mounted roller spun as she reached to it without looking, sliced a length, whipped the ribbon round the crackling base of the flowers, bound it tight, took and opened scissors and, speaking all the time to me as she did so, cigarette still in the corner of her mouth, shredded the last six inches of the synthetic fabric so that it curled up into itself as if she had seduced it.

"This was a great town years ago, Kaiser. Not that I remember it then, but I remember hearing my mother talking about it. A port town of merchants and strong farmers, she called it. One lived off the other. No-one wanted for anything. Before de Valera we had the pig trade, the best in Europe."

She flicked her head and ash fell among the cuttings at her feet.

"My parents were estranged, I lived with my mother. But I knew everything about my father's family too. They were pig men. They left Monument on Sunday nights by train and headed up country to the fairs, one fair every day of the week in a different town. Graiguenamanagh, Athlone, Ballinasloe, Boyle. They bought the pigs and their drovers loaded them into pens and shipped them down to Monument, Ballinrobe, Letterkenny, Sligo town. The men that remained at home were here to take the pigs off the trains and herd them into the boats. The pig boats left for Fishguard twice a week, even up in White City you could hear the creatures squealing as they sailed away down the Lyle. On Saturday nights the travellers arrived back home. They washed and changed and went out for a drink. Every Sunday morning they were at eleven Mass in the cathedral with their mother – my grandmother – spick and span to a man. There were eleven of them and except for my father who was a sailor, every one of them was in the livestock trade. Ten big, strong men that could tell you your weight at a glance. All dead, Kaiser, all dead."

Mrs Rice drank water from a plastic bottle, then hefted flat boxes from the floor onto her table and took out furls of perfumed lilies. Her hair was fading from deep red into a lighter but more interesting shade. She wore jeans which tapered out several inches above her slight ankles. Lighting another cigarette, she squinted through drifting eddies of smoke.

"My father's father drank whiskey by the quart, retired at thirty-five, left his sons to do the work. He was said to remember every pig he'd ever bought. Perhaps that's too much to believe, but

48

what is true was that he'd made enough money to buy land outside Monument – if only we had it today – where he fattened cattle. He told his sons when they walked along the street to keep their eyes on the pavement because that way they might find money that had been dropped. Never spent a tuppence where a penny would do. Drank whiskey morning, noon and night. Never drunk, by all accounts, just reached a certain stage and sang and after that went to sleep. He'd spent his whole life travelling around Ireland by train and that was the way he'd learned to pass the time – drinking whiskey."

Mrs Rice gathered one by one tight-headed gladioli for tall vases on the floor and slipped them into their water, pausing to give each flower its moment of consideration.

"One day – this was before the first war – my grandmother got a severe pain in her chest. She has to go to Dublin to a specialist, the doctor said. My grandmother was in her early twenties, had already had three children. They set off one day, the two of them on the train. By the time they reached Kilkenny he had a quart of whiskey drunk. Why do you drink so much, she asked him? I'm sick with worry that you're going to die, he told her. They reached Dublin and walked all the way to Parnell Square. My grandfather told the doctor how worried he was, how no treatment would be spared, how much my grandmother meant to him. The doctor told him he was drunk, to wait outside. My grandmother went in to be examined."

Mrs Rice put on rubber gloves and grasped vases in pairs and lifted them down from the uppermost shelves and ran the spout of a watering can across their rims.

"After minutes my grandfather was called in. 'Sir, your wife has a serious blockage in her chest, I must operate if her life is to be saved,' said the doctor. 'Operate,' said my grandfather, 'operate.' 'My fee for this operation is sixty guineas,' the surgeon said.

Grandfather blinked. He looked at my grandmother. 'Get your hat', he said."

Mrs Rice paused and made a gesture of helpless mirth with her shoulders, her gloved hands, one with a secateurs, in frozen admonition.

"'Get your hat'. On the way home he drank one and a half quarts of whiskey. Her illness was never again mentioned. She lived to be eighty-nine."

December rain had ridden the night over the swelling ocean and now swept in gales across the town and into the foothills of the mountains. We hurried up the lane off Skin Alley and then into another entry leading to Palastine. At the door, Jasmine paused and smiled encouragement. Then she lead the way in. Don Pascal's was a rambling, low-roofed enterprise, a strictly *cognoscenti* spot because only those who knew it could ever find it. Don Pascal himself was everything you could wish for in an Italian *padrone*, he spoke the Neapolitan version of English – "You like? Es good. Si, si, no probleme" – was swarthy, greasy and fat, most accommodating, histrionic, wore a frosting of stubble and a pigtail of grey hair tied with a black ribbon, except that he was not Don Pascal from Naples at all but Pascal O'Dowd from Milner's Street, his Irish father having given him his name and nationality, his Italian mother everything else, including his love for cooking. The Don made a big fuss over Jasmine and led us, one hand aloft, down through the room chock-a-block with Christmas luncheons to a table at the back near a little courtyard. He arched his eyebrows at the sight of me in his restaurant.

"A lil' drink to start?"

Water, I saw Jasmine mouth and Don Pascal lumbered off, clapping his hands to a waiter and shouting, "*Ferrarrella!*"

I would have been happy just to sit without eating and admire

Jasmine – a wish that was enhanced by the fact that she knew this and, I could see, was happy about it. I tried to exclude from my imagination what her breasts looked like but images of their cherry-red tips kept intruding. I now realised that from the moment of our first sighting, when we had first breathed each other's air, a small but powerful twinkling had occurred and that I could bestow a sort of posthumous inevitability on what was unfolding. A waitress, a New Zealander I think by the shape of her words, seized her moment and there was an interlude during which Jasmine asked questions on my behalf about Penne Arrabbiata and Scaloppine Valdostana.

"Kaiser? What did the Celts eat? Reindeer?"

I wondered if, after an hour, my perception of her would be quite different and more muted from the way it had begun, if the edges would get knocked off the starkness of my need, or if other sobering factors would come into play. I need not have worried.

"Kaiser?"

I told her that reindeer had left Ireland in the Ice Age.

"Didn't the Celts drink wine?"

"Yes. Imported it from the Mediterranean."

"The first Beaujolais Nouveau race," she said. "The Celts were way ahead of everyone, weren't they? How did they dress? In deer skins?"

I told her how pelts and hides would have been old hat. How loose tunics tied with toggles, tied tight around the waist, would have been all the rage. How cloaks were worn and dyed according to rank, and fixed on the shoulder with a sun disc, or perhaps just a beautifully intricate, golden and ornamented brooch. How hair was worn long, but with lock rings, gold, cone-shaped ornaments that were threaded through the tresses. As the New Zealander ground out pepper from a large mill, Jasmine twirled spaghetti into a gleaming clump and laughed. She had a way of leaning back her

51

head when she did this, so that her teeth emerged as features in their own right. I realised how integral to beauty flawless teeth and gums were, how alluring. I wanted to touch her wrist, to feel her skin, to say, "You have a mouth so succulent that I would die to get into it, not just with my tongue, but actually get in there, one elbow after the other." Salads had been laid in front of us, plates of green leaves no doubt flown in from Israel or somewhere similar. Jasmine was describing a holiday she had been on in America.

"LA," she said.

I imagined beaches full of equally wonderfully chested and dentured beauties in bikinis, girls who were most likely taking the day off from being models, or air hostesses. My need seemed wholesome and sparkling, like Jasmine, everything about her was made of clean, smooth planes, already I wanted to imitate her gestures to her, to have no higher purpose than to make her laugh, as she was now doing, to have free range over every rim and duct of her, to possess her – by which I meant, exclusively, even at those times when I was not in theory possessing her – an outrageous position, I knew, towards someone I'd met but weeks before. Yet as she turned to me now and smiled again, I wondered how outrageous, since the light cooking in those deep eyes had every pore of my skin baying.

"Kaiser?"

"Sorry?"

"Glane. Know much about it?"

I told her that nowhere in the world was as beautiful on a good day. That Deilt people had been going up to Glane for centuries and bringing home water from the spring in bottles, which they sprinkled around their houses in winter. It cured everything, I told her.

"What do you mean by 'everything'?"

An old woman near Baiscne who couldn't walk had had her

sons carry her up to Glane, where she bathed in the spring and then cantered home, I explained. And all the mountain farmers used Glane water to cure cattle of red water, or if a calf couldn't get up and walk, they'd rub the water on its limbs and often the calf would trot out to meet them within the hour.

I had never been the first there with the telling remark, or the answer; but something was moving here, beyond what I knew would be the sensational and memorable first smack of our bodies, beyond taste of tongue, beyond the full of my hands, the feel of hers on me, beyond the sound of her quickening breath; something beyond all that was moving.

"Kaiser?"

I could watch her mouth for ever.

"Where did you learn about your parents? I mean, where does your information come from?"

I realised that the answer to her question would not come to me, that as far as I was concerned, the information had always been in my head.

Jasmine said, "Beagle's were the solicitors for the Grainger estate. Mrs Grainger died leaving everything to Vanessa and then Vanessa died. Bohall House was sold and as far as I can make out, when all the expenses and fees had been taken care of, there was nothing left." Jasmine's face was suddenly full of concern for me. "Do you remember having anything to do with Beagle's? Mr M. Beagle, for example?"

I shook my head.

"Are you sure, Kaiser? He was your legal guardian – do you not remember him? 'Mr M.' he was known as – Kaiser?"

When I saw his name float from Jasmine's mouth, just for the smallest instant, as if a crack had opened in a wall, I thought I saw something; or caught an old smell. Then nothing, again. I told her so.

53

"Mind if I ask Beagle's about you?" she inquired. "They must still have files from that time."

I smiled. "If that's what you'd like."

Jasmine smiled back and we walked out of Don Pascal's, into the winter sunlight.

6

I knew I'd find him in the library that Saturday morning: I'd been told he was coming in to paint the doors.

"Feel like a coffee, Kaiser? It's chilly out here."

It was meant to seem like I had just happened to be walking by the library and had seen him. The truth is that I wasn't at all sure that I should be embarking on this venture in the first place. What did we discuss? The past, I suppose – I can't remember. Let me put down what I saw: a well-built man in paint-speckled overalls with a way of looking at me that made me feel warm and wanted. Square of face, sorrowful of eye. I liked those dark eyes and his almost but not quite black hair. I wanted to bury my fingers in his hair. I liked the sinews in his neck, the breadth of his shoulders and the shape of his long fingers. We used those ridiculous plastic spoons. I laugh now, every time I think of Kaiser stirring his coffee!

I think I'll suggest to him that we have lunch between now and Christmas. A long, lazy Christmas lunch somewhere nice. I want to get him on his own again. I want to see the texture of his eyes as he smiles at me.

I've been looking into the old Binn's Street School records and the Demijohn Street archives from the time Kaiser was a small boy. There's quite a lot of material. The authorities in both places were dependent on government subsidies for survival and were thus forced to keep a chronicle of daily life.

*   *   *

1968

He is raised in the orphanage in Demijohn Street, now defunct. Every morning he goes from there to school in Binn's Street, the first mention of his name on the register occurring in 1964. He is a partially deaf boy, so a strict itinerary is mapped out and can be found in the orphanage records for that year: same side of the road, across Ladies Walk, look left, look right, look left again, through the park and past the Bishop's Palace, into Binn's Street. If he is still able to hear traffic, then he may hear birds singing in the park as he makes his way through it.

His teacher in Binn's Street is a Brother Flynn, whose great-aunts had years before run a drapery establishment in MacCartie Square. Brother Flynn's voice was said to be deep and rolling.

" . . . Kaiser? Kaiser!"

"Brother?"

"Answer the question, Kaiser."

If only Kaiser could hear the question clearly, he could give the answer. Most days are spent out on the line, holding his arms at right angles.

The orphanage in Demijohn Street is run by a religious order, one of whom is known as the Big Man. All the kids reckon that even the principal is afraid of the Big Man. For four or six weeks at a time he goes away, then he comes back and is in charge again of the dorms. I can imagine the scene.

"Sssh! Here comes the Big Man!"

His temper is something to behold. He can swing boys by the hair of their heads. He can punch the air out of their bodies so that they cannot breathe for five minutes. But the Big Man has his favourites too. He comes up at night and sit on their beds and tells them stories. He doesn't like Kaiser. He thinks him deliberately heedless, that Kaiser likes to ignore what he is saying and that when he keeps his head in a book it is only to slight him. One night in the washrooms as Kaiser is getting ready for bed, having washed his feet in the basin as he is meant to, he is sitting by the warm pipes, reading. The Big Man erupts over him. His eyes crazy. Kaiser wants to tell him that he has finished washing; but his tongue is slow. The Big Man catches him up by the front of his pyjamas and runs him back into the wall.

"Always. Trouble."

He beats Kaiser's head against the pipes.

"Always. Always. Trouble."

White stuff is coming out of the Big Man's mouth. He keeps hammering until Kaiser sees three of him. In the infirmary next morning Kaiser watches the lips of the boy in the next bed as he speaks. Before that he could watch and hear, but now he can hear almost nothing. At last he gets what the other boy is saying. The Big Man has gone away. This time he doesn't come back, but his voice is the last distinct one Kaiser ever heard.

"Always. Always. Trouble."

"Kaiser? Kaiser!"

"Brother?" He watches Brother Flynn's mouth.

"We have a new boy coming to us tomorrow. I want you to look after him."

Brother Flynn reckons that Kaiser represents the least threat to this important newcomer.

"This is Tim Pender-Goode."

The boy is very wide and fat and very frightened. Because Kaiser is older than him he sits across the aisle in the higher class – but if Kaiser wished he could reach his hand across and touch him.

"You sit over there, Tim, there's a good lad. Across from him. He's called Kaiser. He's deaf. Kaiser? Kaiser! Tim is going to ask you if he wants anything. You have to shout with Kaiser, Tim."

Imagine the scene. Tim doesn't look at Kaiser as he sits at his desk. For some reason Tim keeps his hands in his pockets. It is only later in the playground when Tim thinks no-one is looking that Kaiser see the overlapping scars on his left hand, long lips behind the knuckles of the third and index fingers.

Tim is a very lucky little boy. For although his daddy has left home and gone away, Tim is used to being in London for treats with Ollie, his mummy, a tall, beautiful lady who owns a newspaper. It is Christmas two years before and Tim, a chubby little chap in short pants, has just spent three hours in a big, big toy shop with trains that whizz in and out of tunnels and a real Santa Claus and plastic tube-guns that fire ping-pong balls. Tim's mummy has bought him one of these guns, and a spaceman's suit, and a toy camera and a sheriff's hat and badge and a little red-bearded man on a trapeze who leaps up and over a bar when you press down a lever. These purchases will all be delivered back to the big hotel where Tim and his mummy are installed, but in the meantime, for a very special treat, Tim is being brought for a ride on the London Underground.

Tim holds tight to Ollie's hand in the press of Christmas shoppers entering the station at Oxford Circus. His mind only ever grasps what has been promised next: supper in their hotel, where all he has to do is mention the word pop and a fizzy glass is brought to him by a nice man or a woman; then the pantomime, in which there will be, Tim has picked up, a real, wicked witch, a person about whom he alternates between nervousness and excitement; then afterwards a visit to a real soda fountain, where Tim will have his favourite of all favourite drinks, a fizzed-up strawberry milk shake. Tim, often bored at home, loves being with Ollie, where there is always something new happening. They pass the ticket checker and Tim ducks ahead of Ollie onto the down escalator, then turns to his mummy a few steps above him and grins.

Ollie looks down on the top of Tim's dark-sandy head and sees her life's ambition. Although she knows he will soon have to go to school, she has already breathed the flavour of her ambition into his young nostrils. Lacking a father, Tim must leave the female atmosphere of Pig and Litter and learn the society of men. Ollie hopes that he will have learned a few of the assets that she, in private, admits to possessing: a little of her charm, a little of her guile, more than a little of her toughness. She does not own the *Gazette*, she is simply trustee for her own lifetime. Her grandfather, Boss Pender, passed first over his own sons, and then over his granddaughter, making her custodian for "the male heirs of the next generation". There will only ever be one.

They sail in gentle motion down into London's core, mother and son separated by no more than three steps of the moving steel and wooden staircase. Ollie is gripped by a powerful sense of her own good fortune, a physical and not unerotic sensation, in which the calamity of the life of her own father, White Pender, seems somehow to emphasise the bounty which Ollie has stepped into. An alcoholic, a semi-vagrant, the butt of sub-editors' jokes in his final years, White Pender is still the nightmare from whom Ollie thanks God she has escaped. Her escape makes her shiver with gratitude. Her father shaped her attitude to men, allowed her to throw out Wilder Goode, the sponge who became her husband, equipped her to deal as an equal with the best of them in Monument. She is passing all this onto Tim, her only child, who, as she watches, wriggles downward through the people standing below him on the escalator, onto the unimpeded last dozen steps and begins to jump.

"Tim . . ."

Ollie sees Tim pitch forward, his hands like little windmills flailing for balance. She cannot utter. For the first time since she took him wet and bloody from the midwife, she cannot control what is happening to him. Tim flings out his left hand and falls face down and slides forward in this position as the stairs flatten out and are devoured by the steel teeth at the bottom.

"TIM!"

It is Ollie who drags him free. Ollie, frantic, it is who beholds Tim's young blood in its arching spout.

School is now out of the question. Eleven operations. The best man in Ireland, so small he stands on a special wooden box beside the operating table as he carves exquisite slices of Tim's buttock flesh and gums them down on the mangled hand. Ollie moves up to Dublin and into a room in the Shelbourne Hotel. By day she sits beside sleeping Tim's hospital cot so that when he awakens she can prevent him from tearing at his dressings with his teeth. By night, they strap him down.

Because Tim has only just enrolled in Binn's Street School, he has few friends other than the children of *Gazette* employees – in no way enough for a proper birthday party. His mother has a wonderful idea. She invites all the children in Demijohn Street between the ages of seven and ten to the party and hires a bus to take all of them to a picnic up in the mountains, in a place called Glane.

"Kaiser? Kaiser! What did you give me?"

Kaiser hands Tim his birthday present and watches him rip the paper off and drop it to the ground. A leather wallet. Kaiser probably nicked it from a shop on Long Quay. "Oh." Tim is surprised. He opens the wallet and sticks his pudgy fingers into folds, then rubs it against his face. "I'm going to fill this with lovely money," he says. "More than you'll ever have, Kaiser."

The bus is shiny and sleek, a bit like Tim himself, who sits up beside the driver for the trip, disassociating himself from the others. A thin boy with large, mournful eyes, not someone Kaiser has seen before, makes his way over to sit beside him and tells him his name is Albert Tell.

Ollie has gone to a great deal of trouble, for when they all march up the hill in double file, Tim again at the head of affairs, and cross a big field of fragrant meadow and reach a cottage, there are balloons tied to trees, and rocking-horses and swings and slides, and – the Demijohn Street gang cannot believe their eyes – a long table set out with more cakes, candies, buttered currant bread and more bottles of pop than any of them has ever seen. They sit down and, from instinct, begin to stuff handfuls of sweets into the pockets of their short trousers.

Tim has, by the time everyone is seated, assembled around him a few of the slower boys from Binn's Street. They all shriek with laughter everytime Tim calls down the table: "Al Tell! Al Tell!"

Glane cannot have changed much since those days. Insects beat their thousand-fold wings, slaves to the sun. Heat lies in crusts on the back of Kaiser's neck, his bare arms and head as he creeps on all-fours along the top edge of the meadow. On the cottage terrace far below, Ollie and an old woman in an apron whom Tim calls Aggie-Aggie are clearing the debris of the birthday party while Tim and his friends play hide-and-seek.

Kaiser knows with unexpected instinct that Tim – the sought – is up above the cottage, not downhill of it where everyone else swarms. Dropping, shrew-like, he burrows sideways on his elbows. Smell of the earth, down near the yellow grass stems, cool stones and micro-systems thrown into sudden disarray. With the surprise of the jungle he almost crawls on top of them. Tim's back, broad as a sail. Albert Tell, naked and bound to a slender fir tree, must have looked to Kaiser like an early Christian martyr. Albert's mouth is stuffed with his drawers, which are bound in place by his kneesocks. He sees Kaiser. Tim's concentration on his target is absolute. He has assembled a heap of small stones and one by one is pitching them at Albert's almost invisible genitals. Thwat! Each time Tim's missile hits the mark, Albert's big eyes implore Kaiser from their sockets. Thwat!

* * *

My mother came to see me last night. By the time she left, I was once more acutely aware of all the reasons I moved out of home and into a flat on my own. She wants to control me. She knows that I am seeing Kaiser and she is horrified by this fact.

"Of all the men you could find in Monument," she said.

Perhaps it's this kind of remark that reinforces my determination. I'm not going to listen to rumours or hearsay, least of all from my mother. I'm going to pursue what I embarked on and then, when I'm through, I'm going to make up my own mind.

* * *

For three years from the age of eighteen, when he leaves Demijohn Street, Kaiser lives in a converted seminary in County Roscommon. He has spoken to me at length about that time, not all of it bad. He recalled it very clearly.

Each day, he is tutored in metalwork, in rudimentary joinery, in block laying, plastering, grouting, roofing and plumbing. He is also chosen, along with a handful of others, to study book-keeping. Unlike the real world, in which matters are seldom resolved, I imagine he finds some balm in the calming symmetry of that prosaic craft, in the coolness of balance sheets, where every action eventually finds its place, where every deed, no matter how irregular, is fixed within a greater equilibrium.

Everything in County Roscommon drips: walls, gutters, the very land. Funny, but whereas words are a struggle for him, I have learned that water has remained distinct. In Roscommon it rains for ten months of that year of 1978 and in the summer, when he walks out in meadows that sink beneath his feet, he can hear the trapped water brimming up in the footprints behind him. A land of lakes and hills, it has been deserted by people. The saving of hay – or the failure to save it – is the chief reason put abroad for this forsaking: more than anything it breaks men's hearts to leave their hay ruined in the damp fields, year in, year out, so they have slunk away from all this spoiled grass and wetness.

* * *

1978

Mr Stamp has a lot of the Big Man about him: his angry face, the way he breathes. Bolted early to fat, he wears a spotted dicky and waistcoats of suede. There was once a Mrs Stamp, but she ran off with a County Roscommon farmer, it is said.

"Kaiser? Kaiser!"

"Mr Stamp?"

"Your sheet-metal project is a week overdue."

Kaiser tells him he is doing his best, that everyone else's project is behind as well.

"I'm talking to you, Kaiser, to you. And don't give me any more of that backchat or you may find yourself without a certificate at the end of this year."

There are persons on whom Kaiser has this effect, why he never knows. Even on the rare day of sunshine a shadow settles on Mr Stamp's seal-like countenance every time he sees him.

Frances works as a barmaid in the village pub to which most of the students find their way during weekends. She is tall and blonde, with a teasing smile, with one eye blue and one green, and with a musky, home-produced tang. She finds Kaiser amusing. She holds up her long fingers to tell him how much he owes her for a drink and when he smiles at her, she laughs, her incompatible eyes a-twinkle. I don't need much imagination to recount what happens next. One night, in the passage by the cigarette-vending machine, they come to a halt, buckle to buckle, and – with no more than primal instinct as justification – kiss. But come next day when he smiles her way, Frances turns her head; were it not for the singular taste of her saliva, Kaiser might well wonder if their encounter was not all in his head.

Kaiser's interest in the pre-Celtic, Bronze-Age Irishmen with whose lives he had so regaled me over lunch in December, and which began in Monument, continues in Roscommon. He learns about their daily lives, where they slept and made love, what they hunted and ate, and how they set on fire the rock faces to extract their copper. He comes to understand something of their gods, their superstitions and beliefs, their attraction to dark woods such as those at Glane. His accumulated facts, many of which he amasses in Roscommon, are too numerous to discuss here, but a flavour would include: detailed descriptions of archery equipment, including archers' wrists guards made from sewn calf hide, arrowheads barbed and tanged, how the shafts of arrows were made from birch, how the heads were bound to the shafts with gut from sheep, and the ash bows themselves, their varying lengths, decorations, weight, tensioning and accuracy in average circumstances.

Frances is going out with Ted, a farmer's son, a big, open-faced, ever-cheerful lad with red hair and the majestic, questing nostrils of an African king. Over the weekends that stretch through that final winter, Frances and Ted melt into Frances and George, and Louis, and Seamus, and Frances Butterley and Willie O'Driscoll invite you to celebrate the occasion of their marriage, on a windy day in March, but on whose eve Frances memorably baulks, leaving a caterer to sue for sixty-five portions of stuffed chicken and ham, and Frances back on the market. Yet through all her many boyfriends she has always smiled at Kaiser on the weekends he comes in, her long legs looking ever longer as a night wears on, her lap ever compact, her hair gold and sweet-scented and her eyes flickering their signals like the fore and aft beacons on a ship.

"Kaiser? Kaiser!"

I see Mr Stamp standing beside him, his face dark.

"What has this stuff got to do with book-keeping, Kaiser?"

Kaiser explains that his research into the past is just a hobby.

Mr Stamp shakes his head. "It's hard enough to ensure people like you will not be a burden on society, without having to compete with the likes of this nonsense."

Kaiser apologises.

Mr Stamp's chins quiver as he addresses the class, his sharp-edged words at odds with his wobbly flesh: "This place, for all its warts, represents the best, perhaps the only, chance you have of a decent life. But I too have my responsibilities to society, the piece of paper we issue here is me giving my word to the outside world. My word is my bond, not something I give lightly, believe me."

When Kaiser begins seeing Frances, it is like unfinished business: after all, nature's memory is there to guarantee the survival of the species, but even so, following their first night when she asks him to walk her home, they might have left it at that, their mutual curiosities indulged and the call of creation faithfully honoured. However, Frances, to be fair, is everything promised by her kiss. Need flattens all before it. In the weeks that follow they go at one another with gusto, albeit gusto circumvented by propriety. Since

Frances's family live in the village and she does not wish their alliance known, this leads to illegal hours spent in damp woods, in the hay sheds of departed farmers and, once, under the tarpaulin of Mr Stamp's lake boat. Frances, by all accounts, operates with ferocious urgency. Although she remains on the outside the same bright Frances of months before, when they are alone and her desire has been answered, she sometimes becomes fussy in small things, such as the way Kaiser speaks, or listens, or has kept her waiting. Being Kaiser, he probably outlines how the Celts cooked meat, how they made water troughs of oak and then lit fires and preheated stones in the fires and put the stones in the water to boil it: how they wrapped the meat in straw and cooked it in the boiling water. Frances, if some lingering problem from the pub continues to vex her, insists on diagnosing it, rehearsing in detail the failings of people he doesn't know. If he shows interest in her employers, avaricious publicans, she is quick to accuse him of taking sides. He tells her about the clothes worn by the Celts, loose tunics tied with toggles, tied tight around the waist with horsehair, belts set off with tassels, also of horsehair, the sleeves not sewn but fastened together by small, fine-carved and polished bows of wood. Frances is impatient with Kaiser's handicap, hates repetition of casual phrases, tries, after tiffs, to wound him by speaking bleak, grey words, as he calls them, from the side of her mouth. Often weeks go by without them seeing one other. They enact a couple of false endings, tense and tearful. Then, in the pub, at the end of mellow evenings, Frances becomes re-established as leggy, blonde and beautiful Frances, whose saliva in his memory has been replaced by her inventiveness in tight situations. And although in self-righteous moments he has forsworn her to himself, when he returns those nights alone to his room in the industrial school, and awakens at four in the grip of powerful and seductive images, it is to Frances he turns in order to toss his problem out of mind, and sleep. A

66

week later he finds himself across the counter from her, and sees her disparate eyes swimming to him over the head of a pint, and puzzles at the very notion that this tangy, desirable girl could ever have had attached to her suggestions of petulance.

Mr Stamp's certificate becomes the main concern of everyone in the class. The certificate is their only hope of a job, it will allow them to take their place in the world. Most of them there, if not from backgrounds such as Kaiser's, are from broken homes, or the homes of petty criminals, or their lives have evolved from tragedies unspoken and best forgotten. What unites them is a desperate desire to get away from the past, to be like the people who walk the streets of the village and who can dwell on the future without looking over their shoulders. Mr Stamp's certificate will be their passport.

Kaiser begins to catalogue Frances's traits. The way she always eats meat, her smoking even as she eats, her insistence that she is allergic to certain smells (petrol, coffee, anti-freeze have been mentioned), her basic parsimony, the way she shreds beer mats with her fingernails and holds her knife (like a pencil), how she never finishes a book, how his archaeology bores her, how boxing on TV consumes her interest (glistening, muscular, ebony bodies), how she refuses to accept that he really is deaf, insists that Chinese are savages and that Down's syndrome children should be terminated at birth, never washes her cup, farts in sleep then denies it, rubbishes Willie O'Driscoll, walks on the outside, is left-handed, intones. Where Kaiser believes himself joyfully spontaneous, Frances is fretful without plans. She seems to think that his efforts to engage her in philosophy are attempts to prove himself at her expense; existentialism is fodder to Kaiser. She hates mornings (dawn is his favourite time), only comes into full equilibrium with her senses at dusk, by which time as a rule he wants to crawl away and sleep. It suddenly seems that he and Frances differ not alone in every crucial respect but in every respect. Dogs for him; for Frances, cats. The Beatles versus The Doors, glass against plastic, Guinness and Murphy's, Libra and Scorpio, heaven and earth. Not only has Kaiser got a woman different from himself but a complete and opposite one; and since he respects himself in the main, he realises he can never grow fond of his antithesis.

They might proceed, who knows, as do many marriages, without boundaries of time, growing to accommodate each other like disabilities. Nor is their final parting provoked by any single incident; one weekend Frances informs him that she is going to work in England, and Kaiser, despite the undoubted joys contained between her hips, her tight, responsive breasts, her deeply lubricated mouth, and her incompatible but equally beautiful eyes that once twinkled at him with amusement, kisses her cheek and wishes her well. She tells him they are throwing a party for her in the pub and asks him if they are still friends enough for him to come to it. Kaiser assures her that they are.

"Promise me you'll come, Kaiser?"

Kaiser promises.

"'First there were the nomads who began reaching here from around 6,500 BC. Who they were is preserved in our myths. The Tuatha de Dannan, for example, brought druidism with them. They were wizards and sorcerers, high priests with great power. Blood sacrifice was major in their societies.'"

Mr Stamp looks up from Kaiser's notebook and his cold eyes linger on the class with theatrical amusement.

"'Every Samhain they took one-third of the first-born and slit their throats at a stone idol. The memory of those events still live in us. They are in our blood,'" he concludes and shuts the book.

"So. So this is what is going on here. Instead of the project that might lead to a job in sheet-metal working, you are more interested in the pursuits of savages. Is that right, Kaiser? Kaiser!"

Kaiser opens his mouth, shakes his head.

"Then what's this?"

Kaiser wants to explain, but is too slow. He shrugs, then smiles in a way he hopes may find Mr Stamp's better nature.

"Take that smirk off your face!" Mr Stamp's breathing signals big trouble. "Think this is a joke – eh?"

Kaiser shakes his head.

"So, gentlemen, Mr Kaiser looks likely, does he not, to be the first certainty among you to fail to obtain his certificate."

"Please, sir . . ."

"Perhaps the only one among you to leave here no better off than when he entered. But is anyone surprised? Really surprised?"

The class sniggers. Mr Stamp wheels.

"Two weeks remain, Kaiser," he speaks so that Kaiser alone can see the words. "No weekends off. Go near the village or put one foot out of line and the only piece of paper you'll get from me is one saying you're a moron."

Kaiser is two hours into Frances's farewell party before he remembers he is not meant to be there. All her old boyfriends have turned up, the place is thronged. Frances herself is due to sing in a moment. And then Kaiser remembers. How will he explain to Mr Stamp that his absence from the school is an oversight rather than an act of willful disobedience? It never crossed his mind that he should not come into the village. After all, he promised Frances he would be here.

Despite being the third week in May, rain is falling like sheets of zinc. He leaves the pub and begins to run. His vision becomes distorted, a function of the rain in his eyes and of his anxiety. The certificate is all he can think about. He runs on, choking. At the bend outside the village, he slips and falls down a minor embankment, grazing the left side of his face and his arms in the process. Climbing out, looking as if he's been in a brawl – this is the word used later – he lurches up the avenue. It is Saturday night and with any luck Mr Stamp will be out. Easing in the back door he walks in involuntary puddles across the kitchen. He will change, take a quick shower and be at his project within minutes. He closes his eyes and thanks God for his fortune. Halfway up the dim, back stairs the lights come on.

"Jesus Christ."

Kaiser wants to tell Mr Stamp that he can explain, although he knows that he will be unable to.

"You smell of drink. You've been in the village." Mr Stamp narrows his eyes. "Have you been in a fight? Look at the cut of you! You've been . . . fighting!"

Words won't come to Kaiser, the old problem. He struggles to get them out and into coherent fashion.

"I should have known."

Kaiser stares at him.

"I should have known, Kaiser. I was warned about you. That everything I did would be a waste of time. And now this. I gave you another chance and this is the way you treated it."

"Please . . ."

"I don't like you, Kaiser, you're too sly, can never find words when it suits you, always pursuing your own agenda, making little of the work we do here. You're not fit to represent this school in the outside world. I want you out of here. Tomorrow. I never want to see you again."

Kaiser begins to plead, but Mr Stamp turns his back and goes up the stairs ahead.

"Sir . . . please . . ."

His deaf back. Kaiser grabs him by the arm. Mr Stamp spins around, alarmed.

"Take your hand off me!"

"Please . . ."

"Take your fucking hand off me!"

But if Kaiser lets go, Mr Stamp will not listen to what Kaiser is trying to make him understand, if not by words which will not come, then through the shapes of Kaiser's intentions: that there has been no malice in his going out, that he will work right through the night if Mr Stamps wants him to, that all he wants is for Mr Stamp to hear him out.

"Jesus . . ."

"Sir . . ."

Mr Stamp swings and catches Kaiser on the left ear with his fist. Oh, the pain, not so much from the blow as from the finality of the position. Kaiser's head sings. He sees the man's mouth crammed with all the filthy words that are tumbling over each other. Then Mr Stamp hits him again. Kaiser cannot believe what is being said. He begins to cry with terror. Mr Stamp keeps pounding his head. Kaiser grabs him two-handed and flings him down the stairs. He sees him fall. He sees the noise made as the banisters break under Mr Stamp's weight and then he beholds the explosion of Mr Stamp's skull as it meets the flagged floor of the kitchen pantry and the future ebbs out in a dark pool along the cold tiles.

Seven

From the Proprietor's suite in the *Gazette* building, the tumbling sweep of the damp town, including the Lyle from above Small Quay to the first river bend, was fastened against the blue-black evening sky like a sheet of stage scenery. Outside, in the small, paved roof garden accessed through double-glazed sliding doors behind her desk, her veiny-grey hair snapped at by the wind, her broad face pearled with rain drops, Ollie Pender-Goode was striding up and down. The criss-cross of little paths through minia-ture shrubs meant that every so often she arrived back at the door to her office, where, before turning to resume her circuit, she looked in and considered me with the thoughtful gaze of a predatory animal.

All was quiet below. Only Philly Dixon was still in; as well as overseeing production, the buildings themselves were also in his charge, and in this role he prowled about at this time, checking grilles and skylights, his face wearing an anxious expression.

The Proprietor's suite, by far the largest office in the building, with its own special lift from the underground car park, and its comfortable armchairs done in chintz, its heavy curtains, its brass table lamps and its bathroom facilities, was more like the drawing room of what I imagined a country club to be like than an office. All around on shelves and sideboards were displayed framed and signed photographs, mainly of Ollie, the young Ollie with Dev (he was as tall as her, but only just), with J.F.K., with the Pope, the maturing Ollie side by side with people somewhat familiar and emitting the dull glow of their now faded celebrity. Pics too, but not as many, of Tim.

I turned my attention to the wall opposite the Proprietor's desk, where hung three portraits. Two were big, square, classical pieces in ornate, gilt frames, clearly a pair, and dominated the centre; the third was more rectangular and longer and had been hung to one side. The pair of portraits, their subjects top half alone seen, shared a common, gilt plaque, mounted on the wall equidistant between their two images:

JAMES AND EVIE PENDER

James had founded the *Gazette*, as everyone knew, sometime in the late nineteenth century. Before that, from the age of sixteen, he had worked in a Dublin newspaper, sweeping the floors around printers' upright desks and watching the speed of these men as they shucked lines of words together backwards. He had come to Monument, founded the *Gazette*, fathered a son and died in 1900.

The third painting showed a man standing, walking stick in hand, his countrified outfit that of a city man who had dressed with care for his part as the rural rambler. Portraits err on the side of flattery, but no amount of obsequiousness on the part of the artist – there was no signature – could cloak the arrogance of the subject, the disdainful eyes used to hegemony.

Beneath, the panel said:

OUR BELOVED PROPRIETOR
1881–1965

From down on Small Quay I could sense the deep steam blast of a ship's horn, indicating that her master was anxious to make that evening's tide; I could make out seagulls gliding along the contours of the water, settling in apparent contentment and watching each other with lidless, parasitic eyes; I could taste the radio

73

static coughing from the cabins of cargo ships, and imagine the voice of a pilot, guiding a vessel out to sea through the dangerous waters of the estuary.

The doors shimmered to and fro.

"Kaiser." Ollie put her mobile phone on her desk. She looked at me once more, as if seeking some sign that would impel her to a decision. She shouted, "How are you, Kaiser?"

I told her I was well.

"Good," said Ollie, in raised voice, "very good. I hear nothing but good reports." She appeared to make her mind up. "You're very good with your hands, aren't you?"

"Depends."

"I mean, I've seen some of the jobs you've done around here – not machinery jobs, I'm talking about that window you put in on the ground floor between the outer office and the filing room, for example. And you rebuilt the canopy over the loading bay last year. Why I'm bringing all this up is, I have a cottage on a property out at Glane I'd like you to do some work on – that's if you'd like to, of course. Think about it. I'll have everything you need delivered, all the materials. Glane is a lovely place. You'll like it, Kaiser."

I already knew the cottage at Glane. Apart from being familiar with it from the days when Tim had had his birthday parties up there, I had often gone for walks up to Glane and admired the workmanship of the cottage, its courses of stone, laid by men with knowing hands, its glinting granite window sills and lintels. Following the death of the artist, Mr Tom Pender, in the early 1980s, it had become derelict. Ivy had grown up the walls and into the roof timbers. The bricks in the chimney had, from lack of pointing, crumbled, causing the whole chimney to sag at a dangerous angle. Some of the window frames needed replacing and inside, where water had leaked down, the carrying beams above doorways were past salvage. This was the kind of job that came naturally to me: removing each slate, starting with the ridge, then working down, saving the slates where I could, prying the rotten lathes from the seasoned roof timbers; then, when I had cleaned those timbers down, runging the new lathes, tacking them home and rolling out long, spongy sheets of redolent felt. One evening on a weekend Jasmine came out to see how I was getting on. She liked all things old: books, buildings. As I slated, Jasmine rummaged everywhere, inside and out, lighting up with surprise if she found anything that pleased her.

"Kaiser! Look at these! Look!"

From where I sat a-straddle the roof I looked down and saw her holding up what looked like an artist's sketchpad.

"There are dozens of them," Jasmine said. "They were in the tool shed. Books of pressed flowers, writings, paintings. He must have put them in there before he died."

Later, we sat out on the little terrace in front of the cottage, watching the sun in its journey all the way to the horizon.

"I've been onto Beagle's," she said.

I looked at her. "Still . . . researching me?"

She smiled. "Yes."

"And?"

"You're a big mystery, Kaiser, that's for sure,"

That evening the wind was due west and so strong we could lean into it. Nevertheless, we walked out on the hills, tufts of heather in the air all about us. The wind skittered us along the ridges, Jasmine had to cling onto me or she'd have been blown away. When we got back inside and barred the door of the cottage, I went to make the tea but found myself aroused. I was unable to take my eyes from Jasmine and realised I was savouring her teeth again, like a man who has stumbled on a previously unconsidered aspect of sexuality. As she turned away from me and stood looking out of the window down the valley, I crept up behind her and quickly bound the rounds of her shoulders beneath my arms. She cried out in fright, a jagged, flame-red cry of terror that burned through the very walls of my heart. She freed herself from me and turned, her eyes wide. I had not meant to startle her.

"Jasmine . . ."

"You gave me such a fright, Kaiser!" She was trying to find her breath, to compose herself.

"Sorry. Sorry."

"It's OK." She brushed her hair back from her face and smiled, but I could see I had shaken her.

"Sorry."

"It doesn't matter."

"I just . . . I wanted to . . . I love . . ."

Jasmine said, "I know, Kaiser, I know."

But I'd ruined the evening, that was clear. I went home cursing myself for having been so stupid.

8

Up to last weekend I thought I was making real progress with Kaiser. I believed I was getting beyond the received wisdom of Monument – if such exists – where Kaiser is concerned, and was getting to know him for himself. I went up to Glane where he is working on the old Pender cottage. I loved just to sit and watch him work, the sureness of his hands, his absorption. He is really beautiful. Later, rummaging in a shed, I found a box with sketches and paintings. They must have belonged to old Tom Pender when he lived here. I showed them to Kaiser. He loves old things like that, anything with a connection to the past. Afterwards, as we walked along a mountain ridge, a wind got up and blew heather from the hillside. I held onto Kaiser, a good feeling. He was steady as a house. But then, when we went inside the cottage, as I was standing by the window looking down over the valley, he came up behind me without warning and caught me in a vice with both his arms. I screamed. I know that I over-reacted, but still, for that brief moment, all my former fears about Kaiser surged to the surface and I was terrified. I'm sorry now, for his sake, for the look of hopelessness that seized him when he saw my reaction to his advance.

I have a lot more work to do.

Something my mother said the other day rang a bell. We were talking about Kaiser and for some reason had gone on to discuss the Pender family, in particular old Mrs Cushy Pender. My mother

77

said: "Or Cushy Phibbs, as she was then." I had not known before that Mrs Pender's maiden name had been Phibbs. I have come across the name Phibbs, of course, in my archival work at the *Gazette*. But I am incorrigibly suspicious of my mother. I asked her if there was any connection between Phibbses and Kaiser. She hastened to say there was not, but she went funny across the eyes as she did so. It was her use of the word "then", I think, that alerted me most. Cushy Phibbs, as she was *then*.

In 1938 the Phibbs affair gripped Monument. Only one *Gazette* report at the time mentions it, but from the way you can still hear it referred to by people, there's no doubt it was an unparalleled sensation. So this is my new line of inquiry. 1938 is the date of the Phibbs affair and a key link to 1938 is provided by none other than Albert Tell. Poor, persecuted Albert. His mother, Lilly Tell (née Coad), had been Boss Pender's long-time secretary. (Her nephew, Dick Coad, still practises as a solicitor in Monument and has produced a book, *The History of Monument and District*.) From the early 1970s until 1986, Albert was the racing correspondent for the *Gazette*. Many thought he got the job only because of his mother, and yet Albert was a tireless student of form who became a handicapper *par excellence*, his most celebrated success being his spring double nap in 1982, which landed attentive *Gazette* readers with a 350–1 windfall and helped put Albert at the head of the tipsters' table in Ireland for that year.

Albert retired early due to reasons of ill health and now lives in Dublin. From my days in the library I remembered that he was the custodian of all his mother's old diaries and papers from the 1930s, which he donated to us a few years ago.

*   *   *

She can tell you more about the *Gazette* than Boss himself. A tiny, energetic figure with flaming red hair, eyes that miss nothing, and the gait, as they have it in the printing shed, of a little bantam hen. Lilly Coad works from a desk in the office beside the Proprietor's, pays the wages, brings the money to the bank and recruits or dismisses within the paper as she sees fit. No invoice is paid without passing Lilly's scrutiny. With a natural eye for value, she can cast columns of figures whilst at the same time listening to a conversation. She came to the *Gazette* from a teeming family in Balaklava, Father Whittle himself wrote her reference and recommended her as a girl of exceptional ability. By the late 1930s Boss's reliance on Lilly is complete, he signs books of cheques for her to dispense, allows her to deal with the minor grievances of employees and often has her take his place in meetings with people who want free ads put in for their charities, that sort of thing. Lilly loves the *Gazette* almost as much as she loves Boss Pender, people whisper. Lilly doesn't care what they say. She is fierce in her determination to maintain the Pender family's values, something that comes also from her own background. Tom and White, for example, will not just be functionaries garnering ads or writing facile copy. If Lilly has her way, there will be a proper connection to their father, something Lilly can orchestrate. She loves all the Pender boys. Black is so like Boss it hurts to look at him.

It is summer and the Lyle is sluggish. Either side of the narrow channel, above the ugly flats of mud, the brown banks and fields curl in the heat. It is a dead burning, people are praying for the winds that will bring the rain. Cattle are parched. No-one remembers when hay has sold so cheaply.

Hart noses the Vauxhall in between the whitewashed piers and up a narrow driveway overhung with trees. Flies dance like silver sparks where the sunlight beams through. Black Pender stretches his arms out either side of him in the back seat, a sense of lazy luxury, in the process embracing the shoulder of his twin brother; who looks over, one eyebrow arched in mock surprise and they both laugh. Despite their different colourings and their self-explanatory names, people still confuse them. Sometimes they trade on this confusion. At a dance, for example, if dressed similarly, they will test a girl's powers of observation, dancing alternate choices with her and pretending to be the same person. In dinner jackets, in the dim lights of a hall or marquee, the Pender twins are uncanny but perfect replicas of one another. It isn't true, of course. White is still and always will be the broader and by half an inch the taller. He lost a side tooth on the rugby field, but this is only apparent if his mouth is fully open. But the internal man, whoever inhabits White's handsome, eighteen-year-old body and head, is still the person whom his father, Boss, observed – or had wished there – over fifteen years before. Which has left White on the ground floor of the *Gazette* with the subs and canvassers and Black upstairs beside his father. Not that White overminds: the twins draw identical wages and down on the ground floor no-one is going to say anything if White Pender traipses in an hour late on a Monday morning or leaves early to play golf on a Thursday afternoon.

A house is coming into view as the drive curves around, a farmhouse of two storeys wrapped in winter jasmine, small windows peeping out, the hall door ajar. They make a wide turn and draw up.

"Sound the horn, Hart," commands White.

He is unable to grasp what it is that makes them different. Times were when he wished himself to be sickly like his brother used to be, for he assumed that was why their father's attention had always been for Black and he did not possess the generosity of spirit needed to allow his brother such a monopoly. The more he tried, however, to get Boss's attention, the further away he drove the old man. Then, when Black's health improved, when the outward contrast between the twins shrank, White tried, like a peeping Tom, to see what it was that set Black and him apart. He could see nothing except traits he considered faults. His brother's indulgence of fools, for example. His ponderousness. But these aside, the twin he had grown up with, eaten thousands of meals with, now looked the mirror image of and went nowhere without, this symbiosis of himself whom White ought to have understood as well as he understood himself remained for him, at core, a mystery.

"You sure she's expecting you?" Black asks.

White winks to his brother. "You bet."

It is, in the end, in their relationship with Boss Pender that their divergence is most explicit. White sees their father in no different light than do the paid hands on the *Gazette* beside whom he works – a powerful man, a distant figure, someone who operates on a higher plane, a fearful god-type whose wrath if invoked sweeps all before it.

White's ally is Lydia, their mother. If he was a person whose pleasures came from giving as well as from taking, he might see another side to his mother beyond that which he forever seeks to exploit. That side, of course, is her habitual guilt where her sons are concerned, her feeling that this fair-headed twin son's treatment by his father springs in some way from a failing in herself. She blames herself all her life for the intangible, for not having performed acts which she cannot even identify but which she thinks would have redeemed her son in his father's eyes. Unable to alter the visceral, she indulges in an unending campaign of subversive support of her son's weaknesses, diverting money to him from her household budget, lying on his behalf and, this is shameful, disparaging his twin brother when comparisons arise. White maximises the opportunities which come from this

81

ongoing agony in his mother, and in the process compounds his own defects.

But could he see Lydia Pender née Albutt other than as his accomplice, White Pender might be able to recognise the magnitude of the tragedy that his parents' marriage represents. Lydia, having met Boss in circumstances of biblical significance that day in Coleraine, has never shaken herself free from that particular disability. Everything she expected of a great man has come to pass, except his love. She is a woman who needs a connector to the outside world, a vessel that can enclose and protect her from the vagaries of fortune and runaway horses. Alas, Boss has neither the time nor the interest, not the love in other words, to nurture this needy side of his wife, and so she keeps herself in Pig and Litter, too inward looking to make confidantes, her only companions servants, and observes without even a keen sense of resentment, just numbness, the looks her husband exchanges on the stairs with girls new to the kitchen.

A terrier pup is running towards them. White nudges his brother. The dog lies on its back on the warm pebbles, pink-tongued and big-eyed in front of the open-top car.

"Oh Dev!"

As if her silks are wings so that she appears more to fly than run from house to car, stooping down, her knees now apparent through the light fabric, a young woman is gathering the pup.

"Dev?"

She looks up at White, immense blue eyes beneath a tight, blue scarf tied behind the ears, eyelashes as long as miniature brushes. Black sees their blonde tips glisten where the sun glances on them.

"Sam's name for him." She laughs. "Says neither of them are pure-breds."

She drops the dog inside, draws out the hall door. White steps out and holds his arm for her as she climbs up on the chrome

82

running board. As Black scrambles over the seats into the front, he glimpses a man's pale face staring down from an upstairs window.

The car's engine revs.

"Go to Glane, Hart," says White.

The first stretch of road plunges beneath a canopy of beech, their boles slate cool.

"My brother, John," says White.

"Miss Phibbs."

"Call her Cushy," says White.

She looks from one to the other, both in their button-down caps.

"I expect some people can't tell you apart," she says.

"What's Cushy short for?"

"Helen."

"Helen?"

"Just as Black and White are short for John and James."

White leans back and sings at the top of his voice:

> "*Only say you'll have Mister Brallaghan,*
> *Don't say nay, charming Judy Callaghan!*"

The road swings around to the east and climbs, leaving the trees and breasting the first of the many foothills. Old Phibbs was once a policeman who married late but into land. Had two children, ten years apart, then his young wife died under a wagon of hay. The son, Sam, manages the farm, but the old man is still alive there somewhere; now and then there is talk in some quarters of Monument, after drink as a rule, of "going up to settle with that old polis bastard, Phibbs". Sam, the son, keeps his own company, goes to the service held every Sunday morning in the church outside the gates of Main in the hope of finding himself a wife. A brooding, pale man with the reputation for a terrible temper.

Black is pulling back the iron gate by which one enters Glane;

Hart drives through. White makes Hart drive off so that Black has to scamper along behind, cap in his hand, mouth open. Cushy stretches back as if to catch him. He can see, flailing along, how the situation excites her. They stop and he clambers up, slouches in the front seat and pretends to be exhausted as she makes her sleeves into two fans, batting the air near his face.

The trees have shot in the new plantation, where once the track climbed as if through a forest in miniature, now it is dark and dense, twenty-five years of growth, even on a day as hot as this one there are sections of the track that are ever in gloom.

"Have a go, Hart!"

Hart looks back, his face doubtful. It is normal to park before the section where a long segment of shining white rock, maybe twenty yards in length, forms part of the steep path; although once before he did what he is now being asked to do.

"Have a go, I say!" White repeats.

Hart advances the engine to a roar, throws forward the gear lever and floors the pedal. The car sails like a long insect up the rock. Cushy shrieks.

"Don't tell the Boss!" White cries, face alight.

"Oh boy," says Black.

Hart stays with the Vauxhall when they park. Black carries the linen bag with sandwiches – egg and cucumber – and tea. White, his arm crooked for Cushy's hand, makes remarks in the paddock about the cattle that have thundered down to gawk at them, and then tells Cushy, as he lifts her up and in, that the oak trees here are known to speak with the voices of the dead.

"I told my brother you were bringing me shopping in Monument," she says, legs drawn up beneath her on the rug laid beside the pool, gazing at the rosary beads that impend from the high rocks.

"Was that him at the window?" asks Black.

"'Spect so."

"What's his problem?"

"Hates you lot."

"Oh."

"Nothing personal. He can't help it." She drags back her scarf so that her hair falls around her shoulders. "What a spooky place. I love it."

"The Lyle begins here," Black says. "Right . . ." – he flicks a stone into the pool – ". . . here."

"Then where does it all come from?"

"Good question, Mr Genius," White says.

"Its tributaries," Black replies. "This is the highest headwater."

"No thanks, honestly," says Cushy, declining another sandwich from White and lying back, a cigarette in her mouth. White's eyes flick for approval to his brother as Cushy lights up. Clouds of smoke hang like curtains in the damp atmosphere. "What exactly happens here?" she asks.

"At certain times of the afternoon, about now in fact, giant frogs with the faces of the Catholic saints crawl out from the water here and hunt for Protestant blood," White says.

"Ugh," says Cushy and blows smoke from fluted lips at the pool. "What else?"

"Not much."

"Mother was a Protestant, you know," says Black.

"Was she?" White's surprise is genuine.

"Not a subject we discuss at home," says Cushy.

"Came from Antrim," Black says. "Wonder what they're like."

"What who're like?"

"Her family."

"Like her, I suppose," says White.

"Sam talks all the time of idolatry," says Cushy, looking around her. "Good thing he can't see me now."

"It's all a load of old rubbish," White says, on his elbow beside her. "Pagan rubbish."

"You're so sure," his brother says.

"So are you."

"Don't presume," says Black. "Now pass the milk."

"Oh my God, what's that?" cries Cushy and grabs White with both hands.

Had it not moved, the high figure would be indistinguishable from a tree: tall, straight and unyielding. Black stands up.

"Come out of there, you rascal! We see you!"

"And so you should with such young eyes," Boss Pender says, stepping down beside the pool. He removes his peculiar cap with its peaks back and for'ard and inclines his head. "Miss."

"Father, we didn't think, we never imagined that you, I'm sorry if we . . ." says White, red-faced, rumbled.

"This is Miss Phibbs, Father," says Black, and to Cushy, "our father, Mr Pender."

Cushy reaches up her hand, and as she does so the gossamer of her sleeve falls back revealing the length of her bared arm, shocking white as if marble.

"Cecil Phibbs," says Boss Pender, breathing in sharply, taking her hand. "I knew your mother."

Black sees Cushy search his father's face, then take her hand away.

"More than I did," she says and crosses her legs beneath her, drawing on a fresh cigarette.

"You boys enjoying the Saturday?" Boss asks, jovial.

"Hart said you'd told him he wasn't needed," says White.

"Thought we'd introduce Miss Phibbs to Glane," Black says.

"Capital idea." Boss beams down at the trio. "No tea left for the old man?"

Black, who has often observed him like this, in particular when he wants his way, realises that White is seeing a new side of their father. White is all at once the slack-jawed employee, a different person from the man who commanded Hart. Black, who is often with Boss at his desk, who has sat beside their father in the snugs of alehouses with Boss's cronies, people like the teetotal yet convivial Mr Wise, a Jew, and Mr M. Beagle, the state solicitor, and Bernard Love, a man preoccupied with women, Black has seen his father operate. Never asks anyone for discount, pays them on the nail, expects the same from Love and Wise, who advertise their teas and hams in the *Gazette*. Trades what he had to the full, which is power. Beagle never has a quibble with what is reported on his court cases, local politicians get even-handed treatment, the town as a whole is understood with a high level of respect by Boss Pender's paper. But when he wants something – as when the *Gazette* wished to buy out its ground rents from the town, or in the matter of prompt medical attention, or being first with inside information – Boss becomes the person he is now.

"The boys tell you about this place, Miss Phibbs?" he asks, propped up on the ledge behind, hands on his tweed-trousered knees.

"Just that Prods are in danger from blood-sucking frogs," Cushy drawls.

Boss's good humour drowns, just for an instant.

"Which one said that?"

"Oh, I can't remember," Cushy smiles. "Can't tell one from the other, they're both identical in every respect as far as I'm concerned – don't you agree, Mister *Gazette*?"

Boss rocks back in stage surprise.

"Mister – what?"

"Oh dear," says Cushy and giggles. "Have I been very rude? It's what we call you at home."

"Is it indeed?" says Boss, amused, playing his tongue at the inside of his cheek. "Is it indeed?"

"You covered much ground this morning, Father?" asks Black.

"Quite a bit, most of it when you two were probably still asleep," replies Boss. "Had Hart drop me outside the gates of Main, then I walked right up to Dollan." To Cushy: "I could see the Lyle all the way out to Eillne and beyond, right into the delta and then the sea. And they tell me that there's those who don't believe in God."

"And who would they be?" Cushy asks.

"A lot of them that's beyond in America," says Boss, "people of easy virtue who don't want to think there'll be a Judgment Day. Those who fly in the face of nature. The fallen. People without shame – I've read their newspapers. I've read their books and burned them after, page by page."

Sunlight steals in through chinks in the oak canopy.

"Which of you two made Hart bring the car up this far?" Boss asks the boys, his eyes black as olives.

White runs his tongue across his lips.

"I think Hart himself suggested . . ." he begins.

"I did," says Black. "Thought, what's the point of a car if you have to walk?"

Boss throws his head back, laughing. "Damn right too, if you'll pardon me, Miss Phibbs. A machine is only as good as what you can get out of it, eh?"

"I'm hopeless with machines," Cushy says, "I'd be a disaster in a business."

"It's the men, not the machines, Miss," says Boss. "I've read storybooks, you know, that say one day man will be replaced by a machine. That's sacrilege. Man is made in God's image. Is God a machine? Was the man the Jews nailed to the cross not flesh and blood? Yes, by golly He was. Not a machine, that's for sure, not by a long shot."

Sun has found its way through directly on to Cushy's face. She stretches like a cat.

"So the Phibbses talk about me at home, eh?" Boss says, jocular. "What do you say about me, Miss Phibbs?"

"Oh, you wouldn't want to hear," says Cushy, eyes closed.

"Oh yes, I would."

"You sure?"

Black has never seen his father teased before. It arouses him.

"Yes, I'm sure," Boss says, clearing his throat. "Tell me."

"Just how rich you are," Cushy says and smiles. "Sam used to wonder what it would be like to be so rich."

"You can tell him that money is nothing," Boss says.

"Not when you have so much of it," says Cushy.

"We mustn't keep Hart," says Black, moving to gather up.

"Sam says there are people who think money can buy anything," Cushy says.

"And do you believe him?"

It seems to Black that they are aware only of each other.

"I believe everything my big brother tells me," Cushy says.

Boss stands up, takes off his cap again, inclines. "Get these young bloods to take you in and see the *Gazette* being printed," he says. "Gets the blood moving, that. Every issue is a new birth." He put back on the cap. "Miss Phibbs. Boys. Cheerio."

Watching his father stride away, soon lost in the trees, Black can imagine how, as a young man, his father must have charmed the ladies of his day.

89

Nine

During that last February as Love's whistle blew for one o'clock Jasmine and I would meet outside the front door of the *Gazette* and walk out to Dudley's Hill, wolf whistles flying like darts through the air behind us. We liked to be along the river, down below Church's warehouses and out on the banks, which in a few strides turned into countryside from where we could watch birds, flying in tight packs just inches above the water. I told Jasmine about the problems I had put behind me, about the times I had had to go away and the years I did not want to remember. Jasmine told me about herself. She was the youngest of Mrs Rice's four children. The other three – a daughter and two sons – lived in England and in Dublin. Her father had one night taken the Fishguard boat without bothering to mention he was going. At the start he came back every few years like a landlord inspecting his property, in this case his little girl. A big, handsome man, spoke with a strange accent, brought her gifts and promised he'd soon be back for good. For a week after he'd gone Jasmine used to cry herself to sleep.

"You ever see him now?"

"He last came here when I was fourteen."

"Sorry."

"Yep."

With my thumb I wiped away her tears.

"Thank you, Kaiser," she said and kissed me.

When she spoke about her mother, Jasmine often became restless.

"She's a very difficult woman to live with. Not that I live with her any more – believe me, I couldn't. Side by side with that, she has a heart of pure gold. She'd die for me. She's a perfectionist. Look at her shop. What's more perfect than a flower?"

Jasmine's eyes found the middle distance.

"They say history always repeats itself. Her own parents were separated – her father was a sailor, her mother had been a teacher and got jobs bringing up other people's children. Worked here and there, mainly in big country houses around Monument. A bitter woman, by all accounts, who always considered herself above the people she worked for. There's more than a bit of her in my mother. I mean, what does my mother go and do? She goes and marries a man who walks out on her – just as her own father did."

A sea-going freighter glided down-channel, nuzzling the river into silky folds.

"I suppose she had to be hard on us. It's not easy for a woman on her own bringing up four kids. It goes without saying we'd no money, except for the scraps we'd get sent from my father and the children's allowances. So she went and started a flower stall in MacCartie Square. The first day she went down there one of her neighbours lent her a wheelbarrow and she wheeled it all the way down and filled it with flowers. In her mind it was a huge thing for a woman in her position to do. Her mother had had fierce notions about herself, and although she was now dead, here was her daughter selling bunches of primroses by the side of the street."

Jasmine rested her head in her hand so that the light caught the angle of her raised cheekbone.

"We all helped. After school every day. All day Saturday from as soon as I could walk. We had to carry all the flowers from the railway station to MacCartie Square, and then bring them all home that night. She'd be up at six in the morning, getting us ready, pinching the flowers out to their best, loading up her handcart."

Jasmine smiled.

"When I was twelve she took a lease on the shop next door to the one she's now in. Eight years later she bought her own premises. But the woman whose husband walked out on her over twenty years ago is still the same, she is still up at six every morning, her house is swept and polished by seven, her shop is open half an hour before anyone else's. She smokes sixty cigarettes a day and a hundred on weekends if she goes out for a drink. You couldn't live with her. No wonder my father went away. And yet, Kaiser, if I had a big problem in my life, if I needed something very badly, or if I was in big trouble, I think I'd go to her. Because no-one would fight more fiercely for me. God help her enemies and God protect her friends."

I watched Jasmine cut the gluey, weeping stems from daffodils and hand them to Mrs Rice. No matter how hard she worked in the *Gazette* or was tired of an evening, Jasmine was never tense in the same way as she was in her mother's flower shop. Her face was a set of concentration, devoid of other expression. If she missed a beat in her delivery, her mother's failed expectations would be shown in a tiny gesture of impatience, such as the raising of the corner of one eyebrow, or a flick of ash, or a break in her even breathing, any of which would make Jasmine recoil as if she had been slapped.

"The Santrys were always great people for flowers," Mrs Rice observed, as if drawn by daffodils to other memories. "I bought dafs from Mrs Rosa Santry every spring for years, she'd load up the back seat of her car with them and carry them in here to me herself. Invited me out to Main, any time I liked. Not that I went, but she knew I liked horses, that I'd been brought up with them. A lovely woman, she could have been a film star. Of course there's no shortage of talk about her and Chud Conduit, but whose business is that, I ask? Not mine. The Santrys seem to be happy and there are few who can claim that, believe me."

Jasmine dipped for a fresh armful and the bare small of her back, a delicious indentation, was on display to me for an instant.

"Her son is a very different kettle of fish," Mrs Rice continued. "His grandfather Bensey wrote out a cheque for £100,000 – which even now is a lot of money, think of what it was then – and bought Beagle's for Kevin Santry. Old Mr M. never had a chance to spend the money, though, God rest him." She looked over at me, her eyes searching. "Do you remember Mr M., Kaiser?"

Jasmine's attention was on her daf stems. I shook my head.

"The state solicitor. Are you sure?"

I saw Jasmine shoot out a glance from her place at the bench. "How is Kaiser meant to remember something that far back?"

Mrs Rice turned her back to me and I could see that she was saying something to Jasmine.

Jasmine cried out, "Mother!"

Mother and daughter froze over the mounds of green butts on the workbench. Jasmine's expression contained an intensity new to my experience, whilst her mother went through an elaborate process of shock at her daughter's tone, followed by grievous offence.

"I do beg your pardon," Mrs Rice trembled. "I was merely trying to make polite conversation, but I can see that my efforts are not appreciated."

10

I've begun to see Kaiser again. We have put the incident in Glane behind us and every other day now we go for walks at lunchtime down along the river. For someone with such bad hearing, he's a wonderful listener. I found myself telling him about my father and my childhood. We sat on the river bank as a boat went downstream and I told him how I used to cry myself to sleep as a child, wishing Daddy would come home.

Kaiser said, "I'm sorry, Jasmine," and then he wiped my tears.

Through Lilly Coad's diaries, I am beginning to form a distinct picture in my mind of how people like Cushy Phibbs must have thought and reacted to events in 1938. Lilly wrote everything down: appointments, telephone conversations, expenditures. At the end of each day, in a pocket-sized green, velvet-covered diary with a brass clasp, one for each year, Lilly entered a record of that day's events. The world she describes is in many ways an idyllic one. The people she wrote of can have had little idea that it was all about to end.

*　　*　　*

LILLY'S STORY

1938

Black learns from his father not only charm but the anatomy of business and how to lead men, how to drink, how to be tough with friends and not lose them. White learns none of these things. What

94

charm he has is superficial, he will always be led in a business about which he will learn nothing, he drinks like the other subs and canvassers to get drunk, and if he is crossed in drink, or out of it, he nurtures the grievance into immortal hate. At first girls prefer him to Black, attracted to his seeming cavalierness; but when they discover there is no more to him, they make their retreat.

Black's love for his father has been well-established – for what son would not reciprocate the passion his father had shown that night years before when they had driven up to Glane in snow? Black's love has developed into deep admiration for Boss's achievements, the considerable scope of the Pender family in Monument, the serious commitment to the duties of inherited privilege and worth. He sits by his father's side as Boss writes the editorial – the "we", prerogative of kings and country editors. No-one knows Boss Pender, it is said, like his son John, known as Black, but even Black acknowledges that his father's mind sometimes defies knowing. You might think you knew what he was thinking, but then he comes up with the most unexpected suggestions or approach. Such a versatile brain. Even Ma Church, whom many say has the quickest mind in Monument, concedes she has no grasp of business like Boss Pender.

"Your father terrifies me."

Black is smiling at Cushy. He loves her ability to put on an act, a kind of courage he has not come across before.

"I would never have guessed."

"I just play the tart with men like him." She blows smoke at the river. "Unsettles them. Didn't you notice? He went on the defensive straight away, huffing and puffing about easy virtue and hell's fires. Funny how some men are afraid."

In the two weeks since Hart drove the Vauxhall up to Glane they have met twice, each time as now at the place where Small Quay joins Long Quay, where trawlers dock and unload their

95

catch. Black has mentioned it to White, offering his brother the chance to assert his position which comes from having met her first; but White managed to turn a seeming indifference into an illustration of his own lack of taste.

"She'll tease you until your cock falls off," was his response.

She is, Black knows, someone who thrills him by her outward lack of regard for the conventional, yet a deeper, calmer side to Cushy emerges when there are only the two of them, a woman with a keen mind and a good sense of where the right balance lies in an argument. She is vivacious in her point of view, the effect of which is to make her beautiful. No woman Black has met has been possessed of such perfect limbs; when Cushy walks down the quay-side with him, parasol on her shoulder, people turn their heads.

"Do you *want* to step into his shoes?" she inquires.

"I have two other brothers."

"I know, I've met one."

"You haven't met Tom, the eldest of us."

"You like him, I can tell from the way you've just said his name."

Black narrows his eyes as sun glistens on the tin hull of a belching mud dredger. Towards Tom he feels a great duty, something to do with knowing that although Tom Pender is his nine-years-older brother he, Black, is the one who will have to make do for all of them.

"Yes. Very much."

"Some men would be ashamed to say that."

He laughs, thinks of Tom, the decent plodder, his big, guileless face as he cadges advertisements from Monument's shopkeepers.

Cushy asks, "Do you *love* your newspaper?"

"I know what I love," he says, eyes ahead.

"Really."

"Yes, really."

"Hmm, how interesting." She intercepts the smile tugging his mouth. "I'm being serious!"

"So am I."

By one of the Church warehouses slings of jute bales swing through the air and drop to gangs of bare-chested dockers.

"That first time in the mountains, at the pool. You didn't seem as convinced as your brother White that all the old stories about the magic of the place are poppycock."

"I'm not."

"Any good reasons?"

"Just one."

As he begins to tell her, he isn't sure where the story about him having been brought up to Glane is coming from, in the sense that it is not an event he can ever remember discussing with Boss in recent years, or even growing up – he does not understand how he knows the details. It is as if he is describing something miraculous about a sick child to whom he has no connection, another person. He cannot put himself back in the position he is recounting, nor see his father then as a younger man, nor remember the details that are part of the narration. Yet he knows everything as one knows a creed, the words come to his tongue from long-laid down beliefs and his assurance in his own, marvellous history is beyond challenge. By the time he has finished they have walked all the way back to the end of Small Quay. Cushy makes her parasol fit both their heads, hiding them from the town.

"That was beautiful," she says, and kisses him.

Black falls in love truly at that moment. He will, for as long as he lives, cherish his sense of happiness, and the pleasure that came from sharing the precious, and the peace arising from the sudden certainty of the future.

All business in Monument ceases for August 15th, the Feast of the Assumption of the Blessed Virgin Mary – after early Mass, for the weather is good as a rule, people swim downriver from the town, and lie out on the banks, or bicycle up into the mountains or out to Eillne or to Leire or to Sibrille, where they set out picnics on the scalding rocks and watch the sea through veils of heat. Beginning six years before, so as to establish some traditions before the boys grew into men, Lilly has always arranged a picnic for the holiday and, with the authority that he expects her to exercise, has told Boss that he too must come, an obligation he accepts. No point in suggesting it to Mrs Pender, for if she came he wouldn't, Lilly knows, and the whole point is to get him out for the day with Tom and White. Black too, of course, not that that is needed – but this is a *family* day. Lilly had made up the first picnic, and come with it. Another tradition. August 15th is a day of holy observation.

The presence in the car of Miss Cushy Phibbs, when they pick her up, gives Lilly mixed feelings. Jealousy is one, she admits, chiding herself at the same time; still. A mother might be jealous in the same way, seeing her fine young boy divert his attentions to another woman, and Lilly is mother on the Feast of the Assumption. There is, too, the discomfort that comes from six people squeezing into the big car along with Hart. Boss doesn't seem to mind. He sits in the back with Black, White and Tom, Lilly and Cushy go in the front.

They are driving out to Glane. Although the town seemed baked of life, as soon as they reach the foothills breezes play down between the channels of the trees and rinse their faces.

"Hardly today, Hart," Black says as the white bone of the rock in the track appears.

White laughs. "She can do it."

"Not with this load," says Black.

"You'll all have to use the legs God gave you," Boss says.

Lilly has had everything wrapped and packed into two wicker hampers. Black and Tom take one, White and Hart the other.

"Not the wood," White says. "It's too dark."

"The cottage, then," Black says. "Father?"

"Very well."

"Everyone, please, a moment!"

Lilly has taken out from her bag a box camera in a velvet case.

"Oh Lilly!"

They put down the hampers.

"Around the car, please," Lilly says. "Miss Phibbs."

"No, this is a family photograph," Cushy says.

"Today you're part of the family," Black says. "You sit in." He opens the passenger door and Cushy climbs back into the front seat.

"Tom, stand here. Push over!" White is standing with his chest puffed out, his white linen suit, his white teeth.

"Mr Pender, you go around the back please."

"Lilly . . ."

"Just for a moment." Lilly goes back a step. "Now I can't see you."

"Take the wheel, Father."

"Hmmph."

Cushy gets out, Boss climbs into Hart's seat, a place he has never been before, and Cushy gets back in beside him. Boss places his left arm along the back of the leather.

"Good!" Lilly cries.

Hart leans in to polish the headlamp just as Lilly presses the shutter lever.

Cushy, legs crossed beneath her, is peeling an apple. She is sitting a little to one side on a corner of the shaded rug, angling the knife so as to get the skin to fall all of a piece. The others are discussing the use of photographs in newspapers, or rather, listening to their father laying down his opinion on the subject – that in the future there will be more photographs than newsprint – hardly a picnic topic. The secretary woman, like Cushy, is also sitting a little apart,

99

but attentive to every word. Hart, the driver, has wandered up behind the cottage, a sweet retreat with granite sills and lintels, but rough inside, Black has said, a place woodmen use to cook their meals or to shelter in if snow cuts them off in winter.

"Consider Balaklava," Boss Pender is requesting his three sons. "Balaklava can't read, in the main. But they can see photographs, they can understand a composition with the Lyle in the background and Oscar Shortcourse selling his fish on Small Quay."

The lads laugh.

"That's what'll make 'em buy! *That's* what I mean by the coming revolution!"

Insects drone and click, but otherwise, as if the heat has blanket-like stifled all other sound, behind the dronings and clickings and the soft voices of the men, a huge silence grips the afternoon. It reminds Cushy of another summer. Had apparently been standing in the yard that day when the loaded wagon wobbled in, no memory whatsoever, a blessing everyone said. Was it? Cushy often wonders. She once thought that she had an image of her mother, fair-haired like herself, smiling over her – which had to be before it happened. Then a blank. She would have preferred to risk not having the blessing and be able to remember what she must have seen that day. But nothing exists of it for her, not even the aftermath, or her father's grief, for the child had been removed at once, even before he came home off duty.

Brought to Dublin, to his two sisters, the Misses Phibbs, maiden ladies in a good red-brick house in Ballsbridge. 1924. One was tall and nervous, the other small and nervous. Had never recovered from the day of the telegram six years before, "His Majesty the King offers you his personal condolences," it had occupied the central position over the mantelpiece, a dreadful moment framed and hung, he had had sandy hair and had been known as Bob. Cushy's father was, in fact, their step-brother, their senior by more than twenty years. Sent up money from Monument for Cushy's keep. Such was the high state of the Misses Phibbs' anxiety that when Cushy was seven they sent her to a boarding school 500 yards distant in Ballsbridge. Couldn't bear the day-to-day responsibility. One of them, the small one, died from pneumonia and was buried six weeks before Cushy was told.

All of which made her father a man with the same name as herself but little more. Once only he came to see her, up in Dublin for an agricultural show, brought her a heavy box wrapped in silver paper. A big, stubborn-looking man, the policeman's way of looking at you. When he had gone she unwrapped the gift and found that he had bought her embroidered linen table napkins. The fact that he suffered a stroke in 1929 – put down to the stress of being one of the few R.I.C. men who remained in Monument after independence; bullets in the post – meant little to Cushy, whose school holidays were spent in the homes of schoolfriends or with the surviving Miss Phibbs. She knew that Sam, her brother, already a man, had taken over the running of the farm, quite a respectable enterprise of ninety-seven acres by then, land had been added over thirty years, although people often wondered aloud where the old policeman had got the money. And then, just a year before, Cushy's schooldays had come to an end and she had come home because there was no place else.

"Home" was a word. She was expected to wash and shave her father, something that all but made her swoon, but Sam let her know of all the years' work that had gone into her schooling and now she could at least replace the woman from Deilt who did for them. Hated her brother for that, but not as much as she hated the man whose daughter she was. She had known nothing of the male body before, now she despised it. The crevices. The dead white flesh like baker's dough. He couldn't speak but somehow preserved his authority in a low, brute-like groan.

She found in her brother a man with almost no resources. Twenty-seven years old, a decade her senior, could scarcely read and couldn't write more than his name. Had never been further than thirty-five miles from home. Low sized – from their mother – but strong, he was cruel to farm animals. Burned for the want of something – what? Companionship, a woman. Not just any woman, but someone from the same background as himself – a landed Protestant, in other words. The highlight of his week was Sunday worship in the church at the gates of Main, to which he turned out in the same greasy brown suit, brown shoes well-shone, and doffed his cloth cap at every marriageable woman who passed him. He was a joke, of course. In the end, all he could count as his own was the house and the farm and his belief that, as a Protestant landowner, he was superior to all Roman Catholics, whom he referred to as mackerel snappers.

Cushy cuts the apple. She longs to get out. She doesn't regard her duties as obligations and has no intention of ending up as a housekeeper for her father and brother. Religion means even less to her than her family, which clears the way of a major obstacle. Now she is concentrating on trying to see if the son in this case can be truly separated from the father.

"Newspaper talk."

Black is sitting beside Cushy on the rug as Lilly begins putting away cups and plates in the baskets. Boss Pender is looking at his pocket watch.

"It's so lovely up here."

"I think I used to want to be a shepherd, just so I could live in this cottage."

"You still could be."

He looks at her and she savours the difference in his eyes from his father's. A matter of intent.

He says, "Let's stay awhile."

Hart has come up and shouldered one of the baskets, White and Tom take the other.

"Very well, but tea at six sharp, mind!" says Boss, working his lip beneath his moustache, a little display of disapproval.

Black and Cushy stand and watch as the group, suddenly small in the meadow below, climb through the "V" of the white boulders. Lilly's concerned face looking back up. And White's voice, bell clear despite the distance:

> "*Only say you'll have Mr Brallaghan,*
>   *Don't say nay, charming Judy Callaghan!*"

Black takes out a tin box with cigarettes.

"What do you think of us?" he asks, blowing smoke every way.

"I haven't thought about you much," Cushy says.

"My father likes you."

"Oh?"

"I can tell. He wouldn't have come today unless he liked you."

"May I see the cottage?" asks Cushy.

A wall of stone and mortar separates the cottage from the field. They walk around to the back, where beside an iron gate there is a stile of smooth, slender rocks set like pegs into the stonework. He goes over first, then stands, his arm held for her, which she takes for a moment, then skips ahead of him to the low back door. She expects it to be heavy and creak, but it swings out on good, oiled hinges. Something Cushy finds disconcerting. As if, she thinks, everything one encounters is an extension of the *Monument Gazette*.

"Ow!"

Black's hand to his head where it met the door lintel.

"Let me see."

"It's nothing."

"Let me see."

Already there is a wren's egg, rising.

"Sit down and I'll find some water."

Each of the two small windows are open shutters on a dazzling, rectangular world. Straw in a corner, in the shape of a cot. Cushy finds, back near the door, a stone well, brimming softly from its centre, the action of the spring breaking the water's surface like pouting lips. She unwinds her scarf and folds it pat, plunges it into water.

"Just sit still."

She holds the wrung scarf to his forehead, sees the innate structures of his face, the bridge of his nose, the contours of each pore and cuticle. His hand on her neck. They kiss as she continues to press the wet swab, realises she has never tasted someone's tongue.

"Cushy."

Not so much passion as exhilaration sweeps her, the prospect of sudden freedom, an unfolding of future time unconsidered before now. Black stands up and, kissing all the while, lifts her and carries her over to the straw.

"Wait."

She wants, then, to have it done in a way she will later look back on and be proud of. Nothing hole and corner or furtive. She stands up and unfastens her dress at the back of the neck and allows it drop. She slips off her chemise and knickers. Unclips her hair. Kneels.

"Cushy."

She wants him to see her as she is, inviolate, for her aspirations involve no other person and every step they take together will be a first for both of them. Black stands and goes to the windows, which he shutters; then he takes off his own clothes and bids her stand up so he can spread his shirt and jacket on the straw. Cushy, for the first time ever, has a sense of only herself mattering, by which she includes Black, itself a wondrous extension; but answerable to no-one, whether maiden aunts or friends or the rules of schools or the prudishness of her brother. She feels at once given up and in control, a contradiction if she tried to analyse it, but plausible. He strains against her, his mouth tireless. Cushy kisses him and sees the wings of his strong shoulders and the deep dive of his back. It occurs to her that he is as different from his twin as two men can be. He whispers all the while, mainly her name, but also words telling her he loves her, to which she says, "Ssssh," frightened by the sheer possibilities, some old shibboleth she's picked up, she has no idea where, that to voice the sublime hastens its destruction. She lets him on, his ever-more frantic caresses, reminds her of a colt, but stops him short, penultimately, saying, "Don't ruin it," not from any sense of doubt but because she wants that done in a proper bed not on a pile of chaff. He spends himself anyway, and she uses the scarf again, and then they lie together and, although she doesn't at first believe it, he goes to sleep.

Later, she opens one of the shutters. The sun drenches him, his golden face. It is a moment Cushy will never forget. With the certainty of youth, she believes she will always remember that stone shepherd's hut for its moment of beauty.

* * *

FEBRUARY 16TH

I've been speaking a little to Kaiser about my mother – not that I've given him any hint about her attitude towards him, but I wanted to talk to him and tell him how I felt. So I told him about how my father left home, and how my mother set up the flower stall in MacCartie Square and how we her children helped her. Why did I tell him all this? I think that's what you do when you love someone: you want them to know everything about you, the good bits and the bad. Kaiser, of course, has told me about his bad times – but there is so much he doesn't know, or can't remember. Which is another reason I'm keeping going, trying to find out what it is about him that my mother is so anxious to conceal.

I all but overlooked my discovery of a few weeks ago in Glane. Now old Tom Pender's sketchpads and exercise books have thrown fresh light on the matters under consideration. Tom, who never married, was a private, artistic man and rarely went near the *Gazette,* with the exception of a few months in the early 1960s when his father became indisposed and he worked as *pro tem* editor. During that short time he surprised the staff with his knowledge of local history and his recall of past people and events. His must be a gentle narrative.

* * *

TOM'S STORY

1938

His days are spent in dreaming. Often when he is meant to be around town, portmanteau beneath his arm, garnering advertisements for his father's paper, he is down along the river banks, searching the hidden places for flowers, whose heads he presses between the pages of his notebook. At home, later, he crayons their likenesses into a sketchpad. He sees the river and the town differently from his father, his brothers. They perceive only the uses to which Monument and the Lyle can be put, but Tom has always been suffused with the deep beauty of the place, the wonder of the mountains, the diversity of the flowers and birds and insects and the reflection of light on water. It is this translucent magic that he tries to capture in the sketchpads. He sees the crest of a river wave shot through with a spear of sunlight and he wants to keep the moment for ever.

He loves his father, but his nature does not allow him to tell Boss how much he dislikes the chores he is obliged to perform. His confidences are spread around between the shopkeepers and offices of Monument, where he presents his shy face once a fortnight to ask for their notices, and in response to questions allows small portions of his secrets – but never enough for anyone to form a complete picture – to emerge. So some of them know about his pressed flowers and more about his crayon books and still more, those whom he believes are interested, share his thoughts about his walks out at Glane, or about the idiosyncrasies of the other people he has canvassed that day, or about the men he has met with his father, or about his mother's health. She is a concern of Tom's. He sees her growing paler by the day in the big, dark house on Pig and Litter.

An August so benign that Monument could be forgiven for feeling blessed. The loggerheads in politics between Ireland and Britain, the great new wealth reported from America, even the occasional skirmish on the northern border of the new Free State seem of no consequence to the port town south of the Deilt mountains, fed and watered by its river, at peace. The grain comes in so dry it goes straight to processing. Money for farmers. They drive into town and go shopping in Love's for their teas, or in Shortcourse's for their meat or in any one of a dozen outfitters for the quality winter clothing advertised in the *Gazette*. Monument hums. Only those forever given to complaint say it is time for a good clean wetting.

Boss compliments Lilly about the picnic, a surprise to Tom since he thought his father had been edgy that day, didn't speak a word all the way home, but now, two days later in his office, as Lilly arranges his post in front of him, Boss says: "Must do that again, Lilly."

Music to Lilly's ears, of course, Tom knows, since he understands how much it means to her to get his father and the boys together. Tom thought Miss Phibbs's presence had put an end to that, and the fact that she and Black had not come home with them was another fact he knows Lilly did not approve of, believing that family outings of that kind should end as they began. The reason too for his father's homeward silence, Tom believed. But now, evidently not. "Must do that again." How wrong one could be.

So this last Friday afternoon in August has been put aside, the boys informed, including Black, although he has been hard to find these hot afternoons, Tom has twice seen him down on Small Quay, bicycling out towards Deilt. Miss Phibbs, Tom is sure.

He hears Lilly checking the proposal with Boss, making sure she has not picked it up wrong.

"Shall we be bringing Miss Phibbs, sir?"

"Just like the last time, Lilly. Just like the last time."

"I'll see that she expects us."

He is a funny man sometimes, his father. Tom often feels he does not know the old man at all, that sometimes he is like a stranger. From being close to his father, Tom can tell the moments when the stranger appears. It happens across the eyes. As if some other person has, for the duration of several seconds, taken over his father's soul, someone whose mouth ebbs from the determined straight line of Boss Pender's to a weaker, more curling config-uration. The father sees his son with coldness if at all when this occurs. And then in another moment they are back to the galleys or the columns of figures that make up the *Gazette*'s circulation. The change produces in Tom an instinctive caution, no lessening of love or admiration but the rooting of a basic concern, as one reacts to an emerging disability in any loved one, a hedging against future, unspecified events.

"I've ordered Hart for one o'clock," Lilly tells Boss.

Friday is a good day, the court isn't back sitting yet, none of the main page layouts is ever done till a Monday morning. Lilly tells Tom she reckons his father liked the tongue sandwiches from the last day, she saw him eat six or seven of them, so she is going to go up herself to Balaklava and will have Shortcourse's press her two fresh, calves' tongues, she will even bring a knife with her for the butcher to sharpen. On Friday morning at half-past eight, Boss and Tom have their breakfast together in the upstairs dining room. It is served to them by the new girl, Agnes, only fourteen or fifteen, who speaks with a slight hesitation. Tom likes Agnes already, finds her good-natured and eager to learn.

Boss has an appointment with the bank; he goes there straight from Pig and Litter and brings Tom along.

The manager of the Monument branch of the Munster & Leinster Bank is stooped and wispy-haired, wears winged collars and goes by the name of Dodd. Now he stands a sherry decanter and two little crystal glasses on the red leather of his partner's desk, unstops the slender decanter and fills the glasses with the oily amber liquid.

"To good health," says he.

"And good fortune," says Boss and raises his glass.

"Aaaagh," goes Mr Dodd with satisfaction. He has small, clever eyes. He enjoys above all this ritual with his successful clients when the business is concluded. "This young man will be as tall as you soon, Mr Pender."

Boss glances at Tom. "Ay. I'd like to see him flesh out a bit, though."

"Time enough, time enough," chuckles the bank manager. "Isn't this weather just a tonic?"

"We're going on a picnic later," Boss says. "Meself and the boys. Lilly arranged it. You know Lilly Coad."

"To be sure, to be sure," says Mr Dodd. "Sure, you could give her the keys of the paper and go away for a month and she'd run it for you. Where will ye go?"

"Ah, up to Glane, I'd say," says Boss. He consults the slim watch, once his father's, which lives in the lower pocket of his waistcoat. "Mustn't delay, as a matter of fact. Due off at one from Pig and Litter."

They stand up and finish their drinks.

"From our point of view, work away," says Mr Dodd, dropping his voice and using their proximity and the little glow of camaraderie given off by the sherry to press Boss Pender's arm. "Work away! Machines are the way to the future. Don't ever be short."

"Good to know who your friends are," Boss says and they shake hands.

"Without a doubt," Mr Dodd nods. "To be sure." They walk together out the pink-veined marble floor of the bank to the street door where Hart sits waiting in the Vauxhall. "I envy you Glane on a day like this," are Mr Dodd's parting words.

The bank was in MacCartie Square. Hart is told to go to Pig and Litter. He drives them up through Moneysack and across Milner's Street. It is ten to one. Tom wonders if the others might be waiting in the *Gazette*, he has heard Lilly making the arrangements; but although it is on the tip of his tongue to say so, he never does. Parking on Dudley's Hill in the usual place opposite the entry to Pig and Litter, Hart gets out.

"Go in and tell them we're here," Boss says from the back seat. To Tom, "You see that Mr Dodd? A glass of sherry, a pat on the back? A nice man, don't you agree? But d'you think he'd like me if it wasn't for my money? Never let a bank manager inside the door of your house. They're worse than the Jews that crucified Christ. Scum of the earth, every man Jack of them, never forget that as long as you live. Eh?"

Hart was back.

"Just the missus," he says.

The shrill whistle for one o'clock sounds from Love's yard

down on Small Quay. Boss checks it with his watch, puffs air.

"One o'clock is one o'clock," he says. To Tom, "I'm going to give these bucks a little lesson in punctuality. You get out and wait here for them. I'll send Hart back for ye. Hart!"

Tom gets out and stands by the roadway as his father is driven down Dudley's Hill. Then he makes his way to Candle Lane.

They wait until ten to three; Lilly cannot prevent them opening the hampers. At last Tom sees the car. He remembers the time because he asks Lilly, "What time is it?" and she tells him. Hart is perspiring.

"Where in blazes have you been?" Black demands.

"In Glane," the driver says. To Lilly, "You'd all better look smartish. He says there'll be hell to pay."

"Why did you go without us?"

"We waited – at Pig and Litter."

"Lilly?"

"I'm sure I said here," Lilly says. "What about Miss Phibbs?"

"We picked her up," says Hart.

There is a further delay of fifteen minutes whilst they find White – for Lilly doesn't dare alter the formula from "just like the last time, Lilly".

"What's the form like, Hart?" asks White, getting in up front beside the driver.

"Good," Hart says. "Had me drive up the rock."

"Had you *what?*"

"Drive up the white rock."

"I don't believe it!"

Tom says, "He can't be too bad, so."

"What did Miss Phibbs think?" asks Black.

"I think she liked it," Hart replies.

The full heat is gone from the afternoon as Black leaps out to the road gate; three-forty.

"Go on, Hart!" he cries, leaping in.

The long car winds uphill through the pines, stones rattling against the underbody. A kestrel rises from the path in front of them, from a clump of brown fur and raw flesh, the way of all nature. Tom is apprehensive. He has thought of discussing with Black the small but significant side of Boss's character that Tom cannot rationalise, that side of Boss that has made of their mother a nervous relict of the young woman in framed photographs, taken outside the cathedral.

As soon as they see Boss, striding downhill on the path beside the white rock, Tom knows that he was right to hedge his optimism. Their father's face is as dark as the deep recesses in the woods on either side. Hart pulls up. Boss raises his stick and brings it down full force across the bonnet of his car.

"Is this the respect you have for me?" he shouts. "Is this the way you treat my offer of a nice day out?" He is purple. Stick aloft, he drags open the front door. "Get into the back!"

White, eyes wide, scrambles in on top of Black, Tom and Lilly.

"Get me home," Boss hisses, "before I lose my reason." He turns. "I'm sure it's not your fault, Lilly, I'm sure it's these fellas tom-acting around. But you know how precious time is, you know how I insist on just a few things in life and time is one of them."

Hart, turns, inches back downhill.

"Father . . ." begins Black.

"What do *you* want?"

"What about Cushy?"

"Hah!" Boss shakes his head. "Took herself off home by foot an hour ago, couldn't be bothered waiting any longer, no more than me."

"I'd like to go and find her. Pull in, Hart."

Boss swings around, his whole madness gathered in the thrust of his face. "You'll come home with me, now, Mister," he hisses, "along with these two wretches and you'll work for the rest of this afternoon and for tomorrow too, because you have to understand one day that all this –" he makes a wild gesture "– doesn't come from gallivanting around woods after some lassie who's gone home because you let her down, all this comes from work, work, work – and from the grace of Almighty God, Our Lord Jesus Christ. Do you hear me?"

Black, ashen, cannot speak.

Boss turns back to face the valley. They go down.

And when on Sunday afternoon Black rides his bicycle out the five miles of the rising road to Phibbs's farm, the only person he meets there is a woman from Deilt who is looking after Old Phibbs and who tells Black that Cushy has gone away. Black pedals home, bewildered. He does not believe it, he tells Tom. And ten days later, when he receives a letter with a Dublin postmark from Cushy, saying that she can never again see him, Black tells Tom that he thinks he will die.

*　*　*

FEBRUARY 20TH

Although I love my mother, it is a love from which I feel bound to escape. Is that selfish? I once hoped that my mother could be my best friend, but now I know that life doesn't work like that. I tried in the beginning to talk to her about my feelings for Kaiser, but you cannot discuss with your mother – at least it seems I can't – all the different ways in which you see the man you love. It's too complicated. To involve her would mean placing all the years of her life – her loves, her failures, all her baggage and there is a lot of it – between Kaiser and me. It wouldn't work. I love my mother dearly, but I love Kaiser far more.

113

Lilly Coad's diaries for 1938 are specific about one further incident which has a bearing on this story. It involves a lady called
Tessa O'Grady, only daughter of Monument's first registrar, Mr
Daniel O'Grady (died 1976), who for many years was manageress
of the front office of the *Monument Gazette*. Lilly's notes show
that when Tessa first came to work in 1937, as a girl of eighteen,
she was immediately put in charge of the new telephone switchboard, the first of its kind in Monument. By the end of summer in
the following year, it seemed to everyone in the *Gazette* that Tessa
and her switchboard had been there as long as themselves.

*　　*　　*

TESSA'S STORY

1938

Other young women might baulk at being put in sole charge of the
new automatic switchboard, but Tessa is not the baulking type.
She has her father's wide mouth and good teeth, and his hearty
laugh, and like him she tends to organise people. After a few days
her knowledge of and dexterity with the switchboard are being
widely remarked upon. Although only eighteen years old, Tessa
often refers to herself as "not the marrying kind". This is just
her means of defence against the well-known vagaries of the heart:
every night she goes to bed dreaming of Black Pender. His twin
brother has the same face, albeit under a blond thatch, but with
Black the attraction comes from within. Six days a week Tessa
arrives early to work and leaves late, hoping within the span of
her hours to encounter him more. And she does. He always
smiles to her, raises his hat, calls her Miss O'Grady. To Tessa he
is Mr Pender. She puts through his calls. The texture of his voice.

Like everyone who has ever fallen in love, from one day to the next with just one glance Tessa can tell Black's mood.

By the end of September Tessa notices that Black has become inward. Walks through the hall and scarcely notices her. Requests few numbers and, if someone rings him, is abrupt. Tessa mentions her observations to Lilly Coad, Boss's secretary, but Lilly counsels Tessa not to concern herself with such matters, hinting that a breached romance is responsible, a piece of news that leaves Tessa at once devastated and elated: that he has loved another woman pierces her with deep loathing for whoever that woman may be; but the fact that this person no longer loves Black presents, in Tessa's wild dreams, a new opportunity. He will get over it, Lilly confides, given time. Tessa believes she knows more than Lilly. She wants to run from her switchboard and hold him in her arms and give him the comfort she can see he lacks.

The *Monument Gazette* has a life cycle, that of a beast that needs feeding weekly to make it go quiet. No-one associated with the paper can ever detach themselves for more than a brief time from these requirements, they sleep at night with the beat of the presses in their heads; Boss Pender has never taken a holiday.

The wind turns east on October 1st, as if the mere turning of a page on the calendar is enough to guillotine the good weather. Gales tear up the river and scatter roof slates. Reports come in to the *Gazette* of cattle being cut off at the delta of the Lyle near Eillne and drowning. All over the town readers take in the deaths of these mute animals. "As long as it doesn't come inside the door of the house," they remark, and bless themselves, and scurry out between downpours to check the doors of their coal sheds.

Black begins to come in late, his clothes aren't always fresh. A rumour is circulating that he and White got into a fight with a seaman in the Sailors' Rest on Dudley's Hill one night, a place frequented by street women. Black is being led on by White, Tessa hears one of the office clerks say, less and less can you tell them apart.

Strange, but Boss Pender appears to sail above all this turmoil in his favourite son. The Proprietor has never been busier, spending hours on his editorials, drawing his readers' attention to the situation in Germany and Italy, places neither he nor they will ever see at first hand, and copy by copy building up the circulation of his father's newspaper. This is how the Proprietor thinks of the *Gazette,* as being the legacy of a man who has been dead for thirty-eight years, as if the great James Pender is just about to walk into the building.

It is the Tuesday afternoon of the second week in October, a day which has become dim even in the mid-afternoon. The great presses have been running for an hour in their cacophonous weekly begetting, when a visitor presents himself at the downstairs front desk of the newspaper. Tessa sees a thickset, dark-haired country-man in a brown suit. To Tessa O'Grady he looks like a man on the verge of tears, his face is all lumps and knots, the flesh around his eyes swollen. He asks to see Mr John Pender. Tessa requests his name, but when she doesn't catch it, because of his fraught appearance does not ask again. She telephones upstairs to the editorial floor and speaks to a sub-editor.

"He'll be with you now," Tessa tells the visitor, who stands in the centre of the tiled floor, every now and then tugging up his frayed shirt cuffs into the recesses of his sleeves.

The portents suggested by the early dusk are proven by flickering displays of lightning, a series of them over the space of thirty seconds. The details of distant ships' masts are presented to Tessa and the visitor in intense detail. Thunder, then rain.

"My, what an evening," Tessa says. "Those that said we'd all pay for the summer were right."

The visitor stares at her. Then Black appears through the inner door, bringing with him a brief surge of running machinery.

"There was someone who wanted to . . . ?"

"Not someone. Me. Sam Phibbs, you damn mackerel snapper!"

Tessa O'Grady remembers the expression, one she has never heard before.

"Cushy," Black says.

"You dare call her by her pet name? You aren't fit to wipe the dirt from the soles of her shoes, you villain!"

All the knots and lumps are churning in Sam Phibbs's face, hate brought to the boil.

"I'd like to hear her say that," says Black, ashen but holding his ground to the other man. "Where is she? Where have you sent her?"

"Where you'll never find her, hypocrite. You'll never lay eyes or hands on her again. If you try, by Christ Jesus, it'll be the last thing you ever do."

Black takes a step to the rear, looks in consternation to Tessa, but her hands are shaking so much she could not use the telephone apparatus even had she the mind to.

"I don't know . . . I don't understand what you mean," Black says, his breath coming hard.

"You're all the same," says Sam Phibbs, his mouth gone loose, "in your pews every other day, wailing to your damn statues. But then dare an innocent girl from a decent, land-owning family come your way, you're no better than a monkey."

"I don't know what you're *talking* about!"

"Family way, that's what. Family way, Pender."

"How . . . how do you know?"

"She's seen a doctor in Dublin, that's how. There's no doubt."

"What did Cushy say?"

"Never mind what she said. Enough to know that she named you, mackerel snapper!"

Black strides past Phibbs over to the window. He catches his own hair both sides and seems to tug at it. He turns around.

"No way," he whispers. "It's not possible."

"Not just possible, but fact!" screams Sam Phibbs. "Ask the doctor! 'Not possible.' Damn you, you have ruined her!"

Black, aware ever more of Tessa, looks outside at the rain, seems to consider bringing Sam Phibbs inwards to another part of the building, but then just opens the front door and walks out. Phibbs follows. Tessa sees both of them, drenched in an instant, facing each other. Phibbs catches Black by the front of the jacket. Black pushes him back, steps back into the hall and stands there in a pool of water, heaving. Then Phibbs too comes in.

". . . take my word," he says. "I come here looking for nothing from you, just to warn you. Our family want no truck with your like. What you have done you will have to answer one day to God Almighty for, but in the meantime, stay away from the Phibbses, if you value your life."

Black Pender says, "I'm not going to dispute this any more here. But I want to meet you to discuss it."

"I never want to lay eyes on you again!" cries Sam Phibbs.

"If she needs money she shall have it," Black pants. "You too. But I assure you, there was nothing like that between us."

"Fornicator!" screams Sam Phibbs. "And I don't want your money! Liar!"

"Am I?" cries Black. "Am I, damn you, you bigot? You'll not stand in this hall where three generations of my family have given their lives and call me a liar!"

He goes at the smaller man, slamming him backward into the door and then as Phibbs, dazed, clutches the back of his head, Black catches him by the coat collar and seat pants and runs him out into the torrent. He then brings down the bar over the door. He stands, dazed, looking straight through Tessa. Then he goes back through the inner door, for a moment releasing once more the din of the presses from the deep womb of the building.

Tessa is shattered by what she has seen and heard, but she does not know if she should inform Miss Lilly Coad; her love for Black has made her proprietorial about the incident she alone has witnessed, which seems, in Tessa's eyes, to put Black and her on the same side, against the world as it were; and she has learned from her father how to keep a secret. But the substance of what has taken place so outweighs other considerations that next morning Tessa follows Boss Pender's secretary into the ladies' room and tells her everything.

Lilly listens to Tessa's story without a change of expression. Then she says: "You know who he is, of course, Miss O'Grady?"

Tessa shakes her head.

"Sam Phibbs. Son of Old Phibbs, the R.I.C. man. A Protestant, but not gentry. Poor Sam is distracted trying to find a woman to marry him, it's driven him funny, they say. Put the whole thing out of your mind, Miss O'Grady, and get on with your work is my advice, there's the good girl."

Many questions remain unasked and unanswered; but Tessa does not dare put them to Lilly, who has employed her in the first place and who anyway, has by now left the ladies'. And because she does need this job – because despite his great service to the community Daniel O'Grady's pension would not feed a finch – Tessa does as she is told and puts the incident from her mind and returns to her switchboard where, a week later, she takes a telephone call from young Sergeant Lully in Deilt.

*   *   *

FEBRUARY 25TH

My mother is a slave to past forces that I cannot comprehend – any more than she can, I daresay. These forces contributed, I believe, to her unhappy childhood, her bitter mother, her absent father and the fractured family she brought up. They continue to rule her life and are all part of the reason for her total opposition to my interest in Kaiser.

I was helping her the other day in the shop. She'd just got in daffodils from Dublin and we were sorting them together. Kaiser was there. She began talking about the Santrys and the old times. Before I knew it she'd zoned in on Kaiser.

"Do you not remember Mr M. . . . Beagle, Kaiser?" she asked.

Kaiser shook his head.

"Mr M. . . . the state solicitor. Are you sure?"

"How is Kaiser meant to remember something that far back?" I asked her.

Kaiser smiled at me.

"You see," my mother said, turning her face in a way that he could not see her mouth, "he remembers nothing of his childhood. Nothing. And what you remember cannot hurt you. More fool you to try and interfere."

I could not believe that she would say something like that when Kaiser was standing beside us.

"Mother!" I cried.

What she did was so hurtful. I wonder if she has any idea what it is to be in love.

Although my mother has the ability to steamroll me, I have come too far to turn back now. What I am beginning to see – and this is frightening, to say the least – is the outline of a monstrous injustice. Kaiser is aware of nothing, of course – if anything he is bemused by my interest in the past and tells me that I am in danger of being devoured by it. What is strange but wonderful about this process is that each fresh piece of history I uncover has the effect of bringing me closer to him. I came into the canteen yesterday and we – *connected* across a room full of people! I don't care if everyone knows. This has been something worth waiting for, love like electrical current, sparking as it spans a room!

The *Gazette*'s pension records are an obvious place to look for the employees of 1938. Only two are still alive: the first began as a junior reporter in 1938 and his name is Jeff Dunphy. Today a widower, he lives in Rath Terrace, Buttermilk with his daughter, Ms Dora Dunphy. He is very deaf and nearly blind.

But in 1938, as I found out, Jeff Dunphy was a rugby player of some importance.

* * *

JEFF'S STORY

1938

Monumentals won their last six matches of the 1937–8 season and are therefore, this October, expecting great things in the League. Sandy haired, blue eyed, quietly spoken, Jeff Dunphy has a great reach in lineouts, soars as if with wings and grasps the ball into him, keeps his feet when he lands and braces his strong back in the ensuing rucks. Fast too. Last January during the final minutes of a game against a team from Shannon as Monumentals trailed by three points, Jeff floated high for the ball thrown in on his own twenty-five-yard line, caught it clean, jinked back around his scrum-half and then breaking loose like a runaway colt up the centre of the field, ran in the most memorable try of the season.

Jeff is looking out at the drifting rain, feeling the vibration of the *Gazette*'s presses, which make the timber floors, the heavy desks and chairs strain to effoliate. As he stares out of the window, down on Candle Lane he sees a figure hunching away on a bicycle. The rain-soaked man suddenly turns his head and looks straight up at the building. Something has distorted his face, Jeff sees with shock; it is twisted and paper white.

"Jeff?"

Lilly Coad is standing at the door of the subs' office.

"Yes, Miss Coad?"

"You don't look all that busy. Go down to the garage and bring me up the tax book from the glove compartment of the Proprietor's car, there's a good lad."

The shed is roaring. Men who have worked in here since the paper began, when it used to take almost a week to print the edition on the old Cosser presses, have lost most of their hearing. No way at this time down here on a Tuesday can you hold a conversation. Jeff catches sight of Boss Pender on the far side of the line, surveying the spinning rolls of newsprint with ducal authority. Black is with him. As Jeff watches, they both walk across the floor to the door in the corner which leads to the garage. Jeff follows. He goes through, closes the door behind him, then realises that father and son, Proprietor and heir, are standing in the dim garage only twenty feet from him.

"What is it you want to tell me?"

Jeff's ears resound.

"Something shameful."

"Go on."

"Cushy Phibbs – she says she's going to have my child."

Boss Pender's enlarged, dumbfounded eyes.

"How do you know?"

"Her brother has just been here. Like a madman. She's seen a doctor."

"Where?"

"In Dublin."

"Did she come here with him?"

"No, but Father, it's not possible! It cannot be!"

Boss's heavy breathing. He says, "But she told her brother this is the case?"

"Yes."

"So – you had carnal knowledge of her."

Black's voice, a whisper. "Yes."

Boss hits the boy in the mouth with his bunched fist.

"Oh my God," Boss gasps, leaning back against the car, drained, "oh dear, merciful God."

Black is wiping his mouth with his fingers and is looking at his own blood there. "It cannot be!" he cries.

"But is! Is!"

"Father, believe me . . ."

"We'll ask God for His forgiveness," Boss Pender says, hands joined in contrition. "Oh my God, we are heartily sorry for having offended Thee, we confess our sins above every other evil . . ."

"Her brother will not allow me to marry her."

The father pauses, looks sideways at the son. "And you would?"

"In the morning, if she would have me."

"What do you mean, 'if she would have me'? D'you think she's *better* than you? D'you think that they amount to something out there with their few acres, their perished house, their heathenism? Do you? She led you on, didn't she?"

"I cannot bear to hear you speak of her in this manner, Father."

"Yet you come blubbering to me when you have to pay the price of your rutting, eh? I know this girl and I know that she led you on. Hah! They all do. Admit it!"

Black's head in his hands.

"Yes."

"Hah! So then let's not see these people up on any county pedestal. When a woman behaves shamefully nature has a way of making sure she pays. You understand?"

Black inclines his head.

123

"Perhaps you will have to marry her. Sure, the brother says he won't allow it because he wants to extract the maximum price from this windfall. Money knows no religion, believe me. She'll have to turn, of course, and there's no question that she won't. If the need arises, Father Whittle will arrange instruction afterwards. And she herself – has she said that she will marry you?"

"I haven't even spoken to her."

"But she told the brother that you were the father? Yes?"

"Yes – but it can't be right! There must be a . . ."

"Shut up! She has no option but to marry you, like it or not, a young woman in her position. What else is left to her? Shame and scandal. A bastard child. Penury."

Black sighs. "The brother was hot."

"Then we'll let this night cool him off," says Boss. He reaches over in the semi-darkness and fondles Black's neck. "Your old man'll sort this out for you, d'you hear me? Your old man'll sort out everything."

Jeff goes back upstairs, his head in a riot. Later that evening he decides to tell his father what he has overheard, but at the last moment, he told me over fifty years later, when Mr Dunphy sits down and lights his pipe and composes himself to hear his son, Jeff's nerve fails him.

Two sets of people drive the gathering of information: police and postmen. Both groups rove the town and countryside in patrols and deliveries – a correspondent in Eillne writing of a morning to someone in Monument can reasonably expect the delivery of a reply that same evening – and in the process gather news. The *Gazette* acquires this information in return for favours – jobs for the sons and daughters, small ads put in at reduced rates, an early copy of the paper, free of charge – and assembles the drips of gossip, hearsay, rumour and tittle-tattle into a cohesive whole.

If the story warrants, someone may get on a bicycle and go and check the facts, but in the main, items of news are reported in the general and roundabout language of oracles and printed under the byline of *"Our Deilt Correspondent"* or *"Our Balaklava Correspondent"*. These conventions have been long accepted and the fact that no such correspondents exist effects no-one.

Friday, October 14th. Late in the afternoon. A telephone call comes into the switchboard. The caller who identifies himself as the sergeant of the guards in Deilt asks to speak to the Deilt correspondent so Tessa O'Grady puts him through to the upstairs room in which sit both sub-editors and reporters.

Jeff Dunphy is looking at the wall clock. He has rugby training at six o'clock three miles out on the Eillne road, so it will take him half an hour to get home, change and another fifteen minutes to cycle out there; but that evening he cannot leave early since, as luck would have it, the other subs and all the reporters have already left the building. Jeff longs for a cigarette, but the rugby coach has forbidden it and has, furthermore, told both Jeff's father and Lilly Coad that Jeff's smoking habit threatens the entire foundation of that year's campaign by Monumentals. The result: Jeff is not permitted to smoke either at home or at work and has to therefore confine himself to surreptitious but succulent drags when in transit. Jeff is looking at the wall clock, five minutes to six, yearning for tobacco, when the only telephone in the room rings.

"This is Sergeant Lully from Deilt."

Jeff has encountered Sergeant Lully, who is barely older than himself, around the courthouse in Monument.

"Yes."

"Am I speaking to the Deilt correspondent?"

"Yes, you are."

"Do you know who Sam Phibbs is?"

"Who?"

"Sam Phibbs, he's the son of Old Phibbs, the R.I.C. man. They have a farm on the road to Deilt."

"Yes."

"Well, there's something awful after happening out here to him."

"And what's that, Sergeant?"

"He's had himself murdered."

Jeff stands up.

"Are you sure?"

"Strangled the colour blue, what can be surer than that?" says Lully. "There's a murderer on the loose."

Jeff drops the telephone receiver. He looks around the empty room. Then he runs out into the corridor, shouting, and blunders his way along, strange noises in his ears. Halting outside the door of Boss Pender's office, a place in which he has never before set foot, doubt begins to overtake Jeff and he wonders has he heard right. Then, as he stands there gripped by indecision, he sees coming along the corridor from the stairs, Miss O'Grady, the telephonist. From her face Jeff knows at once that she has been listening in and that he has imagined nothing. Her mouth opening and closing pike-like, small, strangled gasps seeping from her, Tessa O'Grady stumbles towards him, one arm outstretched and terror in her eyes.

"He was . . ." she whispers, ". . . here . . ."

Glad to have an ally in what he is about to divulge, Jeff knocks on the door of Boss Pender's office, opens it for Miss O'Grady to precede him, which she does to full effect, toppling inwards, fainted.

Boss Pender is at his desk, reading aloud for Lilly Coad a rounded denunciation of the results of de Valera's economic "war" against England. The presence of Jeff Dunphy in the Proprietor's office, not to mention that of Miss O'Grady on the floor of the Proprietor's office, has no precedent. Lilly hurries to Miss O'Grady, whilst Boss, his face demanding explanations, motions Jeff to approach.

"Sam Phibbs . . . son of Old Phibbs, the R.I.C. man . . . they have a farm out on the road to . . ."

"I know Phibbs."

"He's been found dead. Strangled the colour blue, according to Sergeant Lully."

"Blessed Mother of God," exclaims Boss Pender and blesses himself. "Are you sure?"

Jeff nods, his tongue is stuck to the roof of his mouth.

Boss looks down to Lilly who has propped Miss O'Grady into a sitting position.

"Lilly!"

Lilly Coad looks up.

"Get me Hart," Boss snaps. "You!" He is pointing at Jeff. "Get a notebook and meet me outside the front door in two minutes!"

Boss Pender is known to have covered news stories, such as when in 1922 he wrote extensively about the Treaty, and he also attended the funeral of Michael Collins and in 1928 reported on the visit to the Monument library of the poet, Yeats. However, up to now murder has been quite rare in Monument – yes, people died by the scores in wars, civil and otherwise, but with few exceptions they were never murdered.

Half-past six. In Boss's maroon Vauxhall 30/98, Hart at the wheel, Boss up front and Jeff in the back seat, they head for Deilt. As they turn in a narrow driveway, Jeff fights to take in the details – a pair of whitewashed piers, high banks on either side, Scots pines. A car is already parked in front of the house, a blue Morris Cowley with its high, curved luggage boot. When Hart turns off the Vauxhall's engine, they hear voices inside. Two guards came out: Jeff recognises the superintendent of the guards from Monument and, hopping from one foot to the other, young Sergeant Lully whose call has so reduced the eavesdropping Tessa O'Grady.

"Bad, Boss, bad," says the superintendent, taking off his cap and scratching his head of greying hair. "Pure black he is."

"Where's Miss Phibbs?" Jeff hears Boss ask.

"Not here anyway," replies the super. "We're checking an address in Dublin." He shakes his head. "The father's in there, nearly dead from starvation, God preserve us from it, and not able to say a word."

"Any leads?"

The policeman registers bewilderment. "Divil a one. I've sent to headquarters for forensic lads, but God knows when they'll get down here. A post-mortem too, of course."

"How about you, Sergeant?" Boss asks, turning to Sergeant Lully. "Had he any enemies you know of?"

Sergeant Lully, were it not for his uniform, looks at first glance as if he should still be at school; but then a closer appraisal would take in the shrewdness of his light blue eyes, which bestow on him a wisdom beyond his years. "I could imagine the father getting done like this, but not the son," he says with slow enunciation.

Boss clears his throat. "Mind if we have a look?"

"I hope you've a strong stomach," says the super and leads Boss and Jeff into the house where local women are laying out cups and saucers.

At first Jeff thinks the murder victim is in the chair and jumps when its hand moves. Then he looks beyond, to the hearth, and sees a man's body arched on the spot where it struggled its last. Chest uppermost, frozen in death in its final lunge, from a face the colour of two-week beef springs a black tongue, long and rigid as a door hinge. Jeff, conscious of the other men, makes himself go right up to the corpse and look full into its face. The shock is like a hammer blow. Jeff stumbles back out through the front door and over to the Vauxhall, where he retches beside its spoked front wheel.

Jeff is looking down over the tips of the trees, into the valley and to Monument. On the wall feet away a black cat is stretching in the last of the sun and shooting its claws. Jeff pulls hard on the cigarette and sinks the smoke deep and holds it there with gratitude. His head is clearer now and he is almost sure: the dead man is the man whose face Jeff beheld earlier that week from the window of the *Gazette*. Jeff wonders if Boss Pender should be told. Boss is still in discussion with the super and Jeff is bracing himself to show his mettle and go and have another look to make sure he is right when his ear picks up a motor on the wind. In through the gates creeps a Model A Ford, which Jeff recognises from his stints in court as belonging to Mr M. Beagle, the state solicitor. Mr M. himself steps out onto the running board, surveys the scene from this relative height, then climbs down and makes his way for the house. But two paces short, he halts and turns to Jeff.

"You're . . . young Dunphy?"

"Yes, Mr Beagle."

"Isn't this a terrible thing?"

"Yes, sir."

"Did you know him?"

"Yes." Jeff feels panic. "That is . . . no, sir . . . no, I didn't."

"I wouldn't be surprised if this is a case of mistaken identity," says the state solicitor, nodding. "What do you think?"

"I . . . I agree," stammers Jeff.

It is well after eight before they all disperse. Boss shakes hands with the super, the guard. Sergeant Lully is standing to one side, taking notes.

"Take the sergeant back to Deilt," Boss instructs Hart. To Jeff, "You've spoken to Mr M.?"

129

"Yes, Mr Pender."

"So go home and write your copy," says the Proprietor of the *Monument Gazette*. Then he gets into Mr M. Beagle's car and they drive out of Phibbs's.

The super departs in his own vehicle and Hart helps Sergeant Lully load his bicycle onto the Vauxhall's luggage rack.

"A case of mistaken identity, I'd say, Sergeant," Jeff observes, lighting up a cigarette.

Sergeant Lully looks at him coolly. "Would you, now?"

"That's the way Mr M. has it and he's the state solicitor."

"You have to look at everything that goes on in people's lives," says Sergeant Lully quietly. "You have to look around them and behind them and above them and below them. Then you find out the truth."

"No doubt," says Jeff as they motor out of the gates. He can no longer be sure that the dead man is the same person he saw cycling down Candle Lane in the heavy rain. It could easily be a case of mistaken identity. It would take a long time to look in all the places Sergeant Lully has mentioned and Jeff has to get back to the *Gazette* as instructed and write his first news story.

PART THREE

Eleven

I must have nodded off in the garden of Pig and Litter that Sunday afternoon, for when I awoke I remembered the following, vivid dream: I am lying in bed on a magnificent July day holding in my arms a most beautiful woman. The curved, wedge-like window of my bedroom reveals nature in its full super-fecundity, lazy cliffs where flowers tumble in great swathes, where bees in uncountable masses forage and where kittiwakes and gannets give full throat as they extend their already considerable and redolent colonies of guano.

As if in great sighs of apparent contentment, Gregorian chant creeps out from the room downstairs, the round twin of my bedroom, and below it, much further below, sea sucks doggedly at our foundations. I must be dreaming, I think, for I can hear the music, each surge of placid sound, and I can hear the sea, which, like the music, rises and falls with the tide of my blood.

With aptness beyond words, slanting sunlight brands the naked back of my lover. She sprawls across me at an angle of roughly fifty degrees, her sweet face resting, closed-eyed, on the limp bicep of my left arm, her swarm of ink black curly hair overrunning my pale shoulder onto the lemon-yellow bedsheet. My contented eyes cruise languidly down the golden, edible slopes of her back, across her wide and evenly tanned buttocks, downward to her generous thighs and thence to the healthy "H" at the back of each of her knees; then, because I have always known, I turn my eyes to her right hand that reclines on my left knee. It is filthy. The contrast between the molten perfection of her limbs and the permanent muck of her fingers, this utter disparity, makes bile rise in my chest, an audible gurgle pushing up stinking air into my nostrils and mouth. The woman sits up. She gathers the top sheet around her shoulders and prodigal breasts. She shakes her hair out and runs her right hand through its squid-like mass.

Jasmine looks at me squarely and says, "We're dead, Kaiser."

I have always considered Monument as belonging to me. This, I believe, is what people mean when they refer to a place as "my town". Monument is mine. I share Long Quay with the housewives and old stagers and ordinary folk like myself; we are partners in this riverside thoroughfare, on whose footpaths have strolled countless sailors from other continents, some of whom came here just the once and others who took one look and never left.

I strolled by the Lyle and it occurred to me that since I had met Jasmine my connections with Monument had become even more acute. I saw her everywhere: in the glass of shop windows and buses, on streets from Buttermilk to Balaklava. I heard her, too, in the way that I hear things, in the sigh of the wind, in the rumble of the streets and in the rolling waves of deep thunder caught in the river's silken fathoms. Monument's deep peace had embraced us both. I had never been more happy.

Mrs Rice was in her shop, a lazy tail of smoke curling from her mouth.

"Friendship is often better at a distance, Kaiser," she spoke in the raised tone she kept for me. "I'll tell you a story about friendship – that's if you want to hear it."

I nodded, yes.

"You heard the saying that if a man wakes up four weeks running in the same bed then he's not from Monument? That came from the numbers of merchant sailors that lived in this town.

My father was one of them. His name was Jimmy, that's what everyone called him, his children included."

Mrs Rice spoke between exhalations in subdued tones which slipped from her like soothing tongues and rolled over me in gentle undulations of spent tobacco.

"As a youngster he wanted only to be at sea. This is a story Jimmy told me himself, about his life before he married my mother. He had a friend called Keeneye Flynn, called Keeneye because he once shot out ten bull's-eyes at a funfair in Buttermilk. Keeneye Flynn from Captain Penny's Road, they went to school together in Binn's Street, just like you did, they sat side by side at the same desk, my father, Jimmy, and his friend Keeneye Flynn. Then they left school and they both went to sea."

Each evening, as now, all the flowers were brought in from the street for the night and watered so that within the enclosed shop the air sizzled with efflorescent combustions.

"But they didn't go to sea together. Jimmy was mainly over and back between Ireland and the Mediterranean, whilst Keeneye found himself on tramps between England and West Africa, and as far as India. Then when Keeneye came nearer home and was put on the Rotterdam route, Jimmy went down to the Suez for a few years. They were never in home port at the same time. Sometimes they'd miss each other by only a couple of days in Monument. Jimmy would come home for a fortnight and inquire, 'Any word of Keeneye?' and be told, 'He's coming home on Sunday week,' which would be two days too late for Jimmy who was shipping out on the Friday.

"He was always talking about Keeneye. He'd relate some tale or other from some African port he'd visited – there was one about a tribesman who wore the clothes of the missionary he'd eaten – and then he'd slap his thigh and say, 'I can't wait to see the look on Keeneye's face when he hears that one!' But he had to wait because they never met in over ten years, never laid eyes on one another. Jimmy would leave the price of a large bottle of stout for Keeneye in the pub they both drank in on Dudley's Hill and when he next came home there'd be a half one waiting for him in the same place, paid for on his last trip home by Keeneye. Yet it didn't seem as if Jimmy realised that he and his friend had never met in ten years. To the contrary, he said he always spoke of Keeneye as if they had just had a drink together the night before."

Mrs Rice pulled out a wooden drawer and began transferring paper money and coins into a leather night wallet.

"Then one evening Jimmy was walking down the street in Suez. In later life he often spoke of the sunsets in Suez, he told me the sun filled the whole sky it was so big going down. This day's dusk had come. On both sides of him he could see the tips of pyramids sailing over their oceans of sand, he could see the fronds of palm trees standing out against the sunset and he could make out, over the settling heat and the smell of dogs and spices, the whiff of Arab lamb kebabs rising from an invisible brazier.

"A man was coming towards him up the street, hands in his pockets. Something about him Jimmy thought familiar. The man must have been alerted too for he stopped.

"'Jimmy?'

"My father couldn't believe it.

"'Keeneye!'

"What must the odds have been they both wondered. Who would ever have imagined that they would meet like that, so many miles from home?

"They went to a bar together for beers since neither of them were shipping out until dawn the next day – Jimmy for Bengal, Keeneye going in the opposite direction, for Southampton. So they sat up at the bar, these two old friends from Monument, now men, both of them bursting to fill the gaps of ten years. The potential of the

136

situation was overwhelming. So many tales to tell, jokes to repeat, reactions to gauge.

"And the oddest thing happened, Kaiser. They found they had nothing to talk about. Neither of them had any news about home that was news to the other. Jimmy was a prudish man, so Keeneye's stories – which I never heard but to which Jimmy always rather heavily alluded – about 'goings-on' in certain Chinese ports met with Jimmy's disapproval. For his part, Keeneye probably thought his old, fun-loving pal had become too strait-laced for his liking. Jimmy spoke of his ambitions: going home, getting a land job, settling down. Keeneye wanted none of that. For him, he had found the life he always wanted. A world outside Monument, women – I'm sure – and cheap rum."

Mrs Rice shook her head, took out her keys, turned out the lights.

"They left the bar in Suez a couple of hours later. Next morning they went their separate ways. They never saw each other as friends again. Shortly afterwards Jimmy came home from sea for good, but when Keeneye was home he never bothered to go and see him. He changed his pub. Nor did Keeneye try and meet Jimmy. Never came near him again."

We left the shop together and walked across MacCartie Square, across Pollack Street, along Moneysack and into Milner's Street. I was hoping that Jasmine – who was meant to have met me at the shop – would be making her way towards us from the *Gazette*. I saw from people's momentarily meditative expressions that the Angelus was pounding out from the cathedral.

"Jasmine is a lovely, kind girl, Kaiser," Mrs Rice said, "but she's stubborn as well. Like me, you might say, I don't deny it. My mother said I was like a ginnet at a crossroads."

We passed Coad's Stationers, and a pair of butcher's shops, and a travel agent advertising holidays in Tunisia from £199.

"She was a gorgeous little girl, people would just take one look at her by the flower stall and buy something. Top of her class in school. But then she might get some idea into her head – she'd want to get her hair cut short, or she wouldn't eat eggs because she said she'd be eating aborted chickens – and the Pope in Rome would not be able to persuade her to change her mind."

I smiled at the thought of the determination in Jasmine's face, the way her head went forward and her eyes narrowed when she was fixed on something.

"I'm worried about her, Kaiser." Mrs Rice kept her eyes ahead, kept walking. I could barely keep pace with her words. "All this searching and asking questions and interviewing people. For what? She spends all her spare time at that computer in the library, I know what she's at, she's putting in all the stuff she's found, boxes of it. It's no good, Kaiser, no good."

I thought about my dream and as I did so something powerful and malign fastened itself around my heart.

"Why?" Mrs Rice had walked on, but I knew she'd heard me. I stood my ground. I called out, "Why?"

"Why?" She stopped and turned, then looked back over her shoulder as if she thought someone might be lying in wait there. Returning the few steps, she said, "Because the past is the past, Kaiser, and that's where it should stay. Do you think I don't know about the past? Hah. I know more than you could ever imagine. This is a happy town, people get on with their lives. They don't look back, they don't go rooting, rooting, looking for trouble, stirring up what's long been laid to rest. This is a good town that's put its bad times behind it. People are happy here. They don't want the past opened up. Do you understand what I'm saying?"

I said I did. But then I told her that the future sometimes depends on finding out about the past.

Mrs Rice shook her head with impatience. "Certain people

know what Jasmine is at and certain people don't like it one little bit. I agree with them. I think she should stop. If she doesn't stop, then this is the wrong town for her. And for you. If you don't like the way we live our lives here, then get out, both of you."

I smiled. "This is my town too. I like it."

"You've a queer way of showing it, then," she said, tight and sharp-toothed. "You're no good for Jasmine, Kaiser. She was much happier before she ever met you. You're ruining everything. Go away. Leave her alone. Find someone else!" She was hissing as if her tongue was hovering at my ear. "It's nothing to grin about."

I was smiling because I could see Jasmine at the other end of Milner's Street.

"Kaiser!"

Something had happened.

"Jasmine? What is it?"

It was as if her mother was not there.

"It's Ollie Pender-Goode," Jasmine was saying in tight, worried words. "She's been rushed by ambulance to Dublin. They say she's not going to live."

12

Things are still in turmoil here. Ollie Pender-Goode has undergone a quadruple heart-bypass operation in Dublin; it is still touch and go for her. Tim, in the meantime, has taken over as Proprietor. Everyone is giving him their support, but it is an open secret that no-one wishes his appointment to be anything but temporary.

Kaiser has been moody these last few days. It is as if he has become distant with me. Sad, too. I wouldn't be at all surprised if my mother said something to him about us. The situation with her is most unsatisfactory, to say the least. I'll leave things to work themselves out for a few days and in the meantime I'll plough on with my research into the events of 1938, hoping that a connection to Kaiser emerges.

I have already mentioned that only two *Gazette* employees from 1938 are still alive and receiving a pension. I should say, *were* still alive. One is Jeff Dunphy. The other, when I embarked on this segment ten days ago, was Hart.

Yes, the big, taciturn, vaguely schoolteacherish County Louth man who knew cars and their engines. On call round the clock – *for over thirty years!* It goes without saying that "they don't exist any more", the Harts. That brand of blind loyalty and unqualified service is not a thing of generations past, it's medieval. The various Penders in later life, when they looked back on family occasions would describe who was there, and then, in the way of

140

afterthought, would add, "And Hart, of course! Nearly forgot Hart." Invisible, almost.

After Boss Pender died in 1964, Hart, through the intercession of Tom Pender, got a job in a garage in Captain Penny's Road. He never spoke of the numerous excursions of which he had been a part. Perhaps his taciturn nature sprang from a deep-seated self-protection, an aversion to garrulousness. There had once been a woman, it was said, a girl with whom Hart had been in love, but she died young. Hart never married.

He had so long occupied the first bed inside the door of the male ward that for a good week after his death the nurses on all three shifts, even though they knew he was no longer there, still said from habit as they entered the room, "Are we all right in here, Denis?" or, "Another cup of tea, Denis?", the fact that he had never replied anyway somehow seemed complicit in the ongoing oversight. The ward day sister, she who had but days before arranged the cake, had planted and lit its ninety-two candles, and guided the knife clutched in Denis Hart's large, yellowing fist to sink through the three layers of jam-filled sponge to the applause of no less a person than the bishop of Monument, went through Hart's belongings.

For years he had worn only bed clothes, the standard issue of the County Home. No suitcase existed, so all that remained was gathered by the sister for disposal into a plastic grocery bag and given to a young nurse: a cutthroat, unused in fifteen years since the nurses shaved him with a disposable; a silver-backed hair-brush whose dun bristles survived only in patches; three letters in their envelopes, Monument postmark, all addressed in a childish hand to the same woman, Miss Doe, c/o Monument Hospital. And a tortoise-shell-framed, faded black and white photograph, small enough to rest in the palm of the hand, showing a group of people in and around an open-top car. At the wheel, a domineering man with moustaches, frowning hugely. Beside him, enveloped by his arm along the back of the seat, sits a pretty, young woman. In the back can be seen two younger men, one partly hidden by the man at the wheel, the other a handsome face under dark hair. Beside the driver's door in a white linen suit, his teeth still sparkling white after so many decades, stands another young man, his hair fair, his chest full as a prize fighter's. Appearing in the left-hand corner, face in part blurred, is the head of a further man, and his hand, clutching a cloth. The only surviving photograph of Hart.

I know all this because, unaware that he had died two days before, I walked into the nursing home and asked to see him. A young nurse who heard me asking, handed me a plastic bag with his belongings. She presumed I was his next of kin. I almost didn't take the bag, but she was in a hurry and looking into it I could see some envelopes. This is the result.

* * *

HART'S STORY

1938

She lives in Balaklava, on Victoria Street, the street of a dozen houses that runs into Prince Consort Terrace. Her widowed mother takes in lodgers and Joan, already three years out of school at seventeen, helps out. Although Victoria Street is not much different to any other in Balaklava, Mrs Doe sweeps her step and the pavement before it and is known for her clean household. For such reasons she has two good, permanent men lodgers, one of whom is a quiet, County Louth man named Hart who works as Boss Pender's driver. Came there from digs on Dudley's Hill three years before, in the summer of 1934. Says little. Not around the house much due to his job, but when he is, follows everyone with his eyes, in particular Joan.

She is tall for her age, gets up every morning before six to clean and light the range so that the men can breakfast in warmth. Each of the last summers she has succumbed to the bad influenza: once as Hart was passing the room she and her mother share, he saw her face on the white bolster, drawn and anxious. Now each time she coughs, Hart worries.

In Balaklava there are still gut houses, the residences of people who trade in offal. Sewage is spoken of only by politicians, whole rows of houses leave out their night waste for collection. Everyone owns a rat trap. Water comes from common pumps and runs dry if the weather is good for more than a few weeks. There was once a great tradition of prostitution, but since the departure of the British army fifteen years before, and the establishment in their barracks of the Free State army, the profession has been in decline. Illegal ale houses and gambling dens have been the targets of recent purges: many old people in Balaklava believe that they were better off in former times, even if that was under British rule.

Joan was a child when Hart came from Dudley's Hill, now she is a woman. He has watched her competence and grace flower into a graceful beckoning. She holds towels for him outside the privy when he scrubs the engine oil from his hands before coming in to eat. He has watched how the sunlight is carried in her auburn hair. Her rare dignity comes from her mother and she deserves everything that she ever might desire. Which has become Hart's secret wish: to buy a cottage on the road to Deilt and – with his employer's blessing – to set up home and family there with Miss Joan Doe. Not that he has expressed this plan in words to Joan, or to a living soul. Hart seldom speaks. But he knows that the quiet happiness that enters him when she is present has to be obvious to her, that Joan knows of his admiration and that, like Hart, she will be ready when the time comes.

Mid April, 1938. By three in the afternoon, Hart has already driven Boss Pender to Kilkenny to meet an Englishman who traded in ink, and back, and then waited for an hour in a snowstorm for his employer outside the Central Hotel, before driving him up to the *Gazette*, where Hart has been given the remainder of the day off. He has not eaten since breakfast, but smiles in the knowledge that Joan will know from instinct how hungry he is.

Hart turns into Victoria Street. Fresh flurries of unseasonal snow spiral down between the rows of smoking chimney pots. A north-easter, it bites in the way Hart, a north-easterner, remembers. He has a sense of comfortable anticipation about the evening ahead, sitting by the range in Mrs Doe's kitchen, a feeling that somehow extends for him into the larger arena of his whole life. Food and heat, comfort and women. These alone are the considerations being dealt with by Hart as he reaches to put his latchkey in the door, and the door, before he can reach it, opens. Mrs Doe. Face, flour white. Eyes, red sunk, their surrounds in deep shadow.

Hart, without understanding how he knows, says, "Joan."

Joan's mother's mouth falls open. She says, "TB."

The Monument Hospital authorities had put up a long, airy chalet-like building made from wood and separate from the main hospital, in which were housed ten males and ten females with tuberculosis. Hart makes the journey any evening he can, having garaged the Vauxhall, out Small Quay past Love & Son to the head of the Deilt Road, where the hospital was built at the end of the nineteenth century. Hart can hear her coughing before ever he sees her. He sits by the end of her bed in the tiny room whose windows are always open and watches Joan's thin face. Sometimes she asks him questions about his job, about the Penders. Hart replies by way of remarks. "Tom's the quiet one," he'll say, or "Black'll be as good a man as his father, mark my words." In this way, over the long summer's evenings, he keeps Joan company.

They say the bed rest, the isolation and the six-month course of injections will cure her, but Hart has secret fears. She has been there for over four months, but far from improvement all he can see is a decline. She has come into age the way of women he knew at home who had their children young: spaces have grown between her once tight teeth, her throat is no longer smooth but trenched, and she has become exhausted from her many months of hacking up bile. A sister intercepts Hart as he leaves the ward at seven one evening in the third week of August.

"Denis? It is Denis?"

Hart looks at the woman. They can both hear Joan's coughs from where they stand.

Hart nods.

"She might be better left for a week or so, Denis. She's fighting a big battle in there, you know, poor little angel."

Hart then knows that he has been correct in his secret fears. That night he makes his way up to his room with an ancient resignation, but nonetheless his mind holds to its images of the cottage on the way to Deilt, of him and Joan, of the voices of happy children, of the comfort that comes from the smell of baking and the sound of wood crackling in a fire.

The next day Hart decides that he will write to Joan. At the *Gazette's* reception he asks Miss Tessa O'Grady to get him paper and a pen. Miss O'Grady gives the driver a look, but then hands him the half-used letter pad of good bond that she keeps beside her desk, and the open-nibbed dip pen she holds in reserve in case her Parker fails. Hart will have to buy his own ink, Miss O'Grady informs him.

Although it will take him hours to write anything in his words of printed letters, that night Hart begins. Never before having written a letter, beyond the first words he is lost, nothing suggests itself to his backward hand any more than it did formerly to his tongue. But unlike sitting silently in company where just his presence suffices, he realises the same silence will not work in a letter. Here words are all. Hart ponders for hours. Tries to think of what he has ever said to Joan and remembers that all their chat has been about his job. She liked hearing about his day, who said what to whom, where he drove the Vauxhall. Thus he sets out, each letter of each word standing alone.

*   *   *

HART'S FIRST LETTER

AUGUST 1938

Outside the *Gazette,* Hart hears Boss complimenting Lilly about the picnic: a surprise since he thought Boss had been edgy that day, never spoke a word all the way home, but then two days later, standing outside the *Gazette,* he says, "Must do that again, Lilly."

"One o'clock, Hart," Lilly tells the driver and nominates the Friday of the following week, same place, outside the *Gazette.*

But when Friday comes and one o'clock approaches they are parked on Dudley's Hill opposite the entry to Pig and Litter, having driven up there from the bank, although Hart understands that they are meant to be picking up the others from Candle Lane. It is not part of his disposition to make suggestions.

"Go in and tell them we're here," Boss says from the back seat.

Hart walks into the narrow entry. He is secure in here, something to do with the lack of noise and the scents from the garden. The hall door is covered by a striped sheet to protect its paint from the sun. Hart rings the bell and as the door is opened he hears the hall clock strike out a single, tinny note.

"The lads here, Agnes?"

The new girl is much taller and bigger boned than Joan, and younger. Grey and considerate eyes.

"They all left after breakfast," Agnes says. "There's only the missus here."

Hart walks back out again as Love's whistle blows. He tells Boss.

"One o'clock is one o'clock," says Boss.

Tom gets out and Hart drives downhill. It occurs to Hart that he should have asked Agnes if he could use the telephone in Pig and Litter to ring Lilly and tell her what is going on. But Hart has never in his life used a telephone.

They gather speed and Boss removes his cap and the breeze fluffs out his brown head hair and the wings of his tan moustaches. Flying along between the autumn hedgerows, Hart knows that the Proprietor feels the tide suck of his youth. She is waiting too, this time down at the road gate to their property. As they pull up, Hart sees her puzzled face.

"Good afternoon, Miss Phibbs."

"Mr Pender. Are you . . . where are . . . ?"

Boss's laugh is full of good nature. "Scoundrels don't know the meaning of being on time. They have to learn."

"Oh, then, in that case . . ."

But Hart is already out and holding the far side back door open for her and helping her up.

"Don't be anxious, Miss Phibbs. When we get up to Glane I intend to have Hart return for them. Nothing like a bit of hunger to capture young men's attention, believe me. Hart!"

They draw away uphill, Cushy seated in the back beside him.

"Such a smell of leather!"

"Does it offend you?"

"On the contrary."

The road is empty all the way to Glane. Through the iron gate, up the made track, Hart slows down below the white rock.

"Drive it, Hart!"

Hart looks back at his employer.

"You've done it before. Drive it!"

Hart reverses, then advances the engine by means of the silver lever inset in the steering wheel and aims the car. They shoot upwards.

"Did you like that?"

Hart cannot hear her reply over the roar of the engine.

Parking near the boulders that made the white "V", Hart unpacks the picnic things and they all cross into the meadow full of cattle.

"Glane cattle, Miss. Men come from all over to buy Glane calves."

In places the grass comes to their knees. Beneath the cottage, Hart puts down the rugs and baskets in the meadow, but the steers keep pushing in close, gaping and gasping, so Hart gathers the things up once more and carries them into the cottage itself.

"You'd better go back for the others," Boss says, his eyes on the valley. He chuckles. "Tell them the old man said there'll be hell to pay."

Hart leaves. At the "V", when he looks back up, he can see Boss leaning on the stone wall, overseeing his kingdom like a king.

* * *

HART'S SECOND LETTER

Hart drives them in low gear up the narrow driveway, Black and Boss in the back, a mist making vision difficult. Hart has put up the hood on the car these last few weeks, although outside the hedges are still thick and green, the grasses glisten, only the high tops of the trees lack foliage.

"Leave the talking to me," Boss says, at least the third time for this pronouncement in Hart's hearing.

He is dressed in his tweed mountain clothes, including cap, and carries a knobby blackthorn stick which he has had fitted with an ivory handle, shaped in a slender circumflex and itself inlaid with discreet, silver scrolls.

Matters have grown worse in the hospital, Hart has heard from Mrs Doe. Each day the mother's face tells the driver of the battle of her child. Joan has received Hart's letter and smiled when she read it, Mrs Doe says.

Now Boss is saying, "Better to square him now, then go find her."

"You'll not square him," Black protests.

"I'll square him," Boss says.

Hart draws level with the front door. Black and Boss get out. No door knocker, so Boss clouts the heavy panels with his stick. Hart can hear the blows echoing around inside. Then, teeth bared in a deep snarl, at them around the side of the house comes a one-eyed dog. Boss raises his stick.

"Get away!" To Hart, "Sound the horn!"

Hart sounds out a series of squealing pips. The dog tries to rush in at Black, who kicks out at the creature. Again Boss strikes the door as Black wipes the pane of one of two windows either side of the door and peers in. Even from where he sits, Hart thinks he can see a corpse, sitting propped in a deep chair, the head fallen forward at right angles to the neck.

"Father."

Boss peers in, steps back. "God preserve us."

"What do you want?"

They turn to the voice, which has come from the gable they stand with their backs to.

"Sam, my father . . ." begins Black as Sam Phibbs, shirt unbuttoned halfway to reveal his white chest, work-stained hands hanging by his sides, takes a step towards them.

"I know him," Sam says and his top lip flutters. "But you've made a wasted expedition, Boss Pender. Nothing you can say will end in my sister joining your brood."

"That's all right," says Boss in a cajoling tone. "We'll do whatever you want, Mr Phibbs."

"Then get back into your car and leave this property."

"You're a decent man," Boss says, "so at least hear another man out."

The implied logic creates, if not assent, then at least no immediate rejection.

Boss continues, "Your dear sister has spoken to you, you have spoken to my son here. The facts are plain. He has sinned before God, he has grievously offended you and your family. He will live with the mark of it for the rest of his days." To Black, "Tell the man!"

"I am heartily sorry . . ." Black stammers.

"But life for us must go on – for you, for me," Boss says, his entire concentration for Sam Phibbs. "And even though there are hard times ahead, life need not always be difficult for us just because someone else has made a terrible mistake."

Hart cannot grasp the meaning of what they are saying. Neither is it possible for the driver to know whether Sam is taking anything in of what had been said. Lower jaw thrust out, he stares at Boss Pender.

"You must do only what you consider fit, Mr Phibbs. I have, believe me, always respected your father, whom I believe is unwell – something I am extremely sorry to learn – but the cases your father prosecuted over many years were always reported in a good light in the *Gazette,* you can go back over the years yourself and read them, there was no finer friend of justice and decency in Monument than Cecil Phibbs."

Sam Phibbs clears his throat. "Finish your piece."

"I have come here this morning to make a long overdue contribution to the care and comfort of my old, respected friend, Sergeant Phibbs," says Boss, reaching to his jacket pocket. "Of course you may do what you wish with the money, but I think I know you well enough as a man of prudence and judgment to use it well."

Hart has never seen a wad of cash that thick. Sam's chest is heaving. The money, single pound notes rolled tight, is being held out to within inches of his face.

"Take it," says Boss. "Please. For your father."

Sam, breath short, gives his head a furious shake. Then with a cry, he turns and runs back around the house. Boss, the money still held in mid-air, looks to Black in puzzlement.

"Is this man mad? There's fifty pounds here."

"Ask him where Cushy is," says Black.

The yell brings back to Hart's mind the man in the printing shed whose hand had once taken the full force of the wire stitcher. Men had turned pale at the same sound. It is so distracting that at first Hart does not see the levelled dung fork.

"Watch out!" he cries.

Sam appears to have Boss as his first target, but then he swings right, lowers the points and thrusts for Black's mid-section. Black leaps. Hart sees the prongs going in. Sees Black fall. Sam is coming again, howling. As Boss makes for the car, Hart, already behind the wheel, is priming the fuel tank.

"For Jesus' sake . . !" Hart hears.

The dog too has gone mad, yapping in frenzy, darting in to score on Black's unattended ankles. In comes the fork, low, stabbing.

"Mackerel! Snapper!"

"Jesus . . ."

Black rolls away, gets up on one knee. Sam raises up the pitchfork and drives down, but Black, the dog now hanging from him, grabs hold of the haft. They swing. Sam Phibbs stumbles back and falls. Kicking at the demented dog, Black runs to the car, where sits his father, straight mouthed, still clutching his roll of money. Hart throws off the brake and they vault forward. A lumping motion of the wheels. A high-pitched wail. Looking back, Hart sees that in their departure they have run over the dog.

* * *

HART'S THIRD LETTER

OCTOBER 1938

A bitter east wind cuts up the river. Monument sleeps. Hart drives down Dudley's Hill and into Candle Lane to the *Gazette*, unlocks the gates to the garage area and stops at the pump. One outside light, a naked bulb. Gusts of wind haul rain in veils across Monument. The pump is worked by manual handle; Hart fills three cans, all he can find, and the tank of the Vauxhall. His mind dwells night and day on only one image, that of a fond face in a wreath of auburn hair in Monument Hospital. She will not come home, they all know. Grief impales the driver. His actions are mechanical. Outside occurrences mean nothing to him, not even the sensational events of recent days. Soaked, the car filled, he drives up to Balaklava. It is nearly two in the morning. He changes his clothes, then brings the car back down to Pig and Litter. He will never forget her. There will be no house, no hearth. As he gets out and walks in the entry to inform of his arrival, he halts. Boss and Black are standing ten yards nearer the house. Hart can smell Boss from where he stands, the whole, big, powerful father man of him, the scents of his pomade and powder, his topcoat smell, all the odours that make up the Proprietor.

"Hart. There are some things here to go out," Boss speaks.

They drive in silence, down Dudley's Hill, across Military Parade, past Love & Son and out onto the end of Small Quay and past the hospital. As the road outside the town begins to rise with the first foothills, Boss tells Hart to pull in.

"Give us a minute."

Hart gets out and walks into the darkness behind the car. The night sits on the earth, unmoving. She was in there, dying. He will leave the digs in Victoria Street, he decides. He will not be able to bear the sight of her at every turn. In the deadness Hart hears Boss's voice.

"I can't go any further with you. Hart has been told where to take you, with the help of God you'll be there by dawn. Go to old Wint Albutt, no-one else, tell him who you are, his grandson. Give him this. Tell Wint you need a place to live for the time being, that there's been a bit of trouble. He won't ask you details, tell him none anyway. Tell no-one. I'll send for you when this thing has blown over."

"And Cushy?"

Boss's sigh. "I'll see that that's looked after. She'll be with you in the New Year. I'll send word about her and her child. Your child." Hart hears the car's springs creak as Boss shifts himself. "It's making a frost," says Boss and gets out. "Hart."

Of all the many times he has seen his employer over the years, Hart, as he regains the wheel, thinks that the sight of him that night, the quays lights from Monument behind him, is the way he will always remember the Proprietor.

Black, wrapped in rugs against the bitter cold, sleeps most of the journey, waking once as Hart replenishes the gasoline. They cross the border at seven the next morning, not at an official customs post but by way of a narrow, ever-turning road, where a sluggish river designates the division of governments. Hart's country.

"We're over," he says and despite his grief, whistles in the fresh morning air.

At noon they reach the coast at Gua, a sweep of green, stamp-sized fields. A tiny harbour. Hart can see that although people are inside the whitewashed cottage they are not coming out. Black takes his things – clothes in a linen bag, a small grip – and walks for the half door. Then he pauses.

"Hart . . ."

Hart has remained at the wheel.

"Thank you." He looks into the grip. "I'd like you to have this." He hands Hart something that glints even in the dull light.

Hart takes the silver-backed hairbrush with its thick, yellow-brown bristles. He feels there are many things he wants to say, but he has no clear idea of how to say them. When he looks up, Black Pender has gone inside. Hart believes that he will never see him again.

*   *   *

MARCH 23RD

Something is afoot. I have been getting odd looks from Tim whenever he encounters me – and twice this week he has come into my office and asked me questions about my work. His mother is out of danger and will, they say, be home in a few weeks. However, yesterday I had a most unusual visit to my flat – the clearest sign yet that I am on the right track. The bishop of Monument himself turned up. I had just washed my hair when the doorbell rang. With a towel around my head I answered the door and when I saw this strange man there I said, "No, thank you" – I thought he was trying to sell me something. But then he said my name and I had another look. I knew I should have known who he was, but I had no idea.

"I'm sorry, but do I know you?" I asked him.

"I'm Jack O'Dea," he said, "I'm the bishop."

He asked if he could come in. Yesterday was Saturday and I like to help my mother on Saturday mornings; so I said, all right, but I would have to go in five minutes.

"You work up in the *Gazette*?"

I confirmed that this was the case.

"A great company. And a great family, Jasmine. Good Catholics. There is nothing hidden about the Penders, nothing lurking in the background, they didn't rob or pillage to get what they have, they got where they are through hard work and diligence. They employ a lot of people in this town, more than sixty if you include Monument FM. I listen to it every morning after Mass and I have to say I think it's a tonic. Do you listen to it at all, Jasmine?"

I told the bishop I listened sometimes to Monument FM.

"Who else do I know who works in the *Gazette*? Apart from Tim. A few of the other ladies, like yourself. Of course, poor Albert Tell has long retired. Goodness, time doesn't hang around, does it, Jasmine? Who do I know in the production side? Most of the men I knew are gone out of it now. Kaiser is still there. Now there's a decent citizen for you – I was chairman of the orphanage, you know, so I know Kaiser with years. He's a good example of what can be achieved in a caring community."

I did not offer an opinion.

"Tim's the new generation, of course, and he's trying to bring things as far along as he can, especially now that Ollie is out of the picture for the time being. God has strange ways, but He is most merciful, of that I am convinced. Not easy, you know, running a business like the *Gazette*, oh no, far from it, I know how difficult it is to run a diocese and I know the same problems arise in business. Tim's involved in a particularly big project at the moment – but a most worthy one, believe me, a project of which the Church approves. Of course, a project like that leads to a lot of tension and pressure. You don't want people trying to undermine you at such an important time."

I asked what he meant.

"What I'm trying to say is that, the same as any other normal family in the world, the Penders have had their black sheep. But that was two generations ago, even before my time – eh? That must make it a long time ago. They went to the gates of hell and back though, I know that, the Penders. Look, the world is full of begrudgers who would only love a rumour or a bit of old gossip to pounce on and to try and disrupt the good work being done by someone like Tim."

I asked the bishop if he had a point to make which involved me.

"People are very sensitive, they react to mood, Jasmine. And, fair enough, a man died years ago, but the man who killed him paid a big price."

"And that's all?" I asked, my Saturday morning with my mother suddenly remote.

"No, there's much more, Jasmine," said Bishop Jack O'Dea, DD, settling in.

To the brothers in Demijohn Street, he was a figure of near papal significance. I have heard that they vied with unique energy during his visits to seat him in well-upholstered chairs, to bring his tea in the best silver teapot, on the best silver tray, and to be permitted, down on their knees, to kiss the ring on his finger in which is imbedded, it is said, a splinter of the true Cross.

Situated on Park Road which runs between O'Gara and Binn's streets, the Bishop's Palace overlooks a small, triangular park, its own property, access to which is shared, by concession, with the other local residents. The palace is a square and now flat-roofed, late Georgian building, its original dome (seen in prints) having been replaced, in a rare example of ecclesiastical economy, by a flat lid. The nomenclature involved – "palace" – , the ample grounds, the proportions of the six reception rooms, the size of the basement kitchens, the aspect from the twelve-feet high windows, the ornate plasterwork, yawning fireplaces, internal bell and kitchen lift systems, copper plumbing, horse-sized baths, king-sized beds with canopies, art, silverware, rare china, tapestries, floor rugs, priceless tallboys and other appointments suggest needs and interests beyond the merely spiritual. His Lordship, Jack O'Dea, DD, who lives alone, divides his time between this pile in Monument, a penthouse flat in Dublin, and Rome, where, rumour has it, exists another residence of equal standing.

Bishop O'Dea likes to address those in care when they have attained sixteen years of age. In the course of long but by no means tedious soliloquies, he transfers to them as best he can – as their fathers might have at such a stage – the results of the lessons taught him by life. These include: hints on how to deal with creditors, the essentialness of owning property, the virtues of moderation and the startling shortness of life, even for the old. He speaks of the incomparable advantages that accrue to those with regular bowels. On the issue of women too, surprising for a man in his position, he is expansive. He informs his young audiences that he has always preferred their company to men's. He confides that he can count on the fingers of one hand the days of his life in which he has not dwelt with fondness on the image of one woman or another, and that he will go to his grave regretting that he has not fathered children. Never once has he been known to mention any of the matters which tradition demands of a bishop, save at the end when he always declares he would like to give a blessing; at which point everyone kneels and he blesses.

He sees himself more like a tsar than a mere spiritual leader. He is, in his own eyes and in those of many others, if not at the sole peak of Monument's community, then at least a co-occupier of that position with the key players in the town's society and business: the Loves, Shortcourses, Crosses, Churches, Santrys and Pender-Goodes.

Tim is rattled by what he sees as my trespassing into territory long preserved and closed to scrutiny, and so he enlisted the help of Jack O'Dea in order to try and contain me. This was precisely what this visit yesterday to my flat was about. But why? What are they trying to prevent me from discovering? What is the connection between 1938 and Kaiser and why does Tim see it as such a threat to his business empire?

The bishop wanted me to hear the "truth" about what happened in Monument in the autumn of 1938, he told me. What follows is his version of the truth.

*   *   *

THE BISHOP'S STORY

1938

Black's leg hurts. He has cleaned out the wound as best he can and made a poultice of hot bran flakes and strapped it to it to draw out any poison. Now each downward pedal thrust sends up a shaft of fresh pain; although by the time he reaches the mountain foothills he finds he can bear it. Wind from the north-west bears within each of its gusts rain in pinheads. He has forgotten his cap. He lowers his head and pumps into the final hill before Phibbs's.

Black wishes many things, none of them attainable, all of them requiring an inversion of time. He is terrified. It is as if his inner structures, the rigidity that keeps him upright, a man, has dissolved. Gone are life's certainties: what cannot be now is. As he beats his way to the crown of the final rise, Black regrets more than anything having involved his father. Yet, at the time, terror in his heart, he had been unable to think of anyone else in the world to whom he could turn. Although he loves his father as he loves no other man, he is still his father and to have revealed intimacies to him of the kind Black has has caused the youth unrelenting pain. He longs for a different mother, someone more like Lilly instead of the woman whom everyone sees as in need of constant protection; his instinct has told him that women would know better what to do in the present trouble than any man. He breasts the rise and the lane that turns off to Phibbs's comes into view. He could have told his father that money would not turn Sam Phibbs, a madman, but Boss Pender, who believes in the power of money over even that of love, would not have listened. Black aches for what he wants to do: go away with Cushy, marry, come back as man and wife when no-one can assail them. But he needs to find Cushy first and only her brother can tell him where she is.

They killed the dog here yesterday. As Black freewheels to the front door he sees its body thrown in the ditch. The sight inside of the old man, the nearest thing to a corpse Black has yet encountered, is something he wants to avoid repeating; he props the bicycle up against the wall of the house and makes his way around to the haggard. The affairs of farms, livestock husbandry and the harsh business of survival off the land are all matters outside

159

Black's experience, so he has no idea if the scene behind the house is typical: on a steaming mound of dung a dead calf, still smeared with blood and glistening with the slick of afterbirth, is being devoured by half a dozen cats. All at once Black's leg is in agony and his strength leaves him. He turns to the back door and sees Sam Phibbs gaping out from a window.

"I've come . . . to ask your mercy . . ." begins Black, as Sam Phibbs emerges. "To apologise for my father."

Sam has a dishcloth in his hands. Black stares at the man's bare arms, clotted with blood, at the sinews standing out in his neck.

"Two pound." Sam comes to him, walking like a man asleep.

"I'm sorry?"

"Two pound."

Black can see that Sam is crying.

"Two pounds?"

"Waiting on her all summer. No help, you see. Everything I do is on my own." Sam's uneven jaw. "Ten hours I tried to save him. No use."

Black realises that Sam is talking about the dead animal behind them.

"I'm sorry to have come at this time," he says, "but I have had to come here to ask you where I can find Cushy."

"Cushy."

"Your sister. Whom I love – as I believe she loves me."

"Aaaaaaa . . ."

Sam goes for him. Black is driven backwards into the door, which gives behind them and, aware more than anything of the blood on the other man's arms, is bowled inwards along the floor of flagstones and meets the kitchen table with the backs of his legs. He finds himself lying on the table, Sam Phibbs's fists flailing for his face. Without warning the table collapses. Breath is punched from Black's body. But Sam's head has encountered a plank of splintered deal and he is staggering, hand to his ear, in an unsteady path to the enamel sink. Black struggles up, gasping. He sees a way to end all this. The man's back is to him. Although his eyes don't leave Sam, Black is also conscious, in the lateral functions of his vision and deductive process, of another presence at the hearth by a mound of skinny turf sods. There is a poker. Black begins to circle to it, his perception that he has an opportunity to solve his problems growing all the time. Sam is fumbling in a drawer, something to do with his head wound, Black believes, although it is difficult to tell if the blood is the man's own or that of the cow outside. Then even as his hand goes to the poker, Black sees the knife emerge from the drawer.

"No!"

Hate has blinded Sam Phibbs, for Black, no time to pick up the poker, sidesteps him handily enough. Now Black, back to the window, can see across the remains of the table to where Sam is crouched, knife held out in front, beside the chair containing the drooling and vacant figure of Cecil Phibbs. Sam leaps. Death is established there that morning. Black has an overwhelming desire for the presence of his father. His fear has distorted what he sees and thinks, slowed down the evidence of his eyes, has made him hear things in unaccustomed detail, the ticking of a clock in another room, the moaning breath of the old man. But despite all his terror, he can see that it is Sam who is just about to die. That makes Black cool and determined. Even though Sam has the upper hand, Black can see the shape of Sam's dead body in the hearth. He grasps a handle of something in his right fist as Sam makes another lunge. Black swings the heavy object and meets the incoming man on the temple. Sam looks at Black with momentary curiosity, as if the appearance of another weapon is a technical breach of unspoken rules; his eyes go round. He sinks. Black kneels on his chest and, catching Sam by the throat, squeezes. Long after he is aware that the knife has fallen to the stone flags, he digs deep with his thumbs. Sam's tongue comes out. Black stands up. Sam lies across his father's feet.

No intervening period, no journey, makes up his memory, according to Bishop O'Dea. One moment Black is looking down at Sam Phibbs dead, the next he is at home in bed. Pain floods him. His leg wound oozes thick, yellow pus. His head and face. His hands which ache. He understands nothing and yet, in keeping with the heightened awareness which still surrounds him, he understands all. His father will know what to do.

It takes three days, but then word flies around the town like cholera: Sam Phibbs is dead. Murdered in his kitchen. Boss Pender himself is driven out to the scene. In Monument murder has not occurred in peacetime within memory.

The bishop then produced a copy of an old cutting with which I was already familiar: Jeff Dunphy's news piece.

SUSPICIOUS DEATH IN DEILT
MR. SAMUEL PHIBBS A WELL KNOWN LOCAL FIGURE
CIVIC GUARDS RULE OUT ROBBERY AS A MOTIVE
From our own correspondent
Monument, Thursday October 20th, 1938

The Civic Guards are treating as suspicious the discovery of the body of Mr. Sam Phibbs, a well-known local figure, in his house near Deilt .

Mr. Phibbs lived with his father, Mr. Cecil Phibbs, in their farmhouse residence in Lower Deilt. Mr. Cecil Phibbs was for many years a member of the Royal Irish Constabulary in Monument. He retired when that force was disbanded in 1922.

The body of Mr. Samuel Phibbs, who was unmarried, was found by neighbours last Friday

162

afternoon. Robbery is being ruled out as a motive and the Guards are said to be puzzled by the situation, although one source yesterday told the *Monument Gazette* that the death may be a case of "mistaken identity".

A team of forensic experts is on its way from Dublin to examine the scene and a post-mortem examination will take place.

The investigation continues.

And then next day, in a development that occupies the minds and mouths of the whole town for years afterwards, Black Pender goes missing. A sensation. Implications that need no explaining. People begin to come forward. There is talk of bad blood between the dead man and Boss Pender's son. Sources within the *Monument Gazette* itself speak of a physical confrontation between the two men in the hall of the paper in Candle Lane.

Boss Pender does not leave his home in Pig and Litter for over two weeks. In bed, a broken man, he lies with his face to the wall, wishing for death, it is said. His favourite son wanted for murder. A fugitive. The following week's edition of the *Gazette* leads with an account about the flooding in Eillne. No mention of the story that is consuming the town. Sam Phibbs is buried on Thursday. Private ceremony. On Sunday, his father, old Cecil Phibbs dies. The Protestant women take out all the good delph again. On the death of these two men, the erasure of a male line, apart from the one original news item, nothing further is published. Neither Sam Phibbs nor his father were popular men and in the minds of many people their passing, in some, warped way, represents an overdue balancing.

But in mid-November 1938, a Saturday, a little over four weeks after her brother's murder, Cushy Phibbs marries the twin son of Boss Pender, James, also known as White.

*　*　*

After the bishop left yesterday, I thought long and hard about his version of events. They may be accurate, but I am not so sure. I intend to keep going now on the route I started out on, to finish the job by my own research and reach my own conclusions; and if at the end of it all I find that the bishop's story is the right one, then I will have lost nothing but a little time.

Thirteen

Often during those last winters in Leire I awoke to visions of a world aflame. Standing at my window, arms outstretched, drinking in the chill glow, I saw it die around me in an instant matched with that in which it was born. You could not hope to grasp the multiple expressions of light on rock and sea unless you lived in a place like Leire; light was only ever a thing of seconds, sometimes just a subtle change in peripheral vision, a transient secret. In January the morning cliffs began to take on the blush of maidens. Within the veins of their gullies and crevices pumped the eager young blood of dawn; the wonder of evening light was all overhead and was the chosen way of clouds to gain their glory. As February came in, colours ranged from the deep purple of Easter mourning to blood. Sometimes the clouds lumped like a phosphorescent washboard into infinity; but equally there were evenings when they wept vermilion tears. Let me tell you about what happened when it snowed out there. Flakes as big as your hand, each one crafted to a separate design, curtained down, so that from out along the cliff promontories you could see only the faint glow of our building. The snow married sky and sea and in the process, in the making of this overdue union, took away the voice of the ocean. I could never decide whether to watch it from inside or out; first I stayed in, a delicious sensation, like standing waist high in featherdown. Then I ventured out and stood on the edge of the sea and realised it had become mute. Later, as a rule, the sun exploded, making the rock pools blaze like day stars.

*

About three weeks after Mrs Rice's warning, I had left work one evening and was walking out along Candle Lane. All the talk in the *Gazette* was about Ollie Pender-Goode: after weeks on the death list she had that morning undergone a heart-bypass operation. The odds were fifty-fifty Jasmine told me when I met her in the canteen. Everyone was talking about Ollie. No-one wanted her to die. No-one wanted Tim as Proprietor.

Jasmine told me that she had been very busy in the library, which was why she had not come out to Glane on the weekends or managed to see me on my half-days. As I turned from Candle Lane onto Dudley's Hill, I was beginning to ask myself if all this research into my past was really worth it, if her mother might not, after all, have had a point.

"Kaiser? Kaiser!"

It was the editor, his face cocked in a cheeky grin. I was sure he was going to tell me some good news about his mother.

"Tim?"

"How's that little tart?"

I didn't understand what he meant.

"Jesus," Tim said and licked his lips, "you're some operator, Kaiser! I'd never have guessed. The whole fucking town wants to be into that one." As he walked away, I could see the sniggers rising off his shoulders.

I was, in fact, meant to be seeing Jasmine that same evening, the first in weeks, but a great weight pressed me down and when I awoke it was too late to go out. I couldn't explain it to her either the next day when I saw her, not that she wanted to know, I think, for she turned her head and walked straight past me. That upset me, the fact that she could treat me like a stranger; and yet that night I had to admit that I was the cause of her anger; I had not turned up to meet her, and all because of something Tim had said.

And then, a week later, from where I happened to be standing on the corner of Bagnall's Lane, I saw Jasmine walk out of the door of the Commercial Hotel and get into Tim's BMW. There was no mistake. It was Jasmine. It was Tim. As they pulled away she ran her hand through her hair, a gesture I had imagined I alone was familiar with. I had to get sick. I turned into a doorway.

I could not get up next morning. My head burned. I don't know how long I slept, but when I saw my face it looked red and swollen. Days went by. I missed work. I hurtled through a succession of tunnels. Ollie's big face grew from the end of them like a balloon. More than anything, water was all I craved. When I opened my eyes, Jasmine was beside my bed, laying a cool flannel on my brow.

"I'm sorry, Kaiser," she said in whispers. "I'm really sorry."

"Why?"

"It's nothing, nothing. Trust me."

"I saw you."

"I know, but just trust me."

Even though over the weeks that followed we became friends again, I knew she would always find her way back to Tim just when I would think she had forgotten him.

"I don't want to talk about Tim," she would say when I asked her.

He was no good for her, I told her. Tim was bad.

"I don't want to talk about Tim." She would smile at me. "I want to talk about you, Kaiser."

And so began the pattern of our remaining days. Jasmine and I would be friends as long as we didn't talk about Tim. Her interest in me was what consumed her. Sometimes we were more than friends, but I knew Jasmine was still seeing him, that she was drawn to Tim by that part of herself that wanted to destroy her. Now if ever Tim and I bumped into one another, he looked at me with laughter in his eyes. I avoided him. I began to hate my job.

I saw him several times in the company of the superintendent of the guards, a big man with curly black hair who had risen swiftly through the ranks. One evening as I passed by the Indian restaurant on Buttermilk they both looked up from their bowls and saw me. As I went by the window I could see their laughter filling the air like red weals.

14

APRIL IOTH

Although I know it has hurt Kaiser beyond uttering, I have gone out twice in the past ten days with Tim Pender-Goode. My reason is as follows: Tim knows what I am doing and wants me to stop – as the visit by the bishop made plain. Of course, the reason he wants me to stop – I now believe, but cannot yet prove – is the very reason I must continue. Every time I look at Kaiser's lovely face, I know what I must do. It is as if I have been sent to liberate him – a fanciful notion, I accept, yet this is what love does to you. Love sweeps aside all considerations of danger, it makes the timid bold. Love makes heroes of us all.

Tim fears what I am doing because what I am uncovering may well threaten his position as Proprietor. But he also has an eye for me. So I decided, purely in the interests of my mission, to agree to go out with him in an attempt to make him relax about my research. And it worked. On the first date, after some initial questions about what I was up to, his interest in me as a woman overtook his other reservations. And so I'm going to buy time in this way. It's cold-hearted, I know. He's a most obvious and unattractive man and easily flattered. I'd prefer one minute in Kaiser's company to a whole evening with Tim.

Today, even though I know Tim would be furious if he found out, I went to No. 1 Pig and Litter, where I at last met Mrs James ("Cushy") Pender, Cushy Phibbs, only daughter and one of two children of former Monument R.I.C. sergeant, Cecil Phibbs. I also met Agnes, her maid.

They both remember Kaiser. They remember his visits from Demijohn Street to Pig and Litter, visits made, they say, at Cushy's suggestion. He was a thoughtful child, they told me, quite frail, with very dark, nearly black hair and hazel, trusting eyes. I wish I had a photograph.

She is blind, old and unwell, and her daughter Ollie's illness has weighed much on her. Cushy's life is the truth suppressed. In there somewhere is still the young girl who went on a picnic a lifetime ago and who loved a handsome young man. Boss Pender has been dead for nearly three decades but still she fears him. And she still loves Black Pender. I could hear that love every time she spoke his name. She has lived her whole life crushed by the thought that in another place he was waiting for her. The interview is still alive in my mind as I write this, for those ancient years are as raw and as real to Cushy as if she was just turned seventeen.

*   *   *

CUSHY'S STORY

1938

She has long thought of death. Although the sun shines on the narrow garden and people walk by on the Dublin street without topcoats, Cushy's predominant emotion is grief. It encompasses all the loss she has been powerless to prevent, the demise of her happiness and the prospect of a future defined only by her own shame. She does not want any bit of the child, now obvious to a curious eye, her changed body another source of grief – grief for the unbroken image of herself that she tries to cling on to. If she could close her eyes and by wishing for death achieve it, both for her and the child, Cushy Phibbs would do so.

Only the sign outside the boarding house off the Dublin's North

Circular Road, "Dollan", gives any indication of a connection with the south. Yet the landlady, now in her late fifties, was the eldest daughter of the rector to the Church of Ireland on the Thom, outside the gates of Main, and she was once hurried up to Dublin in circumstances corresponding to Cushy's, and installed in this fine, two-storey red-bricked house with bow windows near the Phoenix Park, and given an allowance. Parentage was never discussed, but the business end of things was put in place by the land agent of the Santrys, and it was rumoured that right up to his death at eighty in 1920 Captain John Santry never came to Dublin without paying a visit to the park. She took in boarders and became a landlady. She kept in touch by letter with her father, the rector, and his successors. A practice evolved between her and the parish of Thom, whereby Protestant girls in trouble could find a safe refuge for their confinement and the months that followed. Surprising over the years how steady the business – a good business too, always cash in hand; the good, Protestant farmers of Deilt always have savings for such emergencies.

Cushy wants to, but is unable to talk to this woman. She yearns most of all to tell her what happened. She cannot. She wants to tell her about Sam's insanity, about how he came into the kitchen sniffing the air like a wolf, and to show her the bruises on her neck and arms. She cannot. A pathetic pride – its realisation another source of grief – will not let Cushy describe what took place. The belt with the buckle, how Sam ripped it off himself, caught her by the hair and beat her until, exhausted, he fell onto his hands and knees. Cushy has never spoken of that until now, she told me. So much she could not then discuss. Late that night her brother brought over the rector and the next morning the rector took Cushy to Dublin.

In the following weeks she speaks only when addressed. She cannot bring herself to talk, or to touch the other woman, or to ask to be held, or to cry. Side by side, however, with all these inabilities, Cushy is aware that the woman knows.

Her bedroom is at the front on the second floor. She sees the landlady leave to bring her pair of whippets into the Phoenix Park, sly dogs that live in a back-garden pen and, if encountered on leads, slink around your ankles. The woman has a smooth, brittle face that Cushy has heard other lodgers admire for its evidence of lingering beauty, but in which Cushy sees only resentment. This will be her, she knows, thirty years on – if she is lucky. Cushy cannot bear to see her own future so illustrated. The sight of the landlady and her dogs, now at the head of the street and about to disappear, sinks Cushy deeper.

Something slender keeps her sane, she cannot describe it, it's like a thin, white light and if she takes her eyes from it she will cease to exist. Cushy looks down at herself and wonders how a child can be in there. So quiet, her body, so undisturbed. It is her mind that writhes in turmoil. A vision of herself as a child persists: in a dress with ribbed stitching and pleats, a bow in her hair. A warm morning out in the yard, there she is, crouching down, peering under a farm cart and calling, "Here, cushy-cat, cushy-cat!" The cat, ever suspicious, advances into view. She gathers it up in her arms. "Nice cushy-cat!" And at this point there is always the sound of a woman's laughter in Cushy's head.

After it happened, for reasons unfathomable yet more real than anything she ever experienced, Cushy mourned for the girl in the pleated dress. She had killed her. Now the vision is added to: a small, naked body, the aura of death, the pitiless momentum of grief. Cushy sees nothing else. She might be struck as blind now as she will one day become were it not for the whiteness on which her mind locks.

Cushy thinks of the animals in the fields around the house in Deilt, grazing in enviable contentment. For reasons she cannot fathom, her brother is the figure of ultimate authority in her life. At other times she can look on him simply as a man of no education, toiling as best he can, someone with whom she has almost nothing in common, who happens to live in the place she calls home and is her brother. But then she saw his reaction to her news, the cloud over his eyes, his loose jaw, and she understood she would never be able to disobey him.

Cushy spends much time in bed, letting it be known in the boarding house that breakfast is not required, a strategy that allows her to rise late, often towards noon, and then when the day's main meal is served to join the other four lodgers. Only women reside in this gleaming and clean establishment. A pair in their fifties who were once suffragettes and who share the large, back room on the first floor, a woman with spectacles who works in Guinness's, and a red-haired girl, Cushy's age, eight months pregnant, whose father is a bishop somewhere. Little conversation. The suffragettes discourse loudly, as if still at a public meeting. The landlady is served first by a woman doubled by arthritis, and keeps an eye on portions. Cushy asks to be excused, returns upstairs, is often in bed by seven. She prays in the moments before sleep that she will not wake up.

Twice she has gone out, once into the front garden when a troop of mounted soldiers paraded past – on their way into the park, there must have been a hundred of them; Cushy wanted to *smell* the horses – and once into the park itself, on a day of warm, late October sunshine, no wind to finish the de-leafing of the trees, the music of a band drew her in. Not so much the bandsmen in red and blue, nor their music, but other people was what Cushy wanted. Young lovers holding hands, a scene from summer preserved into this unseasonal setting, as if people were storing up ahead of winter with music and sun and love.

She thinks every day about Black. She imagines him walking up the path outside, and lifting his hat and asking her how she is now. She will never again have the courage to see him, not after what happened. He will never want to know her again, he would find her repulsive. Now she falls asleep in the November sunlight and awakens not to the image of Black's face but to that of her brother, Sam's.

Cushy hears the gate, assumes it is the landlady returning. She looks down from her window only when she hears men's voices. The tops of two, dark blue caps. Cushy knows enough of policemen to recognise them.

"Miss Phibbs!"

The kitchen retainer is unable to climb the stairs.

"Miss Phibbs!"

Cushy, bewildered, goes onto the landing. The uniformed men, the caps now wedged at their oxters, tower over the old woman. One of them looks up. His green eyes.

"I'm coming."

Cushy is breathless.

"Miss Phibbs?"

"I . . . am Miss Phibbs. What is the matter?"

His eyes are kind, too. His colleague has opened the door to the front room, the landlady's territory, but Cushy is beyond caring about proprieties. She sits down in the hall, trembling, as the door is closed on the staring kitchen woman.

"Prepare yourself for some bad news, Miss," says the policeman.

Cushy is unable to hear him, not outright, that is, for she can capture the thrust of his meaning and that, to her shame, makes her laugh as well as cry. Great voids open beneath her as she listens. Two deaths, two burials. No-one wanted to upset her. She laughs, face wet. Everything looked after, the young man is explaining. The Pender family. Time is skewed for Cushy. For now the landlady and her dogs are also in the hall, but standing back, and the two suffragettes are out on the landing. One of them calls down:

"Does she *want* to go? She's not being arrested, after all!"

"I've explained it to her," says the policeman.

"Ask her again, damn it, man! I don't trust any of you!"

The green-eyed policeman says, "Do you want to come with us, Miss?"

As Cushy swoons, the policeman intercepts one side of her, the landlady the other. They set her down on the oak hall seat and put a cushion beneath her head, another for her feet. Cushy can hear them miles off.

"Who is taking responsibility for this?" asks the landlady.

"Mr Pender, ma'am," says the policeman.

"Miss," says the landlady.

"Sorry. Miss."

"Cushy? Cushy!"

She has never called Cushy by her first name before.

"Cushy, can you hear me? Do you want to go to these Penders? Do you? You can stay here for as long as you wish – do you hear me? For as long as you wish?"

"What does she want to stay here for?"

Everyone turns. There stands the red-haired bishop's daughter, stomach bulging.

"Be *quiet*!" snaps the landlady.

"I will not! I'd go this instant if I could! I can't because no-one wants me. D'you think this is how life should be lived, hidden away here with you people, out of sight of the world, no husband, no father for the child when it comes? Do you? If Cushy has someone to take her, no matter what has happened in the past, she should go if she wants to."

"Her brother sent her here to get her *away* from those people," the landlady seethes. "He gave me a trust."

"Her brother's dead, Miss." The green-eyed policeman nods confirmation. "And her father."

"Oh my God," says the landlady.

"Go with them, Cushy!" cries the girl with red hair. "Go and have some sort of a life!"

Cushy opens her eyes. She will remember forever the eyes above her and, as she is brought out, the faces upstairs looking down; in later years she often wonders if they are all still there.

When the guards drive her not to Monument, but to a village north of Dublin to which she has never been before and will never again set foot in, and she sees Hart at the wheel of the Vauxhall outside the Roman Catholic church, she is not surprised. The guard has, in his gentle voice, in terms lacking any detail, told her how her brother died and about the missing man who is suspected. Cushy looks at him and smiles; for although she has heard him clearly, she cannot take in the meaning of his words. Nor is shock to be seen on her features when, in the porch of the church, White Pender steps forward, grinning nervously, his brother, Tom, in the background, looking at his watch. Tom and the sacristan are the two witnesses. That she is being married in another faith, to a virtual stranger, means nothing then to Cushy; she is making something of her life. No mention is made of the Pender parents or why they are not present. White smells of drink. Later in the sacristy where she has to sign her name, Cushy remembers something she said in the past, years ago, maybe, to his father. She told Boss Pender that if you left out the colour of the twins' hair, they were both exactly the same.

In later years Cushy Pender becomes known as a woman who says very little, who often takes crucial seconds to answer a question, whose eyes can seem empty of interest and who never complains. She has no curiosity for the *Gazette* or for any of the people who work there. She seldom speaks, except to the servants in the house that was rented for herself and White in James Place, in particular to Agnes, a girl only three years younger than herself who started

176

work earlier that year in Pig and Litter, and who, when Cushy's baby is born, comes to nurse the infant and stays. It is as if on that afternoon in November 1938, in the hallway of the house near the Phoenix Park, all the accommodations of Cushy's life thereafter were decided. She could have remained; she left. It was a question of levels. Anything was better, she had decided, than the life to which she thought she was condemned.

As she grows older, long after they moved into Pig and Litter and only herself and Agnes remain, Cushy can often be heard speaking aloud. Names plucked from nowhere. Old days, a picnic. A photograph. A man she still loves but whom she will never see again. She sometimes wonders if he ever thinks of her, or of Monument, or Glane. Despite the awful thing he did, she can never understand why he has not tried to get in touch with her even once, why he never came south. She would swear that he still loves her as much as she loves him – but the truth is that he was just as imprisoned by his problems as Cushy was by hers wherein both of them were condemned forever to love in silence and alone.

* * *

MONUMENT, EARLIER THAT YEAR

She'd been afraid of him the very first day up there, had brazened her way out of it, but he'd made her flesh crawl. It had been even worse the time they all came on the picnic. Every so often Cushy was aware of his eyes on her. Some men were like that. Old stoat's eyes, as her school chaplain had once described them. Anger in there, blaming her for something although she was a stranger, just a friend of his son's. And what he would do to her in that anger, punish her, the way all men punish women, then walk away, dusting themselves off. It's what women want, at the end of the day, what they deserve. How could she tell Black that without offending him? Your father, this great man you love, has old stoat's eyes for me? She wanted the son, but feared losing him if she told him that so early on. Some men got over it, calmed the beast within, the school chaplain again, they were then able to continue with evenness. Perhaps he might, she had thought, but in vain: she had felt his breath on her neck that day as he sat beside her in the car for the photograph, he never in fact touched her, but he might as well have; his breath was worse, she could feel it slide down her skin, across her breasts, lingering there, and then on down to her stomach. She couldn't look at him. She knew if she met his eyes then he would take it as complicity.

The remainder of that day with Black had filled Cushy with such hope that she had in large part forgotten her discomfort by the time Black told her that they were all going up to Glane again.

She's been looking forward to it, but she doesn't want to risk Sam knowing, so she's walked down the lane to meet the car before it turns up to the farmhouse. A cooler day. She hears the sound of the motor growing from the valley. She cannot keep the smile from her face even when she sees Boss Pender alone in the open back of the maroon car.

"Good afternoon, Miss Phibbs."

"Mr Pender. Where are . . . ?"

Boss throws back his head and laughs. She can see gold in his teeth. "Those scoundrels will have to be taught the meaning of time!"

"Oh, in that case . . ." Cushy turns to go back up the lane, but Hart is standing beside the car, holding open the rear door for her. She steps up.

"Don't be anxious, Miss Phibbs. Hart will go back for them by and by. Nothing like hunger to capture young men's attention, eh? Hart? A rug!"

Hart spreads a woollen rug over Cushy's knees. As they drive off, she can smell nothing but the car's leather.

"Such a smell of leather!" she says.

"Does it offend you?"

"On the contrary."

They meet no-one, all the way up to the iron gate. They motor through and as Hart jumps out for the second time to pull the gate to, Cushy looks back and sees Monument in the distance, down below the heat haze, through the vertical iron bars. Boss never utters, runs his fingers along his scalp a few times, drums the fingers of his right hand on the door of the car. They slow to pull up below the white rock, in the usual place, but then Boss leans forward.

"Drive it, Hart!"

Hart's face becomes uncertain.

"You've done it before." To Cushy. "Hasn't he?"

"Yes," says Cushy, "he has, but . . ."

"Well, there you are, Hart, you hear what my young companion says. Drive it!"

Hart halts, reverses the car down the track thirty yards, then opens her up. Cushy grips the seat. The big car meets the smooth incline and seems to stand on its end. Then, with blinding white a-rush either side, they shoot upwards.

"Did you like that?"

Cushy's face is rigid with fear.

"There, there, it wasn't too bad, was it?" says Boss and pats her hand.

They pull in as once before, twenty paces from the white "V". As Hart holds the door, Boss's hand finds, with deftness and for only an instant, the small of Cushy's back. Hart unloads further rugs from the trunk on the rack, and Boss's walking stick, and a small, rigid basket with a hooped handle. Boss puts his hands on his hips and breathes in. Above them, light clouds patch the blueness.

"Are we . . . ?" Cushy begins, determined to keep brazen.

179

"We'll be where they're meant to be," says Boss. "Come along," and he ushered her ahead of him.

Hart stands aside. They cross into the meadow, Boss striding out, measured lengths of his long stick, Cushy next, Hart following with full arms of rugs and the dangling basket. White cattle, moved down from another pasture since the last visit, canter across to inspect them. Boss waves his stick.

"You ever seen the like of them, Miss Phibbs? Glane cattle. Look at the reach of them."

"They're fantastic."

"Men come from the four corners to buy the calf of a pure-bred Glane. Don't worry, they'll forget us in a minute."

But when they reach the place at the top of the field, the shaded spot where they'd last set out the rugs, and where Hart now begins to arrange them, the cattle keep creeping in, huge heads, nostril steam, their flies in great clouds, so Hart picks up and folds everything and follows Boss and Miss Phibbs to the walled-off grounds of the stone cottage. Then his employer instructs him to return to town for the others. Hart walks back down to the car.

From where she sits Cushy can see Boss Pender outside as he leans on the wall, surveying all the land and valleys beneath him. She is terrified of him, yet she does not want to offend him or to do anything which might result in distance coming between herself and Black. She tries to rationalise the two times he has touched her already, once on the hand, once on the back. Each time with meaning. There were teachers at school, a piano teacher in particular, who liked to touch. The hands, in order to instruct, or, rising to stretch his legs as his girls played their nocturnes, the neck. And the plump grocer who had always brought gifts of rare oranges, or, at times, a peach; he liked legs. You learned an attitude, some better than others. Cushy's is to be familiar, to play the game, seeing them as equals – which gives her an invariable power, she likes to think. Like she achieved before with this one. That way she can hide her fear. Cushy lights a cigarette.

What words exactly passed between them on previous occasions? Cushy cannot recall, but now, alone with him, her unease suggests that somehow she is their hostage. She tries to draw comfort from the room she is in, the straw bedding in the corner, its happy resonances. All she can see is him outside. This is different from the other times with him, why she can't say. He is withdrawn, almost morose, as if his true personality is coming through. Twice too she has found him looking at her, his eyes have not changed from those she saw on the last occasion. And for what reason would a busy man drive out here with her alone and then dispatch his driver back to collect the other members of the party? Why did he not wait a few minutes more for them? Although his back is turned, Cushy can sense his tension. Displeasure with how the day has turned out, she hopes.

"I'll set the things out so we'll be ready when the others get here," says Cushy airily, walking out past him to where Hart has left the basket.

She can see, although he doesn't move from where he is leaning, that he is observing her. She listens with straining ears, although she knows it is futile, for the sound of the returning car. Cigarette dangling from her mouth, Cushy sets out plates and knives, cups and saucers on the warm flagstones. It is hot. Kneeling, she unties the scarf and shakes her hair out. Throwing aside the cigarette, face to the sun, closed eyed, she says, "What a marvellous day!"

The sound, for reasons Cushy never understood but will always remember, is like a fat raindrop. A soft plash. She starts. He has left his place at the wall, but she knows him to be standing directly behind her.

"Count it."

Cushy sees the money on the rug, speared by a pin. Although the breath is gone from her, from instinct she tries to keep her outward composure.

"I beg your pardon?"

"*Count* it."

His voice is all from his chest. Cushy picks up the wad, tries to stop her fingers jumping. Pound notes, ten at least.

"What on earth is this for?" asks Cushy, fighting not to swallow.

"A little gift," he says and now, like the piano teacher, he is fondling her neck. "Between us. You know."

"I haven't the foggiest what you mean," says Cushy, twisting her head away and getting to her feet. She manages still to smile at him. "The boys will be here shortly."

"Not that shortly," he says and she sees that he is taking his breaths like a man who has run. "Not that shortly."

"Don't!" says Cushy, but in a smaller voice, and pushes away his arm.

"Miss." His mouth is set.

"I'm going home," says Cushy, turning.

But he has her above the elbow. And as she turns back, in terror now, he heaves her full into him and begins to kiss her neck. "Cushy . . ."

"No . . . !"

He straightens up, her arm still in his grip and drags her inside towards the room of other memories. What terrifies Cushy most is his deliberation and arising from it the knowledge that he has done this before.

"*No!*"

He is implacable, only his eyes show anger. She bends down to his big hand and bites it. Stopping, blinking, as she tries to go back, he catches her with his other hand and cuffs her with the fist.

"Bitch," he speaks, but she has, she can see, aroused something extra in him, a wildness.

It is as if she is harnessed to a horse and plough. She can not resist his strength as he drags her in, her feet skitter and she tries to fall in order to break his grip, but he catches her around the waist from behind and, her heels kicking, lifts her in and over to the straw.

In all the many years of her long life, the memory always ends there for Cushy. Never again, for example, can she see or smell straw without trembling, feeling nauseous. The taste of blood too, not a common thing but encountered, for example at a dentist's, brings her to the verge of panic. She can of course reconstruct, should she want to, not just from the evidence of her body, bruised in ten places as well as violated, or the soreness that means she will not walk upright for three days, or her torn dress or cut mouth. She knows what he has done, but she retains no memory of it. Neither could she, were she asked, describe what it felt like. Not at all. She has no memory of that. She is aware that he took something extra from her that day, part of her personality, because never again will she be the outgoing, cheeky and sometimes provocative girl just left school who captured Black Pender's heart. A comfort lies in such unremembering, an avoidance of pain. She awakes next morning at home and smells the whiskey she drank, also without recollection, once her father's Christmas whiskey; when she goes to inspect the bottle she sees that it lies on its side on the shelf, empty.

Cushy carries these solidified moments at her core into and through her married life. Her intelligence often begs her to try and thaw the cold block within her as a means, for one thing, of making something of her marriage with White. She never can. The physical illness which arises with any proximity to the centre of that day outweighs her best intentions. Even when her father-in-law is dead – over years she has prayed with fervour in her new religion for his death – and he is removed from her life, the shame of admission remains as strong as it did following that day in Glane.

Had she married a man in whom she could have confided there might have been a slow letting of pain. It never happens. She endures White Pender with blankness. She lies as if in cramp, head averted. She cannot talk because she cannot tell him that she feels nothing. Not a question of not feeling pleasure, a question of feeling nothing. He has often withdrawn before she opens her eyes and realises it is over yet again. She blames herself over the years that she has turned White into what he has become. No-one ever questions why Boss Pender's son is a drunkard, the butt of sub-editors' jokes, someone respected not even by the yard boys in the *Gazette*, and who is senile a good fifteen years before he dies.

Cushy's numbness grows outwards and freezes everything in its grip. When she tries to dwell on the memory of Black Pender, such is her frustration at her inability to distinguish him in her mind from his brother that she gives up. And what about Boss, for the twenty-six years in which he lives afterwards? White and Cushy get married and are given a house on James Place, and the baby is born. Cushy never goes near the paper. Or Pig and Litter. On the occasions Cushy and Boss come across each other, such as the family gatherings which cannot be avoided, or at funerals, they never speak. Their distance is assumed by members of the family to arise from the old business between Sam and Black, bitter times at last forgotten by the rest of them but not by Boss or Cushy. She is never alone again in his company. Her husband puts it down to snobbery and in the early years tries to ridicule her for it.

Cushy makes her friends on the Eillne side of Monument, becomes good at bridge, smokes her cigarettes, even at one stage learns to ride a horse. She knows Boss will never come near her – unless she breaks her silence. It is their unspoken pact. And when he is dead there is no point anyway.

She and White do not move into the house in Pig and Litter until 1965, the year after Boss Pender's death, and the *Monument Gazette* is being run by Boss Pender's trustee, Cushy's only child, her daughter, Ollie.

* * *

APRIL 14TH

Cushy had told me so much – but when I read what I had written, I realised that I was still lacking a crucial detail: Boss Pender raped Cushy, but who killed Sam Phibbs?

I went back through all my notes and analysed them anew to see if I had missed anything. The Garda file on the murder, I had established, was "active" until 1964, but was then stood down. Lost, more likely. Officially, they were no nearer a conviction for Sam's murder then than they had been twenty-six years earlier.

Cushy seemed to accept that Black had done it – and didn't care. Black was the murderer accepted by common gossip in Monument. Perhaps he had done it. Perhaps the bishop had been right.

But sometimes in ongoing research like this you get lucky. Sometimes, of course, you don't, and you never make that final breakthrough; but sometimes you do. Two nights after I met Cushy, the doorbell of my flat rang. It was nine o'clock. When I opened it, Agnes Grace, Cushy's companion was standing there. I had no idea what she wanted. She came in and we talked until almost dawn the next morning.

Agnes's story is a vindication of everything I have been striving for over the these past months. It proves, if proof is needed, the utter baseness of Boss Pender. Nothing, to my mind, can ever forgive him for what he did to Cushy. But there's more – more which Agnes has never been able to bring herself to tell anyone, not even Cushy. Agnes too feared Boss Pender. But now at last her words can speak for themselves.

*   *   *

AGNES'S STORY

1938

Mrs Lydia Pender presides over her home in Pig and Litter with a mixture of uncertain authority, high anxiety and sporadic outbursts of temper at one or all of her five household staff. Underlying her character is the disposition of a victim. She lives her life as someone whose expectations have been disappointed. Her husband is a powerful man, whose feeding she oversees three times a day – but they seldom converse. His discourse is with his boys on details of his business, of which Lydia is ignorant. Her only comfort is, and this sometimes makes her smile, in the one area of her marriage which years before, in 1908 to be exact, gave her the most anguish: her new religion. In the thirty years that have passed, hers has been a most consummate conversion. Now she looks on the memory of the unadorned church in County Antrim wherein five generations of her family worshipped and around whose stark walls are buried, and shivers. In its every aspect, at any hour of the day or evening, the cathedral in Monument radiates for Lydia all the warmth and comfort of a home. The very benches are redolent of the constant presence of humankind. The night-lights and candles that are never quenched, the rich, folded pleats that dress the tabernacle, the monstrance on Sunday evenings at six o'clock, bedazzling. The incomprehensible but consoling words of Latin, rising from the priest. Lydia goes to Mass every morning at six o'clock and on the way home buys the bread for breakfast.

Although but forty-two, she reflects the attitude and deportment of someone much older. Her fair hair has turned grey. She has become round and walks with a rolling motion. She fusses over small things, worries that Agnes, the new servant girl from White City Road, will steal the silver spoons, has no idea nor has ever tried to imagine the extent or meaning of her husband's wealth. In all the time she has been his wife, Lydia Pender née Albutt has never read a single word Boss Pender has written in the *Monument Gazette*.

She looks up as Agnes Grace, aged fourteen, whose father worked in the *Gazette* shed as a dispatcher, carries a tray of beef tea in a breakfast cup with a plate of buttered bread fingers, crustless, into the bedroom in which Black Pender has lain for two days.

"Put it down there, child, and mind you don't spill it," says Mrs Pender, pointing to the lace-cloth-covered bedside table.

As Agnes, whose third week only this is working here, places down the tray as instructed, she sees the little sweat drops standing out like glass beads on Black's forehead. Two days she has attended here, has seen him lost in the swamp of dreams, upside-down half the time, he doesn't know where he is, no day or night for him, ten times she must have helped change his night clothes and bedding. When the doctor, all apothecary and lint, lanced the filth in the bulb on his thigh, he screamed. All the different faces in the gloom, swimming. Agnes is exhausted. She wants to go and squeeze out the flannel from the basin on the floor and lay it cool on his pale face, taking care not to let water run onto the linen pillow slip, both linen and flesh the same, death-like colour. His eyes are open, but if he can see Agnes he gives no indication. Mrs Pender is spooning the heat from the cup.

"This is what you need," she says. "Try and sit up."

Fever has taken colour and strength from him. He struggles to please his mother, winces in pain, cries out.

"Oh, God. Come on, girl! Standing there!"

Agnes, big for fourteen, slips her hands beneath the sodden armpits and heaves.

"My *leg*!"

He's gone down to it with his hand, pulls the covers back and Agnes sees the bandage on the thigh, wet through, dark brown. Propping him, Agnes goes to the basin as she has wanted, presses out the cloth and wipes his face.

"Thank you."

It is the first time that a man has ever looked at her like that and Agnes will never forget it. The fusion between them, only for an instant, more than gratitude, already fleeting.

"That'll do, girl!" Mrs Pender, angling the spoon, blows on its contents for insurance. "Keep your ears open for the bell, mind."

And so, Agnes's memory of Black Pender, preserved for the next seven decades: framed in the rectangular gap of the door, as Agnes pauses in its closing, his face pale as the pillow, made all the more so by his hair, you never saw black hair the like of it, and his lips open to receive his mother's spoon.

The room Black lies in has one bed and is on the second floor, down a corridor in that part of the house known as "No. 2", a room to which his mother sometimes retires when her nerves need resting. High of ceiling, with a single, long window overlooking Monument, when the houses were being knocked into one this room acquired a second door beyond which stairs run down to the kitchens. Agnes, fearful that he will not be able to reach the bell, sits on the top step, just outside the door she's left ajar, inside which the heavy, velvet drapes are drawn over tightly on medical instructions.

Agnes is dozing, head on her knees, when she hears a thump. Leaning back, through the crack in the door she can see that he has swung his legs out over the side of the bed and is standing up. Swaying. Steadying himself on the headboard, he unpins his leg bandage and begins to unwind it.

No-one has spoken to Agnes about the cause of Black's leg injury, but she has gathered from the brief words exchanged in the sick room between the mistress and Mr Tom, a frequent visitor, that someone drove a pitchfork into it. Mr Tom is different from the others, Agnes knows. Not just because he is slight where they are broad, but in the soft looks he gives her; a shy man. In the kitchen he is the only one upstairs who never draws the cook's criticism. Now Agnes can see Black turning his bared leg to a free-standing mirror. The entry of the prong has left an opening two inches long, an open mouth – but now dry of the infection that has coursed from it for the past days. As he sits down on the bed, he begins to rebandage his thigh. There is a sense of urgency and purpose to his movements that precludes Agnes's intruding. He limps to a basin and with a jug of water douses his face and sponges his upper body. Agnes can see a dark fuzz of beard around his jaw and throat; his hand travels over it. Agnes glimpses her own reflection in the washstand mirror and shrinks back. He has not seen her. Having found his clothes folded and hanging in the single wardrobe, he has slipped the braces over his shoulders and is once again sitting, rolling the socks onto his feet, then he takes a silver-backed hairbrush of deep, soft bristles from a set on the dressing-table and runs it in long sweeps through his hair. He has put down the hairbrush and is getting up when the door opens. His father is standing there. Agnes draws in her breath.

"I was going to look for you . . ." Black begins.

Boss Pender is closing the door behind him. Agnes realises the impossible. Boss Pender is weeping. He is sitting down on the bed beside his son.

"Father . . . ?"

Boss stretches his hand out and grasps on to his son's arm, but words, it seems, are beyond him.

"What is it?" whispers Black.

Boss shakes his head.

"Cushy?" asks Black. "Father? Is it Cushy?"

"It wasn't my fault," Boss is weeping. "It wasn't my fault."

"What?" The son seizes the father's shoulders. "What wasn't? What's happened?"

"He was mad as a dog. Mad as any man I ever saw. Who am I telling? Look at what he did to you! He'd have killed me. Stone dead. What else could I do? What else could I do?"

"Jesus Christ," says Black, standing up. "What have you done?"

"I did it all for you. There's no sane man hasn't got a price, but this one wasn't sane. Everyone knows that. He'd have killed me, there was no doubt. I had no choice."

Black sits down beside his father as if his legs have given out.

"Have you done something to Sam Phibbs?"

"Oh, Jesus, I didn't mean to, but I know I'll roast in hell for it. He was mad, you know that, don't you?"

There is no transition, Agnes can see, between being boy and man. A boy had gone to bed in this room, a man now sits beside the father he loves, fighting to keep reason for both of them.

"What did you . . . ? Father!"

Boss looks up. Those deep, deep eyes, their depths now obscured. "He's – I think he's dead."

"Jesus Christ."

"Oh my God, oh dear, merciful God. We'll ask God for His forgiveness. Oh my God, we are heartily sorry for having offended Thee, we confess our sins above every other evil . . ."

Far off, a ship sounds. Down by the wharves men work at loading and unloading, sometimes around the clock, Agnes knows.

She hears deep chimes from the cathedral as Black reaches for a towel and hands it to his father. The old man wipes his face, then blows his nose at length. His head is down near his knees. Agnes can see how at the crown the hair is sparse.

Black says, "What is going to happen?"

"They'll take me, O God help me, it's the end of everything. The shame!"

"They can't do that!"

"You don't know the world. The world never gloats more than on a fallen man."

"They can't take you in. You are ..." He wants to say so many things, Agnes knows, to justify his own sense of outrage by speaking aloud this broken man's achievements as proprietor, editor, employer, public figure, man of property; he can find none of them on his tongue. ". . . my father," he says.

"It's over. It'll look like I went out there and murdered him because of you. Because of what he did to you. I'll swing, God have mercy on me."

"They can't do that! I'm in this as much as you! None of this would have happened if it weren't for me and Cushy. Her brother was a madman, look what he did to me! You defended yourself from him, Father, nothing more."

"But I went out there. I went out to Phibbs's. It'll look like I did that to avenge you."

"But I'm in this too."

Why did he say that, Agnes often asks herself in the months that follow? Why did he implicate himself in that way? Because he wanted to, she realises. Because he wanted to be everything this adored man was, including culpable of homicide.

"I'll take the boat," Boss is saying, getting to his feet. "I'll be in England before they find him. Maybe if you talk right to Beagle . . . in a year or so . . ."

"No!"

"I was younger than you when my father died."

"But you're not dead!"

Even then, Agnes understands that worse than any fear is the prospect of what is being proposed: an absent father, a scandal with no Boss to mitigate it, a *Gazette* with no Proprietor, no editor, a nervous mother without the husband her life depends on. A world without his father.

"If you go, I'll come with you."

"You can't come with me. Not this time."

Black, his own tears coming, cries, "I want to come! I don't want to stay! I don't want any of this without you!"

Boss puts his hand on the back of his son's neck. "If only you could bring me up to Glane now. If only you could save me."

Black's breath is coming hot and short in his chest. He springs up. Agnes can feel the sudden hope that is engulfing him.

"I'll go!" he cries.

Boss looks up at him. "You?"

"If I go, they'll think it was me. You don't have to say anything. Nothing changes. You can keep all this as before. People will talk for a bit, but you'll carry on, the *Gazette*, the family, nothing will change. You can speak to Beagle, he'll want some favour or other, no-one will do a deal for me better than you."

"You?"

"It's by far the easiest way!"

"I cannot allow . . ."

"I can go, then I'll come back! I don't mind, Father! All this will still be here when I come back!"

Boss sucks in his lower lip and worries it. "I suppose in a year, or eighteen months . . ."

"Exactly!" Black's young eyes shine. Then he says, "But what about Cushy?"

Now Boss worries the fingernail of his thumb. "Leave her to me. She'll need time. She'll have the child. Then she can follow you. I'll send her. Then in a year or so you can both come back."

"I'll go to England," says Black. "Tonight. I'll need money."

"You'll have all you want," says Boss. "But not to England."

"They'll never find me there, Father!"

"You don't know England. But I know a place they'll not find you."

"Where is that?"

"Antrim," says Boss.

Agnes comes down the back stairs, trembling. She cannot grasp the full extent or meaning of what has happened, she feels deep guilt, as if she is somehow responsible for the deeds she has heard described. It is the same feeling when outside her parents' bedroom door she hears them groaning. As then, the shock makes Agnes want to sleep. Seated at the kitchen table, one eye on the upstairs bell board, she closes her eyes.

"Miss!"

Agnes has been dozing for just a few minutes.

"Oh!"

She jumps to her feet. In her three weeks there Boss Pender has never been in the kitchen.

"D'you know where Black's clothes are kept?"

She stares at this huge man, at his red and angry eyes. She knows what he has done, she has heard it from his own lips. She is terrified.

"Y-Y-Yes – yes, sir."

"Where?"

"In his bedroom."

"Where else?"

"I-I-I-In the upstairs linen cupboard, sir."

Boss picks up a laundry bag from a clothes-horse that stands before the range.

"Just what will fit in here," says he. "Shirts and underclothes." He looks at her. "What's your name?"

"A-A-Agnes."

Boss's hand opens and a folded pound note is lying there. "I don't want anyone else to know about this, Agnes, it might upset them. You hear me?"

Agnes shakes her head, she does not want to take so much money, but he opens her hand and smiling at her for a moment, places the money there. Agnes can feel the strength of him. A pound is what she expects to earn for one month's work.

"You hear me?"

Agnes gulps, nods.

"Go on with you, so, and be quick about it."

The linen cupboard to which Agnes has referred is at the end of a second-floor corridor which lies at the very top of the back stairs of No. 3. Agnes tries to muffle her heels on the wooden risers. The cupboard's two long doors, from floor to ceiling, swing open. Agnes is presented with towering shelves of ironed clothes, sheets and towels. She has ironed some shirts a few days before, Black's or White's, she cannot yet say which, and stored them up near the topmost shelf here, but needed to stand on a chair to do so. Now, as then, she goes to the adjacent room, an old storage room, where she found a chair before. A light. At the door, six inches ajar, Agnes freezes.

He must have come up the front stairs out of the kitchens. She can see him on his knees by the far wall, his back to her, an oil lamp on the ground. The door at the other side of the room is open. Agnes takes a step into the room, but Boss Pender is so absorbed in what he is doing that he doesn't hear her. And now, as she steps to the edge of the pool of light, Agnes can see a square of blackness in the wall above his head, like a picture, with a little door on thick hinges open to one side of it. The sound of coins. Agnes has never seen one gold sovereign before, never mind so many. Scores of them. They rise from the floor in a glowing heap. Boss is thumbing single coins from this heap into a pouch. They look warm in the lamplight. He weighs the pouch in his hand, seizes out a handful from it and puts them back onto the pile; then he draws tight the neck strings. With cupped hands he ladles all the coins from the floor into the open mouth of a satchel. Standing, he hefts it up into the safe, closes the door, which shuts with a metal sound, then turns its lock and withdraws a key.

"I need a chair," says Agnes, but Boss Pender has already walked straight from the room by the other door, carrying the lamp with him.

Agnes hurries back down the flights of stairs with the linen bag full of the shirts and underwear. It is past two in the morning. At the head of the main stairs of No. 1, she halts. Down below her, in the hall, father and son stand in their topcoats. Boss is carrying what looks like a large book beneath his arm.

"Are we ready?" asks Black.

"I've been thinking about what I'm going to say to Mr M.," says Boss. "He'll need to be sure you acted in self-defence."

Black frowns, as if a stride behind his father in the new reality. "Yes."

"I think you should draft a note," says Boss, "something I can then use to your advantage when the time is right."

"You think so?"

"Yes, to clarify it in Mr M.'s mind, if needs be."

"But . . ."

"But what?" snaps Boss. He fumbles for his watch. "Do you know it's past two and we're still here!" He places down the leather portmanteau and opens it. Agnes can see a square of white paper

195

and, in a leather holder, a green pen which Boss hands to the boy. "Hurry now!"

Black unscrews the pen's top. "What shall I say?"

"Say, 'To Whom It May Concern. I, John Pender, say of my own free will, that on this day', no, write, 'on October 13th, 1938, when I went out to Phibbs's farm near Deilt, Sam Phibbs once again attacked me.'"

Black pens the words, but the ink runs dry.

"Here."

Boss has taken up a silver inkwell from where it was set into the hall table. Black sinks the head of the pen into the inkwell, raises the gold lever on the side of the pen, brings it back down, then takes out the pen from the ink and wipes it clean with blotting paper.

"'I tried to defend myself. I feared for my life. We fought, and may Almighty God forgive me, but when we had finished Sam Phibbs was dead.'"

Black looks up. His father's ungiving eyes. He writes.

"'I leave Monument with a heavy heart, but I trust in the mercy and forgiveness of the law to let me return.' Sign your name."

Black signs his name. Boss takes the page, with care placing the ink side on a sheet of inlaid blotting paper, fishes out a long brown envelope and inserts the folded letter. Then leaving the portmanteau on the hall table he slides the envelope into his inside pocket and as he does so looks straight up the stairs at Agnes.

"What in blazes are you . . . ?"

"I-I-I-I have what you told me to get, sir," says Agnes, coming down, the linen bag held before her.

Boss glares at her, his face full of suspicion. Then with a squelch from its draught-proofing the hall door opens and Hart comes in.

"How many cans?" asks Boss.

"Three."

"And she's full on top of that?"

Hart nods.

The clock chimes the half-hour with a single, tinny beat.

"Come on."

Boss stands back for his driver and his son to leave. He looks again at Agnes, standing there, as if he means to say something to her but cannot for the moment remember what. Then he leaves, drawing the door to behind him.

Agnes sits on the bottom step. She has a sense of grief, a new feeling of loss, not for her alone, but for the house. She can sense a sudden emptiness on top of her previous guilt and confusion – as if something precious has been removed. She is also fearful – for herself, her job and, foolish though she knows herself to be, for Black Pender whose shoulders she has so recently propped up in bed, whose eyes last evening she dared imagine were for her. Pain in his face, yes, but also a strange illumination. He reminded Agnes of a saint, she can imagine him now like the figures in the big coloured windows of the cathedral, their faces afire.

And then, as if a vision, the hall door in front of her re-opens and he is there.

"Come with me, Agnes!"

She does not understand. He has taken the leather book from the hall table and is already beckoning her from midway up the stairs.

"Quick, girl!" He winces with the effort. "I won't hurt you."

She doesn't know what he is talking about, but her concern is all for his pain. He goes up ahead, saving the injured leg, his breath short. Then stops dead midway up the second staircase and Agnes collides with him.

"Ssssh!" He catches her wrist, tight, holds a finger to his lips. The silence of the sleeping house, not a real silence but an accumulation of the infinitesimal. He leads her, wrist still held, back down the corridor to a bedroom. Then he opens the leather book and begins to write. Agnes sees the angle of the speckled green pen against his first knuckle. Black shakes his head, writing so fast that the pen blots.

"Damn!" He looks up. "Excuse me." He tears blotting paper from its place inside the cover and soaks up the ink. Then he scrawls some more lines at speed, dries the whole page and folds it.

"Agnes, I want you to do something very important," he says as he licks an envelope. "I want you to keep this letter until I ask for it – do you understand me?" He is flattening the seam of the closed letter with the palm of his hand. "Agnes?"

"Y-Yes, sir."

"You must never open this letter or give it to anyone else, no matter what they say to you. Do you promise me?"

"Yes, sir."

"Say, I promise you, Black Pender."

Agnes stares at him.

"Say it!"

Agnes lowered her eyes. "I-I-I promise you . . . M-Mr Pender," she mumbles.

"No!" Now he catches her by both wrists. "Say what I asked you – and look at me when you're saying it! Agnes!"

Agnes looks at him. "I promise you, Black Pender," she says.

Black smiles. "Thank you." He hands her the letter which bears no name. "I have done nothing wrong, Agnes. I will be accused in the coming days of having done many things, but I am innocent of all of them. I do not understand how these things have come about, but what I do now I do for my family – do you understand?"

Agnes nods.

"I'll be back, soon, and I'll live in this house with my new wife, and you'll work for me, do you hear me? There is nothing to worry about." And then he leans in and kisses Agnes on her cheek, just below her ear.

Agnes remains there for nearly an hour, clutching the letter. Later she brings it downstairs with her to the room she shares with the girl who does the dishes for the cook, and, to the sound of her snoring, takes out the old suitcase that came with her from White City Road and with her fingernail works open a small tear in the material that lines the lid and through it slides Black's letter until it drops.

She thinks much about the letter in the weeks that follow, never more so than when she hears the things that everyone is saying. She wants to cry out during these moments, for she knows it is all lies, but she never dares – from fear, but also from belief that he knew best – say so. That he has said he will return is enough for Agnes. If she is serving tea upstairs to the likes of Father Whittle when he comes to visit the grief-stricken mistress, and if the priest, when Black's name comes up, begins to talk about true repentance, Agnes touches her cheek below the ear with her fingers. It thrills her to do that, for it is something that only she can under-stand, a secret, like the letter, between herself and him.

Agnes the young woman still remembers the love and the promise made by Agnes the girl, but it does not hurt her any more to think about it. Now months often go by without it occurring to her. When she is told that she is going to James Place with Mr and Mrs White Pender and their baby girl, Agnes sees the suitcase for the first time in months, and runs her fingers down the lining of its lid and feels the envelope. She could take it to Cushy then and tell her what she knows; but although Cushy is married to someone else, she is always sad and Agnes feels that nothing but trouble will come from her interfering.

In the following years her secret occasionally comes to mind, but when she is seventeen, Agnes Grace begins walking out with a man from Captain Penny's Road, a baker's assistant, a kind and caring man of twenty-five whose passion in life is greyhounds. He asked Agnes if she would mind leading one on their walks, and soon they become a feature of that stretch of the road to Eillne, Agnes and her baker, each of them with a clutch of dogs.

In 1942 he suddenly goes away to war. Plenty are going from Monument. Agnes is mystified. The excitement in his face. It never strikes him that he might not be coming back. The greyhounds are what Agnes is most sorry for. Sold for half nothing to a dog man from England in 1944, after the news is confirmed.

The two men in Agnes's life become one image. Kind and sad. Agnes preserves a love of walking, something she keeps up all her life, an upright figure, arms swinging, out Captain Penny's Road towards the holy well. She becomes less a servant, more a companion to Mrs Cushy Pender. There often are times, in particular when October comes round again, when Agnes wonders whether she should tell Cushy what she knows. But then she looks into the other woman's eyes and sees such sorrow there that she cannot bring herself to bear the burden of increasing it.

And as for her suitcase from all those years ago with its great secret: when years later she goes to look for it, it is no longer there. Agnes cannot think what became of it. Lost, like an old memory, perhaps, or thrown out during one of the times the house was being repainted, or taken when they lacked a suitcase of their own by another Pig and Litter employee returning home for Christmas, or taking the boat to England, or America, perhaps one of such girls in some far-flung place, now in her old age, still retains in her junk room a small, brown suitcase, stiff with age and never used, in whose tattered lining lies the cry of an innocent man.

Fifteen

I remember the evening we went to the pool in Glane as one of no wind, or if there was it was from the north, for the sky lay flat, allowing a glazed path of egg-yolk to run all the way from Tom Pender's cottage to the dying sun. We had sat outside until it had grown dusk and we could begin to watch the passage of creation. We walked down the meadow and climbed the boulders. I ached for her. Not in any way of crazed and probably in the circumstances blasphemous tumescence, but above all for her unnegotiable presence. Jasmine went to the edge of the pool, where she knelt, cupped and sank her hands, and drank. Her copper hair had fallen forward in a mass, showing me the long nape of her neck. She dipped the top part of her head into the water. Gathering her wet hair in her hands she straightened up, wringing it, and the water flowed out on her shoulders and down her chest and back. Gleaming like a seal, she returned and sat beside me. I reached over to feel her wet hair, then, my fingers damped, I brought them to her lips. We kissed. Her tongue was sweet and urgent. I peeled the soaked sweater outwards and over the rounds of her shoulders and reached around to unhook her, and she half stood, her torso bared, and then swung her leg over my knees and sat on me, still joined at our mouths, her left knee wedged between me and the rock. "Natural" was the word insisting in my head, this was so natural. I broke from her, only because I needed to kiss her breasts, each of them pliant and hard-nippled, and then to lick a path down to her navel and to burrow there like a shrew. With hard nails she scoured my scalp, the backs of my ears, the base of my neck, making my flesh pores open like fields of tulips. I stood again and she locked her heels at the small of my back and we tottered to level ground on the river's infant banks and completed what has been started, human chemistry, never doubted, ratified in blinding proof as above us luckless rooks tried to settle down for a night's sleep.

"Are you OK?"

Jasmine rested her forehead against mine. Her hair must have absorbed gallons of water, for my upper body was soaked through and I could feel moisture running down my back.

"Fine."

"We're all wet."

I made a fire in the cottage and we lay beside it. Jasmine's head lay beside mine on the pillow. She smelled of lemon balm. She spoke softly, each word sculpted by her lips.

"They say Ollie will make a full recovery."

"Good."

Jasmine rolled over and took my face between her hands.

"She seems always to have taken a special interest in you, Kaiser. She gave you your job when you came back to Monument, she gave you this project here in Glane." Jasmine put her elbow behind her head. "Did Ollie ever talk to you about your parents?"

I told her she never had.

"How often did you see Tim Pender-Goode?"

"We were at school."

"Yes, I know, but did you go up to their house a lot?"

"Tim's parties."

"Was Ollie there?"

"She lived there."

"Who else?"

"A maid, I think."

"Agnes."

"Yes. And a very old woman too, wore thick glasses."

Jasmine nodded her head. "That was Mrs Cushy Pender. You see, Tim grew up in that house in Pig and Litter with his mother, who was separated, and with his grandmother. The maid you mention was called Agnes Grace. She and Cushy still live up there – Agnes has been nursing Ollie these last weeks."

Outside the cottage all the colours of the world were sliding into the horizon and seeping away through its long, crimson gash.

"What do you remember as a boy, Kaiser? Before Monument?"

"Nothing."

"Come on. We all remember something."

"Faces, then. High faces. Smell of medicine."

"You were sick."

"Think so."

"A hospital."

"Don't know."

"Accents?" She was propped on one elbow. "Do you recall any specific accent, Kaiser? Can you hear a voice, for example?"

I shook my head.

Jasmine kissed me. "Our memories are hiding in the great meadows in our heads, Kaiser. All you have to do is believe and your memories will come to you, creeping from the meadows. It's true."

I told her I remembered the taste of black and white sweets, the image of an old man upside-down and the devil with fire in his eyes.

"Hmmm." Jasmine sat up and put her hand beneath her chin. "I used to have nightmares about the devil when I was a little girl, thought he was coming to get me – maybe you did too. But a man upside-down . . . What kind of a man?"

I shook my head again. "Old. Upside-down."

Jasmine smiled and stroked my face with the back of her hand.

"Don't worry about it. Leave it all to me and I'll tell you when I'm finished."

Although our love arched out and over that whole spring, I knew in a seldom-accessed recess of my mind that one day I would lose her. We never discussed what Jasmine did when she was away; and when she came back after an absence I was always sure I would taste the dirt of treason on her tongue, but never did. I had so long rehearsed our last day that when it came I did not recognise it. The mountains wore a bright countenance. Light was generous and vast, wind warm. Although I could only imagine what they sounded like, the streams in Glane bounced and glinted in May sunlight and ran in and out of fragrant gorses and heathers on their way down the mountain. Swallows described extravagant parabolas. I could feel the earth in my legs, not just its steepness, but moving miles below us in its very pith where the spring of the Lyle was conceived.

"I'm always tired, Kaiser."

"Then sleep."

"I can't."

"Why not?"

"My body is tired but my head won't rest." She burrowed closer in the bed as if chilled, her face close to mine. "Kaiser. I'm afraid."

I drew back. "Of what?"

"Of the past."

I shook my head. Her face contained an expression I had not seen before. "Do you mean my past?"

She nodded.

I felt my chest buck. "Tell me what you know."

Jasmine looked away. I reached and turned her head to me, perhaps more forcibly than I had intended. "Your mother knows something about me that I don't!" I shouted. "Isn't that right?"

Jasmine had drawn back and her eyes were large and fearful. "Let go of me, please, Kaiser."

"I'm sorry." I took my hand away from her face. "Now tell me."

Jasmine shook her head. "I have promised myself that I won't tell you until I'm certain."

"Fuck you! Certain of what? Afraid of what?"

Jasmine was trembling. "Tim's under pressure financially, big problems."

"What problems?"

"He's paid a lot of money for land out in White City which he's hoping to sell to the government as the site for the new mental hospital. But the deal is taking for ever and the banks are breathing down his neck – big time."

"So?"

"So – you represent a threat to Tim. And, I suppose, so do I."

"Go on."

"I – don't want to say any more."

"How am I a threat?"

"Please, Kaiser . . ."

"Jasmine . . ."

She could stick her chin out when her mind was made up. "Like I said, when I know it all, when I find the final piece – which will be soon, I think – I'll tell you everything. Soon. I promise. Please."

"Now!"

"No."

"Why not?"

"It wouldn't be . . . right to tell you. I could still be wrong, you see."

"Don't care!"

She closed her eyes as if she needed to convince herself she was doing the right thing.

"I'm meeting a key person tomorrow, Kaiser – it's the last piece in the jigsaw, I'm sure of it. I'll tell you after that, I promise."

A vase with wild flowers stood on a table. I flung it across the room, where it hit the cottage wall and disintegrated. I began to shout, more out of fear than anger, I think. I told her I cared for her and wanted to help her, but if she didn't trust me I could do neither. She was crying and saying she could not tell me yet. The thought of her mother knowing something about me that I didn't made it worse and now Jasmine's stubborn face drove me further on. I got out of bed and caught up the table and threw it through the window. The glass explosion was amplified in a million, dazzling fragments of noise.

"Tell me!"

"Stop!"

I overturned the bed in my rage and she tumbled out.

"Stop it! I'm going home!"

"Tell me!"

"Stop it! Please . . ."

I may have caught her arm in an attempt to prevent her leaving: whatever I did, she opened her mouth and let out a blinding white scream. I was shouting. I told her to fuck off back to Tim and to tell him about her problems. I shouted at her not to come back to me again. She went into the next room and I tore the door off the hinges.

"Jesus . . . "

"Tell me!"

I threw the door across the room and it glanced off her arm.

Tears stood out in Jasmine's big eyes. "Please, Kaiser, don't . . ." she was saying.

She left soon after that. I looked out and saw her headlights like moths sinking into the valley. I was soon cursing myself for losing control. I would never do her harm or wish to frighten her. I'd ruined everything. That night, alone – afraid too, if the truth be known, but of what I did not know – I tried to bring down a slow curtain on the day now that my anger was gone, to turn out all lights and to sit in the dark, inducing my swirling thoughts to settle in advance of bed. As a rule this helped me to sleep in peace, as opposed to leaping awake after an hour in a brainstorm of conflicting signals and then taking two further hours to sleep again. But that night the curtain fell unevenly and I therefore plumped for my reserve strategy, which was to go directly to bed chewing half a narcotic tablet for which I possessed a repeat prescription. I drifted off, savouring on my gums the menacing smack of arsenic.

16

I awoke this morning feeling numb. I am still numb. My extremities delay before responding to commands; my thoughts are log-jammed. It is as if everything I have put my trust in has dissolved. The scene in Glane last night terrified me. I thought I knew Kaiser. I thought we had moved into a safe place together. We made love, wonderfully. But then, as if from nowhere, he erupted into dreadful violence and there was a moment when I really feared for myself. What kind of future can there be with such a person? Not much, I fear. And yet, under the numbness, I still love him. Want him. This is crazy. I'm in love with a man I'm terrified of.

Or is it crazy? Seeing it from his point of view, after all, it must be deeply frustrating. Since last year I've been trawling through records and spending much of my free time here in the library – working on him! And yet I've told him nothing about my extraordinary findings. Of course he is frustrated! Add to that the fact that he finds it difficult to articulate ... I'd probably start throwing things too, were I in his position.

The truth is I now do not know what to do. Earlier today I met Mrs Ollie Pender-Goode, the person I was convinced holds the final key to unlock the mystery of Kaiser. To be honest, I almost did not show up for my meeting with her because of last night. I was too upset. And then I put myself in Kaiser's position and, despite everything, went along.

*

Ollie lives in Pig and Litter. All her life she has set the standards by which she and everyone around her has lived. She was once a big, domineering woman, used to command, now she is shrunken, can walk no more than a few steps, and those leaning on Agnes, her skin is pallid, her limbs tremble. Her eyes alone speak of her unyielding spirit, but even they have been tarnished by near death.

My plan was to present Ollie with such a weight of evidence that she would not even try to deny the part I was sure she had played in suppressing the truth. I gambled too on the fact that no-one would ever have told her who her real father was; so I informed her about what I now know of the events of 1938, including her mother's story, leaving nothing out, and of the huge injustice that had been done. The effect was dramatic. Ollie has always suspected that Boss Pender was her natural father but has never been able to talk to anyone about it. She has always known this day would come.

She began to talk. Her descriptions are precise and full of detail. Where she herself was not present, she has been able to relay what happened through the accounts of third parties, especially those in Antrim, with whom she kept in touch. Where there may be other gaps, I have, when it is reasonable to do so, used my imagination to fill them in.

* * *

OLLIE'S STORY

1962

So rare, everyone says, to find hair so black. Raven. Coal. Soot. These are all words people use to describe his hair. Straight and oily, when he brushes it it shines like tar. The same people describe his brother's hair and complexion using altogether different words: wheaten straw, gold, butter. White. Odd that, in a pair of boys born an hour apart.

He looks up from the ridge he is a-digging, across the wall of dry stones to where the boy sits by the cottage door within sight too of his mother. Listless. None of energy or merriment that a toddler should be seized by. A large and round face that dwells for minutes at a time on the nearby North Atlantic. The boy worries him. Sinking in the fork at a judicious angle, he leans back on the haft, lifts. Flesh-white potatoes break the surface, shocking in their summer light bareness. He reaches down and picks their unblemished spheres from the clay, drops them in a bucket.

The sea means little to him. A river, yes, he can understand; where he was raised one of the great Irish rivers flows, ordains the shape of people's lives, they sleep and rise with their river, called the Lyle. He crossed many rivers on his way up here, comparing them to his own, but none, not even the great rivers of the North with their shipyards and frigates, had the same hold on his imagination. And then – the sea. It is as if rivers and the sea are unrelated, like the mighty rivers in America he has heard of that run their course only to disappear down great inland sinks. On this craggy northern coastline of few trees, where hunts the herring gull, where eels can be trapped, of stony foreshores, of driving winds, he has found an entire community living from the sea – taciturn people, few of whom have heard of the Lyle river.

Nothing was ever said, that autumn he had came up, 1938, aged eighteen, a foreigner or as good as. It didn't need to be; they were people to whom the amount of money in question was a fortune beyond imagining. They took it without comment, gave him a room and their name. Dropped the "Black" too, no need for it up here. John Albutt. He had almost smiled. No-one in the hinterland asked any questions. A tight community on the sea.

People took stock of one another during Sunday worship and buttoned their lips.

His mother's father, his grandfather, Old Wint Albutt he was known as, didn't look like anyone John felt he should be related to. A retired crayfish fisherman who rarely spoke, his forebears had come from Staffordshire. Sat in a chair beside the scrubbed slate hearth, occasionally turning the bellows wheel, making sudden sparks, casting and recasting lengths of light hemp through the canon of knots. Jutting, white bushy eyebrows protecting eyes the colour blue. Nose a-drip twelve months of the year. The bowline, the clove hitch, the cat's paw. The sheepshank, a knot used for temporarily shortening a rope, or to bypass a weak spot in a rope by placing the weak part in the middle between two loops. Day after day. He'd lost two sons at sea, both within view of the house, both in the same week of April. One had been tall and stringy, the other broad and short. Eyes like their father. Neither could swim, the policy in these parts, like the holes in their gumboots to let the salt water through. The Becket bend, also known as the sheet bend, a knot used by sailors for uniting two ropes of different sizes.

One evening in early 1939, four months after John's arrival, Old Wint came to him, never said a word, handed him a newspaper. With a rush of pleasure John saw that it was the *Monument Gazette*, hurried to his room, lay on his bed and opened it, but only so that he could read small sections at a time. Like a miser he wanted to eke out the delights. Thirty minutes later he went into the haggard and, on hands and knees, vomited on the earth. Everything disgorged, but even so he stayed convulsing. No-one came out to him. At last, bloodless, he staggered into the kitchen range and as his new family averted their faces, he burned the paper.

The months went by, no-one discussed it. Early the following fall, amidst all the growing talk of war and of the border between the two parts of Ireland being sealed, without telling anyone he took off one day from Gua, his face bearded, his clothes of rough homespun, and crossed into the Free State at the narrow neck of land where Donegal is found. He had no clear plan, and he knew the danger of his position, a warrant out and circulating, but he had to see it for himself. After that everything would flow. When his eyes were satisfied he could begin to think about coming back to Monument and clearing his name.

It took him all of two further days to complete the journey. The train south out of Sligo stood idle in the vast midlands of Ireland for more than half of one day, another engine arrived with the fall of night and he spent the hours of darkness in Athlone, sleeping in a hay barn because he was too afraid to go to a boarding house. On the morning of the third day he saw the peak of Dollan. The trees of Glane flashed with the early sunlight in their reaching tips. He wanted to cry to heaven that everything he had been caught up in was a dream.

Avoiding the main road into Monument he climbed the web of laneways that brought him up into White City and from there he crossed the crown of the town to James Place, which the notice in the paper had given as Mr and Mrs James Pender's address. He thought the town empty until church bells made him realise it was Sunday and everyone was at Mass. Reaching James Place he stood into the shadow of a hoop-shaped entrance way and waited.

As for the child, which had now to be somewhere near at hand, on the one hand he reasoned it could not be his, but on the other, because he had never doubted the fact of her condition, he accepted it had to be. Even in the depths of his despair and hurt, he had never imagined that she had been with another man.

He felt alien, more apart from his town and his accustomed

surroundings than he ever would have thought possible. Perhaps it was the threat of arrest that attended him, or perhaps some deeper alienation, springing from the seed of betrayal, was at work; either way, he had become a stranger.

People began returning from Mass, families, men in bowlers, women in their Sunday best, heads covered. It was the one time of the week in Pig and Litter, the period between the end of Mass and Sunday dinner, that the Pender family had always been together. He imagined his father at that very moment, shaking out the Dublin Sunday paper and commenting aloud on whatever he was reading.

Black saw her all at once. She was on the far side of the Place and he had to step out to get a good view. Alone. Walking slowly, her eyes lowered, Cushy was wearing a light coat and brown shoes with flat heels. A handbag on her arm. She wore a headscarf. Black had never in his life seen anyone so sad. Which was why, for no other reason, he emerged from his hiding place and began to walk towards her, confident that he could put an end to her sadness, that she had been almost a year waiting for this very moment, that all the mistakes of the past would be put right by the mere fact of his presence. But then, even as he was anticipating the smile on her face, he was halted as if by a blow to the chest.

"Cushy!"

His twin brother, White, his face bright, was running up after her, the way she had come, all arms and legs flailing in the white suit that Black so well knew. They were less than a hundred yards from him. Cushy stopped and turned. White reached her and then, pretending the effort was too much, gasping as it were for breath, he leant there in front of her, hands on his knees. Black stared. Cushy stood there, looking down at him. She seemed inanimate. Then White straightened up and offered her his arm. Linked, their faces hidden, they walked to the railings of a house beside the

213

library. Cushy turned her head for a moment. She was utterly dismayed. But the strength had deserted Black's legs. He watched Cushy and his brother enter the house. He heard the door close. Then he turned away and for the final time left Monument.

Had it been otherwise that day, had Cushy been on her own, had Black managed to speak to her and had she told him that, despite all, she loved him still, then everything might have changed. But as it was, far from being buoyed up with hope, his spirit was drowned by what he saw. His old name meant nothing to him. Gua was his home.

After that, time held little meaning. The war came and went. He worked the land six days a week, never a day off. Ten years passed so quickly they surprised even himself.

He married Harriet Hunter, his first cousin, a schoolteacher. Often the way in these small communities, another matter on which there was little discussion. She'd recognised his education from the things he spoke of, his interest in books. She had blonde hair, clear skin. He stepped into her faith. They married in an unadorned church, a brass cockerel on the bell tower where you might expect a cross. Flat, Wesleyan hymns. By midday everyone was back in the fields because there was hay to be saved in the locality.

And nothing for a dozen years. Everyone had lost hope, including Harriet. Terrified at her age, she stayed in bed for the last month of the confinement. Everyone still says she has never quite recovered.

The boy reminds him, as well as of Tom, of – the name will not come. John has tried to make himself get close, find the thread to bind them, work it into one of Old Wint's hawsers. Without success. They are so different, yet the boy's silent face speaks to him of everything he has lost, including love, his name and religion, his river. He worries for the boy's frailness. An old man, a neighbour credited with skills in diagnosis, says it may be "hair growing in". Just as his wife, when he married her, reminded Black of someone, so too now, over a dozen years on, does the boy; not just of Tom, his brother – where is Tom now? – but of an ever-present third party for whom no name or description exists. A source of irritation. The spuds burst through the clay like treasure trove. Spheres that sometimes remind him of women. Feminine, at any rate. Old memories, other days. Laughter. The people up here sometimes chuckle, but the type of outright laughter that had once been common in his life is rare. He glances upwards towards the cottage in time to see the boy topple.

When John Albutt married Harriet Hunter in 1948, her father, Andrew Hunter, the man who had travelled to Monument all those years before for the wedding of his wife's sister but who had risked pneumonia rather than enter a Roman Catholic cathedral, this quite decent farming man had sold, for a consideration of £25, a cottage on the far side of his thirty-seven acres to the newly weds. It was understood that the land would one day be John and Harriet's; but in 1962 it was Andrew Hunter's land.

Still tough times, little money. Everyone cycles into Gua for their provisions or travels by bus for the longer journeys. No-one in Gua owns a motor car. Harriet takes her bike the two miles in each direction every day to her school, brings John books from the mobile library that visits the school once a month, books on history, on farming, about kings of England and France and the American Civil War. John reads every one and Harriet reads most of them. During the winter they sit either side of a kerosene lamp and do not go to bed until their eyes smart.

Andrew Hunter is much confined indoors with asthma, his chest gone into a point, and John works the farm for a labourer's wage. John is forty-two, but is often taken for older. One day

Harriet cuts his hair and beneath the deep layers finds grey. He has tried to plant trees, but has learned the same lesson as have people here thousands of years before: salt kills them. He is good with his hands, he finds, can build drystone walls with the best of them. He acquires and rears exotic fowl: bantams, guinea fowl, Leghorns, Cuckoo Marans, Wyandottes, Buff Orpingtons, Minorcas. Their assorted white and speckled eggs have never before been seen in those parts, let alone their feathers. He wins prizes at agricultural shows for his groomed birds, their foreign quills and plumage the subject of fascination as far as Coleraine and Londonderry. At home he puts all his rosettes and silver cups in a glass-fronted cabinet. Occasionally people from Coleraine come to buy for breeding stock and always leave remarking that John Albutt is a perfect gentleman.

But he has become inward too, is distant even with Harriet, watches with the thoughtfulness of a stranger her preparing eggs for waterglass in August and September. The past is never an issue, never discussed, as if the money discharged all obligations. One day she runs out from the cottage calling him to come and see the long, black car sitting beyond the field they called Diggan's Field, after the man who had sold it to her father, Andrew; she runs out laughing and grabs up the child, shouting in her excitement.

"Look at the big car! Look!"

She runs with the child out into meadow and yelps for the thrill of it as the car slides away. John comes to the door, but stops in its shadow, just long enough to see what she is on about; then goes back in.

"Did you see it?" she asks him later, at tea.

He nods, yes, he has.

"It was so – beautiful!" she says, wound up still.

He looks at her. Then he gets up and goes out into the haggard.

The past is a fester to him. He longs for the river and can find no comfort in the sea.

At first he thinks the boy is dead. Face like linen. The blue lips. He cannot find the strength even to cry out, to call her, a mule once kicked him in the chest, same thing. Winded. He puts his hand beneath the child's head, tiny balls of potato clay run down the alabaster neck.

Then, "*Harriet!*"

The terror. Lifting the wisp-like body into him he crashes through the half-door as she comes out, apron to her mouth. He places the boy down on the deal table and falls to his knees, crossing himself, whilst Harriet goes to the dresser and with steady Protestant hands takes out the vinegar. As she shoves the mouth of the uncorked jar up under his nose the boy makes a death moan.

John grabs Harriet's bicycle and runs out. The doctor lives on the Coleraine side of Gua, a cycle trip of twenty minutes there and back, sometimes when you arrive you have to wait three hours for him to return from the house calls, which he makes on horseback. But for trips to Coleraine after the harvest, or for the every other month provisioning expeditions, Andrew, her father, has a mare, and a trap, which locals smirk at. Very much Andrew Hunter's mare and trap. His wife insists that stable dust is the cause of his asthma, but Andrew grooms his mare every day, feeds her hay and mangolds, a pinch of oats, changes her bedding, bends down wheezing to heft up her big hooves and scrape them to clean hollows. No-one takes the reins but Andrew, bad and all as his chest is. In Coleraine he invests in sulphurs and when he gets home spends hours with his towel-covered head midway into a steaming pail.

John lets fall the bicycle, spokes flashing, runs into Andrew Hunter's house.

"The trap!" he cries, himself caught for breath. "The boy . . ."

In minutes they have her tacked and harnessed. John drags back the carriage-house doors, Andrew leads out the mare. John is too demented to climb up; he grabs up the bicycle again and sets out ahead, legs whirling.

Inside the cottage Harriet has wrapped the boy in grey blankets. His eyes are flickering. Andrew comes in, leans on the door jamb to ease the chest, looks to the table and shakes his head, panting.

"Poor. Wee. Lad."

John gathers up the child, runs back outside and climbs up the two steps. Harriet clicks to the hinged panel. She sees: her father, barely able to take his seat behind the reins, her son, dying, her husband clutching their dying son. Then, without a word or waiting to watch them leave, she turns and goes back into the cottage, where she sets to scrubbing the deal table.

The doctor is at home, thinks at first from the appearance of the party that Andrew is his patient, tries to help the gasping pillar of the community down from the trap, sees in the process the real point of the commotion and performs his examination on the spot. During which the boy becomes conscious.

"Ah, that's the brave lad," says the doctor, probing and pressing.

The boy blinks at the contact of the cold fingertips.

"Coleraine Hospital," says the doctor, grim-faced, then tries to persuade Andrew down, to let his own son aged eighteen take the reins, but Andrew Hunter has never surrendered the reins of his mare and trap, not even to the doctor, so the doctor stands back and says, "Very well. Mind you keep him awake, John, whatever you do! Be quick! I'm right behind you."

Love is not something the people around him associate with John Albutt – although Harriet always claims that he loves her in his own way, as if the level of affection he has achieved is the best he can manage; and he is lovable, not often a trait in unloving men. Andrew Hunter observes his son-in-law as someone for whom demonstrations of attachment are overlaid by caution and reserve; and so Andrew is most surprised to see – when, between wheezing breaths, he is able to take the time from exerting his mare to lengthen her stride – the father of his waning grandchild overcome with such heartfelt emotion. Their dust is seen for miles. Men and women in roadside fields straighten from their work and, seeing the doctor in the convoy, some of the men remove their caps.

But what to say to this stranger child to keep him from slipping away? *Mind you keep him awake, John, whatever you do!* How other than with words can he keep him awake – but what words? He has seen the boy only distantly for three years, has never loved him until now, they have no custom of talk between them. But now, in one of those intense revelations that are the result of love, or more usually, grief, John realises that the person his son reminds him of is himself. Or at least an aspect of himself, one that he has tried to bury, a gentle, unmanly side; and in that moment he clings to the light body on his lap and loves him as he had never loved before.

"You've got to stay awake!"

His words cause the boy's eyes to focus. To lick his lips. Then away again swim the fixity of the pupils.

"Listen!"

Again, twitched from the edge of consciousness, the lad comes back to life, but as if in reply only to the voice, as if his father's voice not the air he breathes sustain him. John props the head in the crook of his arm, takes his bearings from a ruined castle on the landscape and realises they have well over an hour of their journey left. He is not a man of great imagination. His most pronounced ability is his memory and for twenty-five years that has been subject to suppression.

"There was once a very big man with dark, almost black eyes," he begins. "Everyone called him Boss."

The child's eyes flicker.

"From his own father he had inherited not just his newspaper business and his house and property on almost every street in the town of Monument, but also land in the foothills of the mountains in a place known as Glane."

By cradling the child's head near his own, John can overcome the din of the trap's wheels and the mare's flying hooves, and he can hide his tears.

"This Glane was a special place. It extended over thousands of acres. The Boss's father had planted tens of thousands of trees in Glane and Boss himself had planted even more. When the sun shone on the Deilt mountains, from Monument you could see the new trees as if someone had painted the mountains black. But something even more important could be found up there. At the heart of Glane there was an oak wood, as old as Ireland, and there was a pool in the centre of the oak wood that at certain times of the year could cast a magic spell."

At the word magic, the boy smiles.

"You're smiling, and so too did the Boss's son, Black Pender, called Black because of his hair, smile when he heard of that magic pool. He didn't believe in it. He knew that magic was found only in storybooks."

Andrew Hunter knows his mare. By keeping her within an even, reaching stride, just on the bit, she can keep going at the one pace all day.

"How is he, John?"

Despite the dust, Andrew seems to have recovered enough breath to turn around in his seat.

"He's the very best," John Albutt calls, hugging his boy.

They reach a long stretch of the road known as the Heartbreak and now the breaths from Andrew's chest come in a clear, painless rhythm. John can hear it as he speaks to the eyes that flicker from his lap. If asked later what he said, or the nature of the story he told, he would not have been able to repeat it. The words come in a torrent. They tell of another child, long ago, of his sickness, of a foetid, heated room in which the drone of prayers seem to lie like fog, of the doors being thrown wide open all of a sudden. Of being wrapped in a rug by a huge man and being carried out past wailing women. Of the surprising but delicious taste of clear, night air. John Albutt would not have been able to recount on demand the details he recounts in Andrew Hunter's trap: the fear and excitement of being transported in a big car up through a wooded mountain in the midst of a raging snow storm. How the boy sees the snow like a veil across his father's face. The deep sense of love and security the child feels at being carried by the man he so adores. And then, at the end – the sight of the moon and the stars in a pool so perfect that it could well be made of glass. John Albutt will never again remember what he told in such detail, any more than the son in his arms will, in a deep and recessed chamber of his brain, ever forget.

When at last they pull up outside Coleraine General Hospital, two hours have gone by since John's son's collapse. The medical man from Gua hastens in ahead of them; John follows, light bundle in the grey blanket in his arms. Even Andrew Hunter, his mare tethered, comes in, part of the group, reluctant to be separated. The doctor has the nurses set up an intravenous drip of antibiotics, the only treatment for advanced meningococcal meningitis. Then John and Andrew are brought into a staffroom by the matron and given hot tea.

For forty-eight hours the boy battles. After the first day, Andrew goes home to Gua. John finds a church with a cross on the spire and sits for hours in the back, imagining that he is in the cathedral in Monument, hearing in his head boats hooting as they sail with the evening tide, catching the smell of polish in the hall of Pig and Litter, and the striking clock, listening for the voices of his father and his brothers. The matron is waiting for him at the door when he returns. At the sight of her, his knees began to crumble. But she runs out and lifts him up, smiling, crying, "It's all right, John, he's made it! He'll be as fine as anything, thanks be to God!"

He weeps. The doctor from Gua returns and claps him on the back. Touch and go, bedod, he says! But had the lad become unconscious, everyone acknowledges, the result would have been far different.

Seventeen

The heat from the sun had lessened, shadows were spiralling over Candle Lane. I saw the car pull in outside the front door of the *Gazette* and the man get out. Philly Dixon didn't look all that much different: a little whiter, a little rounder. Being Sunday he was wearing a sports coat, trousers of light cord, suede shoes. He'd done well for himself, Philly, his devotion to the paper, which included a check on the premises every Saturday and Sunday nights at this time, had been well rewarded. I saw him go in.

If I could have gone back in time to the first day Jasmine and I spoke, when she came out here and told me about her research and then about her interest in who I was, if I could have revisited that moment, I would never have allowed her to proceed. For another minute of her I would have traded everything on the disk in my pocket. For another minute of her I would have given my entire future, whatever that might be. I don't know what this says about me and my attitude to truth, but my love for Jasmine was the only truth that has ever sustained me.

I had not seen Jasmine for two weeks. In the *Gazette* I picked up from chat in the canteen that she had gone to visit her sister in England. I now regretted beyond words my behaviour in Glane, how I must have frightened her, the way I would have to regain her trust. The sidelong glances of the office girls in my direction were tight and anxious. I saw one of them say that she had met Jasmine's mother the day before and had learned from her that Jasmine might not be coming back. The girl's stare, pregnant with hostility, told me that Mrs Rice blamed me for the outcome of events. That made me ill. Next morning I rang in and told Philly Dixon, the foreman, that I was staying at home. In my mind I saw Jasmine and myself standing either side of a chasm, lost to each other. I looked back on the images in which she was always present and which I held dear, whose evocation had always been currency for me: the taste of her lips, how she would put her hand to my cheek, her words of endearment and encouragement at times of hesitation. I thought about going to see her mother, but I knew I would be unable to disarm her of her preconceptions and so I abandoned the idea. My light went out. Despair hatched in the cantilevers of my chest, in my waters, in the stench of my waste and in the weight of my limbs. I fought not at all, or if at all, then only in actions of helpless and dispirited anger. Thrust back upon only the sum of my own net resources, I discovered a dislike for myself which I assumed had always been there but which now, its hiding place stripped bare by circumstances, was starkly obvious. I gorged on narcotics and played with the idea of the last great engorgement; but a residual sense of duty, it must have been for I can think of nothing else, held me back. I begin wondering if I might have been better off never having met Jasmine, a thought that provoked a fresh spiral of despair, for my life seemed to be a succession of tragedies and the fact that love had once played a big part in it now seemed a cruel fabrication. In dreams alone she came to me. Walking down Dudley's Hill I would discern her molten presence in the street, her lavender-like scent, and she would come alongside and slip her hand through my arm and say, "Friends again, Kaiser?" and we'd just walk on as if no time had passed, down to Long Quay, and watch the ships making ready for the tide.

The day I returned to work it was summer. I had spent the days before in Glane and as I cycled back into town, even though it was still not yet seven, heat lay on the hills, pressing dappled herds down into yellow-flowering meadows. Newborn foals stretched motionless. Sleek yearlings bounced up on sprung fetlocks in mock surprise at my early passage. Being press day I wanted to be in early, to put on my overalls, to get back into the tempo of the plant, into the smells of ink and paper. In town screeching gulls wheeled and flocked in the tangy ozone. Fuchsia was filling in gardens, sun bounced in warm reflection from each leaf of a long hedge of gluey escallonia. I was recovering from myself, which is the way I saw it. I had wounded both Jasmine and myself, I had gone down, but now I was back up again and gaining strength from the magnificent spell of weather.

From early morning the shed roared its weekly proclamation the way it had in unbroken sequence every Tuesday morning for 120 years. In at one end spun the great, blank reels and out, at a distance, flopped folded copies of the *Monument Gazette*. Lunchtime, tray in hand in the canteen, I saw one of the older office women come towards me.

She shouted, "Kaiser? Kaiser! Jasmine was asking how you were."

"She's back?"

The woman nodded, her eyebrows catching the flesh above her nose in worried corrugations. "Friday." She looked about her, then leaned forward. "Go and see her, Kaiser." The loud words.

"Something wrong?"

"She's very down. Just go and see her."

I watched the woman take her tray and join the other front-office people at their table. Once or twice some of them looked over in my direction, bleak signals. I went back to the shed. Two men at the other side of the line didn't think I could see what they were saying.

"Kaiser looks fucked."

"I'm told that little front-office mot he fancies is in the puddin' club."

"Fuckin' eegit."

"Who'll sort her out?"

"Hardly Kaiser."

I made it through the shed and into a toilet cubicle where, athwart the bowl, I was sick into a mint-fresh newspaper even as my bowels opened. Retching, voiding, marvelling even as I did so at the body's versatility, I felt my head boil. Why had she not trusted me enough to tell me? I could hear myself moan. Why had I let my pride get in the way of helping her when she most needed me? I saw the shadows of the outer doors banging, saw in the reflection of the washroom tiles the boots of a man as he stepped up onto the plinth of the urinals. I wondered if there was strength enough in my legs to do what I had to. I saw the sing of piss against the stainless steel and retched anew.

The toilet cubicle shook. Then the door came in.

"Kaiser? Kaiser!" Philly Dixon was standing there. "Are you all right? Jesus, d'you want a doctor? Kaiser?"

I pushed out past him, trying to ignore all the time I'd lost, didn't even think of changing from my overalls, just ran straight out of the shed, across Candle Lane and around the corner into Milner's Street. Late afternoon. Dust was rising. I saw dogs barking, people's heads turned. At the bottom of Plunkett Hill a bus blared and the driver pointed to his temple. I ran up the steps into Cattleyard and across it and down the far side. Choking for breath at the bottom of Half Loaf, my legs were atremble. I sucked for air that wouldn't come, tried to remember the words of a prayer, also unavailable, a wonder that, since daily prayers had been usual for so many years. Her flat off James Place was in through an old courtyard and at the back of one building on its utmost floor. Private or inaccessible, depending on your outlook; 550 square feet. Jasmine had bought it three years ago on a 995-year lease. Why these auctioneer's statistics? I had no idea, they hummed in and out of my head with my strangled breath, balm to my agonised reason. A flight of stone steps ran up to her flat alone. I hit the door with my fist. Shouted. Doves flew in coveys, disturbed. My blows to the door seemed to make me the focus of a thousand eyes. She was in there.

"Jasmine! It's me! Open the door!"

I put my ear to it and tried to hear the essence of the house, but all that I discerned was water. She was in there. My love, my child. Standing back I came to the lock with the flat of my boot. Inwards flew the door.

"Jasmine?"

She would be crying, or asleep, and I could now be the healer. Dead chrysanthemums stood in a vase. Once they had been yellow. Without the amplification of the door's fibres I could no longer hear the water.

"Jasmine!"

Light fell in dazzling slabs through partings in the living-room curtains, themselves puffed every now and then by air from the open, top window. The counter dividing off the kitchenette was bare, its work tiles wiped and gleaming. Beside the oven, knives stood upright on a magnetic bar. I was already planning to return to the *Gazette*, to collect some tools and come back and fix up the front door, when I felt a droning. Meadows came to mind, July rather than June, cattle under trees, air black above them. It vibrated the top of my head. I stepped out into the corridor. The one bedroom was empty, on the quilt of the turned-down bed lay a folded pullover and a pair of her blue jeans. Further on, the other door, that to the bathroom, was ajar. A fan, I then thought, or a hair dryer left on. I pushed the door inward. In an instant they had swarmed into my face and hair, taken by surprise as it were. Bluebottles in their legions. Small, black flies that I crushed by the handful. They kept getting into my eyes so that my view of Jasmine was intermittent. I was shrieking. Jasmine was stuck in the bath in a mould of red plastic. Just head and neck, and the fingers of her right hand and the tips of both her knees showed where the plastic had been cut. So perfect. I knelt down, batting at the flies, although many of them had returned to settle on the red plastic. Her lips, so white, were parted. I could see words frozen just outside them, suspended in the foetid air, yet perfect and untouched by the disorder.

Kaiser, love.

I bit my hand to stem my screaming.

The Garda station was at the courthouse end of Cuconaught Street. I had been waiting for over thirty minutes in the hall where, although outside it was a warm afternoon, the storage heaters were on. On walls around me posters dealt with items as diverse as methadone and sheep-dog trials. The hatch to the general office was unmanned.

"Kaiser?"

The superintendent wore a brown tweed jacket with a yellow hatching. His tight black curls seemed to burst from his scalp.

"Come on up."

The stairs had been refurbished with metal slips on the edges of the risers and steel rails. The super held open the door to an office, closed it behind me and came around the other side of a desk that was bare except for an orange file.

"So," he said, sitting down, "not a bad day." He raised his voice. "Good weather!"

"Nice."

"I'm sorry you were kept waiting, but you know the score, I suppose. What can I do for you?"

I told him I was the one who had found Jasmine.

"I know, I know. What a shame." The super leaned back, his hands stuck into the pockets of his trousers, and looked out of the window. He shouted, "I read the report! Big shock for you! Waste of a life. Of two lives, I suppose."

"Then – it was true?"

He nodded, mouth grim. "You know where she'd been the week before? England." He nodded again, as if to say England was enough. "The Marie Stopes people there. It's where most of the girls in Monument go for the job."

"She had . . ."

"An abortion, no. We've confirmed the facts. She went over all right, booked in, but then checked out before the job. Returned last Thursday night, probably shouldn't have gone directly back to work. Very, very depressed, we've umpteen statements. God be merciful to her is all I can say."

The echoey, metallic bending of his words warped around the room like the shadows of plunging swallows. He was a man who did not shirk eye contact; now his very dark eyes were locked on me.

"I know your involvement there, Kaiser. I'm very sorry."

I said, "I think there was foul play."

A mighty frown harrowed the policeman's brow. "She cut both her wrists to a depth of 2.5 millimetres with a safety blade," he said. "Yes, I'd call that foul."

I asked what the post-mortem said.

The super sighed and flicked open the file with his middle finger. "'Death through misadventure.' I think the family appreciate this aspect of it being kept down. OK, Kaiser?"

He was halfway to his feet.

I said, "Jasmine was not a suicide. She was the opposite. I don't care what the post-mortem says."

The superintendent whistled out a toneless little tune. He sat down again.

"So, what are you suggesting?"

"I think she was murdered."

"And who did it? Did you do it, Kaiser? Did you kill Jasmine?"
I closed my eyes. "No."

"Ah." The super was nodding away, as if that great mystery had been disposed of. "That's you out of the way then. Anyone else come to mind? What's the motive, by the way?"

"She may have been a threat."

"I see. A threat to whom? Do you want to tell me?"

"No."

The point of the policeman's tongue made a lump near his upper lip. "Just like that. Another post-mortem, perhaps. Take her back into the morgue, scrap the funeral arrangements, explain all this to a family already distracted with grief. Why are we doing all this, dear people? Because Kaiser wants us to. And by the way, forget the fact that this poor woman was observed to be in deep depression, that she had recently considered an abortion, that her arteries were in shreds and that there was a razor in the bath tub, forget all that. This is murder now, by persons unknown, motive unknown."

We sat together and the sounds of the building rolled in on me, wave after wave.

"I've always had my reservations about you, Kaiser. You caused a bit of a stir, you know, when you first came back here. People have this preconceived idea of what's normal and what's not. They wanted to know if the streets were safe to walk, that sort of thing. You killed a man, after all. You were convicted of manslaughter for your crime. You were lucky it wasn't murder they stuck on you. You served three years. But there were people in this town who wanted to give you a second chance, one of them an ex-member of this very station. An old man, you probably don't even know him, he was once the sergeant in Deilt when they had a Garda barracks there. Sergeant Lully. No? Well, there you are, for his own reasons, Sergeant Lully always spoke up on your behalf, as did other people, powerful people in the town. So you got your second chance and we told anyone who asked us that you were fine now. Sure, there had been problems, we said, but they were in the past. Now you were fine. And you are. Staying in sheltered accommodation in Demijohn Street. Your trouble is a good few years behind now, Kaiser. Leave it there."

I wanted to tell him that what was lovely was now dead. I wanted to explain how Jasmine had felt in danger because of what she had found out about me, that my existence somehow threatened Tim, that Tim was in financial trouble and that somehow all of these things and Jasmine's death were connected; but since I could neither prove nor explain anything, I knew he would think I was crazy again.

"You're a different man from that young fellow who got into all that trouble years ago, Kaiser. You've got a good job from people who've been very decent to you. I even hear you've been doing up an old cottage out in Glane. Fair play to you. But don't press this one, all right? And remember, although you were given early release, you're only out on licence. If there's any trouble you could end up being put in Leire. Or even worse." The super had come around the desk. "I'm sorry, Kaiser," he said and touched my shoulder. "I really am."

Next morning fine showers had rinsed the town, little local affairs driven by playful gusts off the face of the Lyle. Funerals are popular in Monument. Funerals allow people to spend a short hour or so in their offices, filleting their post of cheques, then to take the remainder of the morning off. The bell of the cathedral drew me from the river, a comforting obeisance. I avoided the main entrance and made my way to the left-hand side door. In the days of now distant memory, between the surf of my adolescence and the imperceptible alluvion of manhood – a time when I could not yet have been technically termed "lapsed" – this had often been my door of late entry to Sunday Mass. Seated deep in the apse I could observe at leisure the faces of Monument composed in their weekly forty minutes or so of worship. By way of the reliable side door I now entered the cathedral and stood a moment beside a ribbed, Ionic column which marked the entry to the baptismal font, observing the growing structure of the buzzing congregation. Jasmine's coffin stood just outside the altar rail, at each of her corners a tall candle in an iron black holder. Never, I was sure, had so many flowers been seen around a coffin, so many they seemed to swell up from the floor and kiss the brass handles. I don't remember the Mass or the words of the priest. My attention throughout the service was on Mrs Rice who, black-hatted, sat at the very edge of the pew, with, beside her, a woman much older than but still not unlike Jasmine, and two big men with sandy hair, and finally a small, elderly looking man with glasses and, despite the goodish day, a coat and scarf. He sniffed without cease. Her father, I realised, the great hero who had made her yearn so much for his return, who had so towered in all his grandeur and might over her youth. It was better she could not see him today, I thought, just as it was better that he could not see her.

Amid the censering and the clunk of chains Jasmine was lifted up onto the shoulders of her brothers and other men and carried down the main aisle of the cathedral. I stepped out. Mrs Rice's eyes and the tip of her nose were the same, sore red. In words that wept she said, "It's all over, Kaiser."

I said, "Did she tell you?"

Mrs Rice bit her lip. "Tell me what?"

"Tell you what she'd found?"

The woman's eyes brimmed and she shook her head. "All she ever told me was that she loved you."

I stood where I was as she walked down the aisle behind the coffin and out into the suddenly sunny morning. A big funeral. A lot of people live in Balaklava. I dragged one foot after the other, spent. It was as if the only good thing I had ever in my life possessed was being marched away from me. One of the last to leave the church, from the top step I could see over the heads of the mourners to the mound of yellow earth that marked the grave's mouth. I wanted to shout out over their heads that something was wrong, although what it was I would not be able to explain. To the left, on the fringes of the crowd, I all at once saw Tim. He was laughing in a hunched-up, trying to be quiet way, listening to something the man he was with had said. This man had his back to me. I could see Tim's laughter, yellow puffs of it, rising. The other man turned. He was laughing too, nodding his black, curly head. It must have been a good joke. I walked down the steps and over to them. I hit Tim in the mouth. He went down. I kicked him in the head.

Following Jasmine's funeral, I was sent to Leire. It was a secure regime, highly waxed and polished, but even in summer's late flush of glory it appeared barren. Located on a post-volcanic, infertile rock and bounded by a sixteen-foot brick wall on three sides and a sheer cliff on the fourth, it was approached by a pot-holed track on either side of which well-maintained, whitewashed stones had been set down to avert visitors from driving into the Atlantic. It had once been a convent, but come the mid eighties falling vocations and economic strictures had forced the nuns of Leire to consider selling up and regrouping elsewhere with others in a similar position, or to make commercial use of their tens of empty bedrooms. Long inured to a life short on laughs, they opened a home for those in long-term recovery. Lo, soon the tens of rooms were filled. Blessed in business by life's talent for mindless tragedy, now Leire's success was doubted by none except those supporting the legalising of euthanasia.

The good men and women who ran Leire wore white collars and black tunics. Smells of food being mass produced eked every day to my senses and, as ever, strafed me with the first shells of grief. We walked from the day room to our meals along a stone-flagged corridor whose light green walls were garnished with random examples of Roman Catholic iconography, including the Infant of Prague, Pope John Paul VI, Pope John XXIII, Blessed Luke Wadding, Archbishop Romero (always a little surprise) and John F. Kennedy. The day room itself was furnished with eight armchairs of tweed seats and backs and of sharp, wooden arms, and three couches of similar, although not matching, design, and a few low tables made of chipboard and topped in veneered marine ply. On the wall was a painting of the Virgin Mary in usual light-hearted pose. A china holder for holy water hung just inside the door. And a crucifix. Other furnishings included a black and white television set, a free-standing ashtray on a pedestal with a black knob that was pushed down in order to consign ash or butt into its tin bowl, a standard lamp that never worked, an (for reasons unknown) electric toaster, a wash-basin, a copy of the Bible, a water vase containing three plastic roses and a wicker wastepaper basket. There were no windows in the day room.

At first they watched me by the minute and sent monthly reports to the superintendent in Monument, then as a hierarchy evolved and patients higher on the scale of volatility were admitted, I was given jobs around the gardens, then down on the farm. I needed a guarantor for this freedom, someone who would stand over my behaviour: apparently the same man mentioned by the superintendent, the man who had once been a sergeant in Deilt, said he would stand over me. I appreciated that. Although I had never met him, it seems his associations with Monument went back long before I was born.

We were presented with a computer by the Monument Lions Club in the second year of my confinement. Located in the library on the top floor, it was a three-gigabyte machine with accelerated graphics plus Caribbean-lagoon-like blue screen, a telephone extension and hi-speed modem. If the idea was to enlarge the world of those in Leire through access to the ether, then the computer was a failure, for no-one but myself ever bothered to climb the forty-eight steps to the library. I spent most of my free time up there, trying to tap into the files which Jasmine had set up in the Monument Library. I could never do so. I could never guess the password she had used. The library in Leire commanded impressive views over the coastal wilderness: jagged coastline with, above it, peaceful fields of cattle, herring gulls big as eagles going on hold at eye level as they took a desultory peep. Each day I tried a new password: every variation of her name and mine I could think of. "Glane". "*Gazette*". The word "love". A thousand others. When she died, I assumed, they had removed all trace of her from the computer. On summer's evenings I could see fishermen between me and the horizon working their lines, as beyond them the sun plunged for warmer oceans.

After three years Mrs Rice came out one day to see me. At first I was startled – her head was snowy white. She laughed at my reaction: "You've got a few grey hairs yourself, Kaiser. I like the beard, though." We sat in the visitors' room and she asked me about myself and how I was getting on and if they were treating me all right and feeding me. The flower shop was still on the go, she told me, although she was thinking of trying to sell it if anyone wanted a flower shop, all the dragging and organising was becoming too much. She had no-one to help her any more. Then she told me why she had come out to Leire: it had been the third anniversary a few months before and she had decided the time had come to put Jasmine's personal belongings to rest.

"Everything was still there the way it was the day she died," she told me. "Apart from cleaning everything up, nothing had been touched."

So Mrs Rice had taken out all Jasmine's clothes and put them in suitcases and given them to the St Vincent de Paul. She had a few items of furniture together with Jasmine's framed photographs and personal mementos brought up to her own house in Balaklava. That left her to deal with the things in and around Jasmine's desk – all the bills and correspondence, bank statements and tax returns and life-insurance policies and books on procedures in libraries, Jasmine's novels, dictionaries, photo albums, framed diplomas, computer manuals, the computer itself with its printer and stationery, maps, journals, two briefcases, medical records, holiday brochures, pens, pencils, passport, chequebook; Mrs Rice went through them all and then either sold or dumped them. Then she gave the keys of the flat to a local auctioneer and six weeks later, along with its remaining furniture, carpets and curtains it had been sold.

"Someone had to do it, Kaiser," she said.

Loss revived in fresh swells of drenching grief.

"I know the next question you're going to ask me, Kaiser – and the answer is, yes, it was all there in a box, all the stuff she had collected about you and which led to so much trouble, and no, I didn't keep it, I brought it down to Small Quay and threw the whole dirty thing into the river."

I couldn't speak, my mouth had once again lost its ability to make the words.

"It was what she wanted," Mrs Rice said. "Read her own

words." Mrs Rice's face took on a kinder expression. "They're all in here in a letter she wrote to you when she was in England," she said and picked up her handbag. "I'm sure she would have posted it if . . . it's not much to have of her, but it's yours." She looked at me then, as if from a distance. "Maybe I'll come out and see you another time," she said.

I told her I would like that and thanked her and we walked out to the corridor redolent of "Mr Sheen", where we said goodbye. Mrs Rice stepped through and the keys were turned behind her. I went up to my room and lay down with Jasmine's letter.

> *June 10th*
> *Dear, dear Kaiser,*
> *. . . The time has come to reach some big decisions. My reasons for them are set out in this letter. After this, I want you and me to go forward, unafraid, our heads high and our eyes only on the future.*

My eye jumped to the bottom of the page.

> *Why did I embark on it in the first place? Many reasons, and I'll tell you of them soon. But in the meantime I'm getting rid of "Kaiser's Gazette".*

I didn't even bother to go to the next page. Clutching the letter in my fist I ran from my room – only at night were we locked in – down the corridor, down the stairs, along the flagged passage-way past the Infant of Prague, the Popes, Blessed Luke Wadding, Archbishop Romero and J.F.K., past the doors to the refectory and kitchens, then, two at a time, or in twenty-four strides if you will, the anticipation an agony in my chest, up the stairs and into the library. My fingers flew over the keys as I logged into the Monument Library's computer. Then, not daring to look with both eyes, rather squinting at the little box, I typed in the words "Kaiser's *Gazette*".

So accustomed had I become to the message "ACCESS DENIED" that when the doors now opened, in great unfolding of icons and graphics, with the vibration of a verbal greeting and with the stacked lists of Jasmine's work waiting there like untouched treasure, I did not at first believe it. And then, as if my heart had waited all this time to thaw, I understood. That moment was the second best in my life, the best being the day I first met Jasmine before any of this ever happened.

PART FOUR

18

MAY 26TH

This has been a bad day. I cannot think. I've done the calculations twenty times and arrived each time at the same answer. It's so – *unexpected*! I cannot assemble my thoughts, it's all I can do to type these words. One way or another, when I've written down this report, I'm going to leave the library, have a stiff drink, and then I'm going to drive out to the chemist's shop in Deilt where no-one knows me.

I have not seen Kaiser since Glane. He has been off work and I have been driving with all my might for the solution that I know is so near. I should go and see him, of course. Especially now. This is no time to be alone.

Today's session with Ollie was the second this week. Because of her health, she can only see me for a couple of hours at a time. I now understand – if before I doubted my suspicions – why years ago she invited Kaiser to Tim's birthday parties and brought him into the house in Pig and Litter, why she gave him a job at the *Gazette* and more recently, got him involved in restoring the cottage at Glane. It is now all so clear to me. Ollie is aware that an old sin is outstanding and feels that Kaiser's presence amounts to a partial absolution. My research is a further opportunity for her to correct the past. She understands what I am doing and accepts my reasons for requesting that she does not divulge these interviews to Tim.

My two hours with her today again brought vividly alive not

only the Monument of over forty years ago, but also the small, County Antrim community in which Black Pender lived the best years of his life.

*　*　*

OLLIE'S STORY

1964

Ollie's wedding is the last time he will be seen in public and the whole town has come to shake his hand. For years he has struck dread into men's very quicks and there are many for whom he is an object of detestation; but today they will all do homage to Boss Pender. His clothes and his linen, all specially cut and tailored for this day, glow. Erect if no longer tall. Vigour in his handshake, colour in his cheeks. Eighty-three years and still his dark eyes have time for the bridesmaids. Oh, how the town declares its pride, at least for today, in Ollie's grandfather. He represents everything that men aspire to: wealth, power, longevity and, more important than all the rest, continuation. His own father came to Monument nearly a hundred years ago and changed the old order; his son carried on, and now here they all are at Ollie's wedding, at the blessing of the ongoing succession, the proof that mere flesh and blood can be transcended. Men find peace in such a sublimation.

It was as if, for that great day alone, he asserted himself over his health, as he did over every other aspect of his life. But then, the day after Ollie's return from honeymoon she calls up to Pig and Litter and is beckoned upstairs by a maid, white as her apron, to his bedroom. He has not been up for a week, Ollie is told. She sees the look across his eyes, not that at twenty-five she has known anything about approaching death before that moment – her

242

grandmother dropped dead without the slightest warning six years before – but Ollie recognises the look as soon as she sees it. The weary acceptance. Beaten at last. His defeated eyes speak to her far more than the novel sight of his big cheekbones, or his listlessness. Smiling, she kisses him, then runs downstairs and calls the doctor.

Ollie has always regarded Boss as her father, or rather, seen herself as his daughter. Her own father, White Pender, with his malt watery eyes, she learned to screen from her mind. Up to her wedding she lived with her parents in James Place, but sometimes she did not even recognise her father. As for her mother, Cushy, Ollie has never heard her speak Boss Pender's name. Some old enmity, Ollie accepts, families are full of such distortions. From forever Ollie has sat by her grandfather's desk in the Proprietor's office. A big girl, tall as him. The very spit of him, she hears them say around the town. And: brains skip a generation, when they think she is out of earshot. She has learned everything from the Proprietor.

Dr Armstrong, a man not far off Boss's age and her grandfather's medical attendant for fifty years, asks Ollie to come and see him. He still practises his profession, albeit at his own pace and with chosen patients of long standing, from his house in Binn's Street, whose front-room surgery with its coal fire and jaded leather chairs and couch, its tables piled high with journals and magazines, its doctor's desk with pigeon holes and kidney bowls and bottles of long forgotten use are deemed irrelevant by the good doctor's patients to his sustained gift for diagnosis. A man who always dresses in a three-piece suit, with a flowering spotted kerchief, whose face affirms a lifetime's liking for whiskey, Dr Armstrong leaps to his feet when Ollie is shown in and catches her big hands in his and reaches his lips to her neck and kisses her.

"The best day out I've had for thirty years," he chortles. "You were the bride of every man's dreams."

"Your present was too generous, Doctor," says Ollie. "It catches the light beautifully."

"Nothing like crystal," smiles Dr Armstrong. "Now, and I will not take no for an answer, we're going to drink the health of the bride."

Ollie sits on the leather fender and the doctor goes to a medical cabinet and takes out a decanter and glasses.

"Where did ye go at all? Remind me," he says, blithely splashing whiskey halfway up the sides of two tumblers.

"Italy," Ollie says, "Rome."

"Ah, I'll never see it now," says the doctor, returning with a beaker of water. "Say when."

He sits into the chair with the long seat and back and raises his glass.

"God bless you, Ollie."

"Good health."

They drink and Dr Armstrong smacks his lips. Ollie knows that questions are unnecessary. No new hope will arise from this consultation.

"I always loved Glane," says the doctor, "just like the Boss. Funny thing, when I qualified first I'd never been out there, never heard of Glane. Then this day I was up in Deilt, middle of summer, I wasn't long qualified. A tailor's daughter, the child had measles – no, I tell a lie, not measles – not measles . . ." The doctor's eyes grow round and unfocused as his mind is for a moment arrested in its sudden image of this faraway, sick daughter of the tailor of Deilt and his own lost diagnosis. ". . . Whooping cough!" cries the doctor. "Whooping cough, I'd bet me britches! Anyway! Out I comes from the house in Deilt and who is standing there with his bicycle but the postman."

Ollie sips her whiskey, feels it and the fire light up her face.

"'Doctor,' says he 'I think you should go up to Glane.' Nothing more, bedad! He's gone off down the street like a greyhound, the rascal, and I'm there scratching me head and it's twelve o'clock and me dinner'll be up on the table here in Binn's Street at one, Mother of the Divine! And I'd never even heard of Glane!"

Ollie remembers everything the Boss taught her: how to be fair but tough, how to use the *Gazette* like a sword if needs be. How to borrow money at the very moment you did not need it. How to keep your purposes hidden, even from the person you sleep with.

"What could I do? The Hippocratic oath, you know. Dinner had to wait! Up I goes to this place Glane."

And what of the past? He never spoke about old days as such, but nevertheless, through the simple process of association, of chance remarks, of seeing old photographs, of learning to recognise the areas that were forbidden to discussion, Ollie as a child became aware of the past as in an outline. She saw it in her grandfather's face at least once a day. His face that the world outside never saw. Ollie was too young then to recognise grief.

". . . two old farmers, two brothers, that was all that was left up there a mile beyond your Glane, but Glane is still the townland. You know the place, Ollie! God in heaven, you know it better than anyone! Pishogues and fairies and wicked dark skulduggery!" chuckles Dr Armstrong and fondles his glass in both his hands. "Oh, God Almighty, those days are long gone, that's for certain."

At some point in her journey from girl to woman, when she was sixteen or thereabouts, one day – or it seemed like that – Ollie realised that her grandfather's entire life was spent under a shadow. It was manifested in his relationship with Ollie's parents, in the way he lived at home, where for him his own wife might not have existed, in his almost total lack of social contact and in his avoidance of the past. He lived every moment of his life for his newspaper. He had an estate out at Glane, said to have once been the pride of his life, in which he had not, Ollie knew, set foot for twenty years. Ollie's first conscious knowledge of womanhood was that her grandfather's life was one lived in perpetual sorrow.

"Anyway, I drives up through the woods – miles and miles of the finest timber – and arrives outside this cabin. When I pulls up I sees just the one old fella, God knows he must have been ninety, lurking around in the shadow of the shed. Come over here! I shouts at him. Is there any kind of trouble? 'Me brother, Doctor,' says he . . . "

She never had the courage to ask him, because when he became aware of her presence, or was needed somewhere within the *Gazette*, the look left him and he resumed as before, bustling and energetic, a man of power and property, the Proprietor.

" . . . into this house I goes. The smell, God, you don't have to be a doctor, Ollie! This old fella was in the bed, eyes open to God. Dead for at least a week I'd say. What, says I, turning on the other fella, in the name of God and all that's holy, what is the meaning of this? This fella should be buried this last fortnight! And he looks at me like an old water spaniel I used to have and he whines, 'Jasus, doctor, I thought he was only bla-guardin'!'"

She'd seen Boss's eyes when he'd first met Wilder Goode, her husband to be. Anglo-Irish from Eillne direction. Couldn't conceal his disdain as he shook Boss's hand. That he didn't own the shoes he stood up in was to Wilder nothing compared to the fact that the Goodes had once owned ten thousand acres. A month before her wedding Boss had taken her aside, given her a cheque for a thousand pounds, more money than she'd ever need for the months after her wedding. Spoke, or rather mumbled on, for half an hour about how she'd always be taken care of, how she'd be his trustee for her lifetime, how she'd run the paper when he was gone. Trustee for the male heir. Her son. That stung Ollie. She knew she'd made a mistake.

Dr Armstrong thumps the arm of his armchair. "'Jasus, doctor, I thought he was only bla-guardin'!'" he shouts.

She came home full of misgivings. Knew, given everything, that she could never love the man she had just married. She decided to tell Boss, to admit she had been wrong. That was her reason that day for going up to Pig and Litter.

"That's the best I ever heard, Doctor," she says. "The best I ever heard."

"Ah, dear oh dear oh dear. Ah, dear God," says Dr Armstrong, wiping the tears from his face and blowing his nose in his ample kerchief and tucking it away with a flourish. "Ollie, my dear," he says, "Boss has only a few months to live."

Despite the fact that she knows anyway, she weeps. She listens as the doctor speaks of inoperable bowel cancer, the long life already enjoyed, the prospect of merciful release.

"When did . . . ?" Ollie asks.

"April," replies Dr Armstrong. "He thought it was bad indigestion. I don't know how he's lasted."

"He came to my wedding. Everyone said he looked so well. He must have known then."

The doctor leans forward and squeezes Ollie's hand. "There's many he rubbed up the wrong way, Ollie, that's for sure, but for me your grandfather will always be a great man."

The kitchens in Pig and Litter are at hall level, the day rooms all on the first floor. Boss Pender is moved down, at his own request, into the big, front sitting room with its three windows overlooking Monument – the room Ollie and I sat in today. It is a room conceived with a coal fire as integral, for the steep bank of forge-red coals in the fireplace is caught and reproduced in the many polished mahogany planes, both vertical and horizontal, as well as in the turned, wooden legs of chairs and in the glasses of mirrors and of pictures, and, in Boss's final days, on the table to the left, laid out in a single setting of silver cutlery, glassware and the other trappings appropriate to the five-course meal which would now never be eaten. There was a glowing, glass-fronted corner cabinet housing china and porcelain figurines, a baby grand piano and a polished up, half-sized Cosser printer from 1870.

Now the room is always in twilight, the red velvet drapes on each of the three windows partly drawn across the lace curtains. His bed is adjacent to but not too near the fire. He can no longer sit up to take in the view he values most. Perhaps it is from seeing him supine, but Ollie notices for the first time the two, bothered ridges that have gathered, like the backs of sea shells, along the line of his brow beneath the skin. His dark eyes themselves, the dominant feature of Boss Pender that most people have always carried away with them, his eyes, which once needed the space of a whole eye socket, are now reduced to small, hard spheres, lacking any distinct colour, leaving the sockets with unused areas of flesh whose tint in some places is livid purple, in others the skin of chicken. Ollie's compassion is without limit. She washes and changes him, won't let the nurse do it. She is amazed at how his bulk has bolted. He cries out when she moves him. Dr Armstrong prescribes morphine.

One day he whispers, "Any news?"

She holds his hand and begins recounting what might interest him, starting with the *Gazette* and working out into the town; but he shakes his head.

"I meant you. Any news?"

All at once she understands. "No news yet," she says. She smiles. "Give me time."

He appears to be on the point of saying something, but then he turns away.

Ollie's practical side – her Pender side – is to the fore, for she knows her grandfather will wish to die as he has lived: with meticulous attention to detail. Thus over the following days she speaks in quiet tones to him about the arrangements, learns his preferences in hymns, describes to him the special edition that will be published, bordered in black, the day of his funeral. The whole town will be in mourning, she says. But she knows too to leaven the morbid with hope and thus she also encourages him to think of the paper as a living thing, something that will survive all of them and which in this instance will be carried forward by Ollie herself. He asks her if she understands the terms of the trust he has put in place: under which she will run the paper and enjoy all its benefits and profits – but as trustee for her lifetime. He wishes the male line to inherit, just as he did. Neither his son, Tom, nor her father, White, are right for the burden and thus the *Gazette* will fall to the male heir of the next generation. Ollie tells him she understands, that he has shown her the trust document. Whatever resentment she may have felt at one time about her ultimate exclusion has been replaced by the satisfaction of know-ing that she is trustee for her unborn son. For Ollie has always known that she will have a son.

And then, one day, racked by pain, he waves away her hand with the morphine and becomes most agitated. Ollie turns to the door, to shout down for someone to get the priest because she thinks this is his time; but in a sharp voice he calls her back.

"Boss?"

"There is . . ." He struggles for the strength to find the words. Ollie puts her hand beneath him and tries to ease him. She can heft him now with one arm. Boss's face contorts in pain and he fights to concentrate. "There is someone . . . I want you to go and bring home," he says.

"Someone?"

Lips scoured white, he grimaces with pain and nods with massive patience.

"Bring who home?" Ollie asks.

"A boy," says Boss Pender.

* * *

SIX MONTHS BEFORE OLLIE'S WEDDING
GUA, COUNTY ANTRIM, 1964

Within the confines of the world of which Gua is the centre, within the stone-walled fields that run all the way to the edge of cliffs, where hay is saved in summer as the sea spumes, where the ocean lives in your ears and eyes and nose, John Albutt has found a kind of peace. He loves his wife and his child. And also, although it has taken all of twenty-five years, he has come to love the place. He has found a virtue in its simplicity which is reflected in the lives of its people. Lives pared to the bone, but none the worse for that. It is as far as can be travelled from Monument, the whole of Ireland and all that is in it lies between the two places. Of the northern community of which he is a part, he has become a silent observer. He has learned that the Albutts and the Hunters say little, do everything in life with one eye on the tide. Old Wint is long dead: John hammered stones out of the January earth to help make the grave. Wint's son, also Wint, fishes for eels and crayfish, within twelve months of the funeral looks the mirror image of his dead father, even wears his clothes. These folk eat in silence and their views on other people in the community are conveyed, at the mention of names, by the motions of their heads. Six years ago when their sister in the south died, Harriet's parents, old Andrew Hunter and his wife alone went down, just as they had fifty years before to see her married. No words were spoken in Gua about her passing, there was no discussion about a delegation, Andrew and his wife just went. John knew they were going and could have gone with them. He chose not to. Nor, when they returned a day later, was their trip reviewed or even mentioned. There had been no border when they had attended her wedding and now, for her funeral, they had crossed it for the first and last time.

John sits near the cliff's edge, his eyes on the sea, and worries about his child. Harriet claims that since the illness the year before last he has become backward. Inward. Doesn't answer you if his back is turned. Harriet too is a worry, the tightness to her face, the tension in her back, the way in bed she puts her hand to her head and sighs. When pressed, she mentions headaches. John tries to soothe her with his hands and voice, and sometimes she comes to him, her face wet, and tells him over and over how she loves him. He sometimes imagines himself in another life: the sound of the presses, the bustle on press day, bales of papers being loaded for delivery, the smell of ink, the feel of that week's edition in the hands, the glowing masthead, the vitality of being associated with this extra dimension to oneself. Always at this point, when the fantasy requires the leap into the personal, of the life surrounding the life, he stops. Not that Harriet could know, but it seems disloyal to her to go any further. It also brings pain. John sees the immense sea and wonders what it means. He is drawn to the cliff in all weathers, in the winter for its honest rage, now in the July sunshine for its scents and flowers. But in the many years he has known Harriet, it was only in the months before they married that she ever came up here to these North Antrim cliffs with him. Knew them too well, she laughed then. Called them treacherous.

It is Saturday. John is walking back down the track and sees the cottage inland behind the lower cliffs, lying white like a fragment of bone. Harriet would be back from Gua, she'd have left the shopping things on the kitchen table, then gone up to her parents' house to collect the boy. Old Andrew often puts a halter on his mare and stands her out and lifts the boy up to sit on her bare back.

John comes down quickly into the small proportions of the place, the cottage with the slate roof, the gleaming paint, the white-wash, the concreted apron front and back, kept and swept like an article of faith. The prize-winning fowl in their coop. A pig in one shed, a calf in another. When the pig is up to John's thigh, Andrew Hunter will take it home and kill it noisily and then lay it out on his kitchen table, and butcher it. When Andrew has the cuts cured he will bring back half of them down to John. Harriet takes eggs up to her father, comes home with her mother's soda bread. When the calf is a year old, John and Andrew together will bring it into Coleraine and stand all day at the fair until at last their price is met. Such certainties of life have become a comfort to John, as are his books, still brought once a month from the travelling library. And the stone walls he builds, which from a distance seem to thread their way along the cliff-tops, people say only those with a natural ability can make them. John goes in the back door calling, "Harriet."

His eyes are still in thrall to the sun, so that he sees nothing at first in the kitchen except the window's frame of brightness, and he stumbles over something at his feet. He looks down and makes out the outline of Harriet's shopping basket. Sugar has burst from its brown bag and is spread in a fan. At the far side of the table, on the flagged floor, lies Harriet, one hand stretched out as if reaching to the window, one of her shoes off. She is still wearing the blue linen coat she always wears when she cycles into Gua.

This time there is no running, no headlong dash to the doctor or to Coleraine. She has been dead for more than an hour. John does not want anyone to see her like this, any more than she would have wanted it. The untidiness. He lifts her from the floor and carries her into the bedroom and lays her out on the bed they have shared for five months less than sixteen years. He removes her

252

coat and hangs it behind the door, and then all her clothes and folds them and puts them into drawers. He takes out the nightgown she wore on their wedding night and dresses her in it. He manoeuvres her into the bed under the sheets and blankets, soft pillows beneath her head, then he goes out and cleans up the kitchen.

Lying beside her, knowing the boy will be all right, John stays with Harriet till dusk. And when the darkness comes, he lights a candle, brings it into the bedroom and kneels down beside the bed and asks Harriet's spirit, which he can still discern near at hand, to forgive him for having loved her only as second best.

Nineteen

I stepped into the recess of a gateway as Philly Dixon, the *Gazette*'s door locked – and tested – behind him, turned his car and drove out by me down Candle Lane. I paused for a moment to inhale the last of the evening air and to feel the distant, tickling tumult of the town. Then I went down the side of the shed and by way of a fire door that sprang to me easily when I levered it, I entered the *Monument Gazette*.

The building dated from 1972, the year in which the original premises were destroyed by fire. Newspapers are tinder-dry institutions, full of paper and glue and ink and chemicals that go up in a trice; in my day, a man found smoking in the machine shed was out of a job, there and then. I could have dwelt among the machines in which I had once found comfort, but conscious now of time, I hurried through the shed without dallying into the area behind the reception, where the automatic telephone switchboard was located. Finding the lever, I threw it to off. Then I went up to the first floor.

The main office was warm from the day's heat. Sitting at a desk I turned on the computer and watched as the system booted up. I would have to present the contents of the disk over one edition of sixteen pages, I had calculated. I slid in the disk, then clicked my way through to load it. The system hummed.

It had taken me a long time to arrange everything in proper order – more than a few years – and I was now going to have to execute my design in a matter of minutes. Nevertheless I was calm. I thought of how diligent Jasmine had been, how painstaking. I was, in effect, her executor.

As the pages of film slid out one by one I held them up to the light and saw the columns set out with their headings and neat spacing. Then, as the final page emerged, I laid it on top of the other fifteen that I had produced, picked up the plastic stack and went downstairs. The print-down frame was at the back of the shed, behind the Heidelberg Speedmaster. I placed the first two films down side by side on the aluminium plate and switched on the ultra-violet light. I doubted the *Gazette* had ever before been printed on a Sunday.

I wondered as I worked how one man could have caused so much destruction. But then what I knew of history always pointed to a man alone, whether good or evil, as being the catalyst by which future generations lived in misery or hope. Boss Pender had been such a man. It had taken the birth of a new century – until now – for his malignity to be excised.

I removed the last of the eight aluminium plates, chemical washed, from the processor and brought them over to the presses. A thousand times I had done this before, felt their wobbly mass between my hands, looked at their silver greyness and never imagined that I would one day be loading them in this manner onto the waiting cylinders. I first took a rag and with a bottle of white spirits carefully cleaned down the surfaces of the line. Pride in my work. You never went to press with a dirty line. Then I dropped the first plate into the clamp at the base of the cylinder on the foremost Pacer, nudged it secure, then gently wound the cylinder around until the plate was wrapped to it tight. It took me fifteen minutes to load all eight. I went to the head of the line and began to strip the outer casing paper from the first reel of newsprint. I needed four and each of them weighed half a tonne. I looked at the wall clock at the back of the line. It was seven-thirty.

As I hoisted the reels one at a time into place using the inbuilt hydraulic, I felt a great tug of loss for what had happened: not just for myself and Jasmine and our child and the ongoing generations, but for all the lives that had lived under Boss Pender's shadow. His three sons, each of whom he had systematically destroyed. His wife. His daughter-in-law. His daughter. And, almost half a century after his own death, his grandson, Tim, who was still carrying out that dark legacy.

The reels sat snug on their axles, the four presses were threaded, the ink ducts filled, the water trays full. I began to run the line to allow the web to settle down. As the rotation began I could feel the soles of my feet remember the noise.

Not that I could ever forgive Tim for what he had done; but I could now understand how, with the same lack of moral courage he had inherited from Boss Pender – if you can inherit a lack – he had felt powerless to do otherwise.

Wiping my hands with a swipe of paper towelling I walked in measured pace down the line, making a final inspection. Then I returned to the end, to the folding machine where the web joined and became a newspaper. I hit the red switch. The web spun over-head, from one end of the line to the other, its tone to me one of comfort. Already, along the belt from the mouth of the folding machine, the latest edition of the *Monument Gazette* was becoming jammed as new papers were added from the line. I lifted off a bundle and placed them down on a nearby table. All the dead faces represented in there, all the dead voices. It was as if the seed of what had once happened had grown down into the earth of Monument and was only now able to burst forth.

20

As I sit here in the library today, I am faced with two decisions. One involves the child in my womb; the other, its father, the man I love. This has all become too much, almost. I need time and space – away from Monument, if possible. I rang my sister in England an hour ago and left a message. I may go and stay with her and try and sort my head out over there.

Funny, but the choice involving Kaiser seems more daunting than that relating to whether or not I am having his child. I must decide whether or not to tell him what I have found out. On the one hand, he deserves to know; but if I tell him my revelations will cause such turmoil in Monument that I doubt our love will survive it. We will both be caught up in a battle by others for their very existence. Some of us will not last out. Our baby will suffer.

On the other hand, if Kaiser knows nothing except that I am to have his baby, then we can live our lives peacefully, somewhere other than in Monument. I want none of what I have discovered – either for him or for myself. The past reeks of death and unhappiness. We will both be much better off without it.

In the meantime, I must write down what is Ollie's final testament, which proves at last everything I imagined to be true. But before I do I should set out how I came to suspect that truth in the first place.

I have my mother to thank for the fact that I became interested in Kaiser. It was her reaction when I first told her I'd met him

257

and who he was that sent me searching. She was aghast. At first I attributed her reaction to her incorrigible snobbery – a matter in which, I would say, she is indistinguishable from her late mother – but then I realised there was something far more complex going on. She *knew* something about this man and she did not want me to discover what that was. I find this extraordinary. She was prepared to take sides against her own daughter to defend a man, Boss Pender, whom she could scarcely have known, and to keep secret a crime which took place before she was born. She wanted nothing to change. Although she exists on the very outer edge of the circles which have as their centre the *Gazette* and the Pender family, she was prepared to go to great lengths to preserve the Penders' secret. I think this realisation has brought me to another decision: if this is what small towns like Monument do to people, then I want no further part of small towns. When this is all resolved, as it soon will be, I'll persuade Kaiser that we should go away.

Last year, however, my curiosity was provoked. I began looking in the files of the Demijohn Street Orphanage – now in the Monument Library – for documents around the time Kaiser would have come there. Almost immediately I found a receipt for £1,000 issued by the orphanage and dated the same week in October 1964 in which Kaiser entered that institution. On the back of the receipt was written, "Kaiser". It was issued to Beagle & Co, Solicitors, and although I was unable to get any satisfaction about this – or about any other matter relating to Kaiser – from Beagle's, I found a payment of £1,000 in the accounts archives of the *Monument Gazette* made that same October day 1964 from the *Gazette* to Beagle & Co. It seemed that the *Gazette* had paid what was then a very large sum of money towards Kaiser's place in Demijohn Street. I set out to discover why.

I wasted a lot of time reading copies of the *Gazette* itself in the four years leading up to October 1964; I found nothing. I looked again at the old payments book of the *Gazette* to see if I had missed anything: immediately beneath the £1,000 payment to Beagle's was an entry, "Hart, petrol expenses, £3". Mileage logbooks for all the paper's vehicles had been kept, including for Boss Pender's car. I established that on the very day that Kaiser was registered in Demijohn Street, Boss Pender's car had travelled a total of 597 miles – 597 miles in one day! That is nearly the whole length of Ireland and back!

Maybe I should have stopped there, but I did not and here I am, nearly one year later at the very end of a story which began on that day I first met him.

I heard a note of caution in Ollie's voice today, or of regret, as if since my last visit to Pig and Litter a week ago she has been discussing my visits with someone else. I would not be surprised. More of the old, defiant and domineering Ollie was evident. Her health is improving and she may well now regret having spoken to me when she was more vulnerable. When I left, she did not go so far as to say that she did not want to see me again – but both of us knew. Following what I learned today, set down now with my usual interpretation of Ollie's details, there is really no more left to be said.

* * *

OLLIE'S STORY

Four weeks to the day on which Harriet died, a car draws up outside the cottage. It is a Wednesday, lunchtime, a local woman cooks the daily meal and minds the child, an interim arrangement. John goes to the door and sees a small, neat man with a trim moustache and dressed in a suit with a fob watch and chain and wearing a grey homburg hat. He raises his hat, introduces himself. John forgets the name as soon as he hears it, invites the man in. He assumes it is something about Harriet.

"I am a partner in Smith & Scannell, Londonderry, sir," declares the man, having declined the offer of tea. "We are solicitors and we represent on this occasion a person from Monument in the Republic who says he should be introduced as an old friend."

John stares. "Old friend?"

"Very old and once very dear," says the man with knowing.

John, still associating the visit with Harriet, says, "My wife has died."

"Ah yes." The solicitor from Londonderry's eyes become downcast. "I am so sorry, sir. I apologise in the circumstances for the intrusion at this sad time, but time, I regret, is not on my client's side."

"Your client."

"He said you would know him."

"Or I might have forgotten."

"He thinks that would be very understandable, but all the same, unlikely. He says that his life ever since has been a torment, but now he begs to meet you before he faces his maker."

"He is . . ."

"Dying, sir. Little time remains to him."

Black's head reels as a succession of past images assail him. "What if I won't see him? What will he do? Will he buy the sight of me with gold?"

"I have not been authorised to make any such suggestion, sir. All I have been told to say is that if in the past there survives even a single memory of happiness for you involving this old friend, that you at least consider granting him this one wish before he enters eternity."

John puts his elbow on his knees and his head sinks down. "I don't wish to meet him," he says. He can smell the polish from the other man's shoes. "Too much time has gone by."

"Very well." The solicitor gets to his feet. "But if following further reflection you see fit to change your mind, here is my telephone number. I can set up the meeting within two days of your agreeing to it."

John sees him out to the door.

"One last thing, Mr Albutt. If you do decide to see your old friend, he asks that you bring your young son."

John blinks. "How does he know I have a young son?"

"The recent death notice," murmurs the solicitor and sets his hat on his head. "I am so sorry for your trouble, sir."

He cannot get the visit out of his mind. In the days following, he sinks into a torpor of retrospection. He could have returned to Monument to clear his name, but he chose not to – both for reasons of deep hurt at Cushy's decision to marry White and for reasons of fear that he might fail to establish his innocence. For nothing had spoken louder those first few years than the absence from Gua of his father and mother and brothers. Why had none of them ever come to see him? His father had hidden him, he had long realised, he was every bit as much his father's victim as had been Sam Phibbs. And then, six months before, the car with the

261

southern registration had appeared in Diggan's Field, and John had felt nothing but revulsion. But in the pellucid aftermath of his grief for Harriet he can separate out the hurt of betrayal and the anguish beyond recounting at the loss of his own potential from the reward of his own son. He has what his father never will – the son he loves. His father has lost everything that he has gained. John's love for the boy outweighs his rancour. Another man with less capacity for love might falter on the issue of injustice, but John is not a man who can dwell on the malign. He loves the boy as he once loved his own father. With shock, he realises more: that when he gets beneath the pain, there still survive, side by side with intense hurt, traces of his old love for his father.

Hay is being made in Gua. All the farms listen every night to their wirelesses, then one day, as though on a common blade, every meadow topples. John drives an open-topped tractor with a rear bobbing attachment up and down the long incline of a neighbour's twenty-acre field, fluffing out the swathes of cut grass. At the centre of him still survives a perverse pride in the Pender family and the *Monument Gazette*. He carries in his veins the blood of a man who created a great institution and he, John, has played his part in contributing to that institution's survival. A part of him still believes, and always will, that his selflessness is, deep down, appreciated by his family. They owe him everything. Any other course of action that long ago night would have been unthinkable – is still unthinkable. Most of the details are gone or nearly gone, but this stark belief remains. John, one eye on the field ahead, one on the hay-bob behind, understands that in over twenty-five years little has changed. But he is also a proud man who has never been able to grasp the course of his life.

I can imagine vividly the situation described by Ollie. A summer's breeze straight off the sea, full of salt and goodness, bathes his face. He has long resolved that he will never cross the border again, and although he can feel sympathy for an old, dying man, his first response to the solicitor – "I don't wish to meet him" – is still his decision. And yet, from that part of John where lies compassion comes a keen appreciation of the old man's desperate need – to lay eyes before he dies on not only John, but on John's son. He can put himself in the same position. Like his father and his grandfather, he sees his own immortality in the figure of his little son, and he has not enough capacity for hate to deny Boss Pender that last comfort. Added to all that, he is intensely curious. Gulls rise up over the ledges, gliding on wall air, peeping. He cannot resist.

They are in the early bus on Sunday morning, father and son, making the long journey from Coleraine through Londonderry, down through Strabane and then Omagh and Enniskillen. Up to dusk the night before he rowed the hay whilst men came behind and baled it. The Gua bales will lie scattered all the long Presbyterian Sunday in the fields, before being stacked on Monday. Two years before he came down here to the border with old Andrew Hunter on a cattle-buying expedition. South of Enniskillen, at a crossroads within sight of the upper Erne, they took tea in a public house near a river, on whose far banks, he had been told, grew the grass of the Irish Republic. Now he is resting his hand on the back of the boy's neck and is watching him eat his way through a bag of bull's-eyes as they sink ever down into the pith of Ireland.

The public house is closed, he hears church bells from the south, the midday Angelus. He told the solicitor one o'clock, but he wants to arrive early, he feels that way he is in control. They make their way down the field to the water. No bridge exists for six miles in either direction, the reason he has chosen this place – or, to be accurate, why he nominated the far bank of the river, knowing that his father will not know the hinterland. He carries the boy through tall grass and buttercups. At the river they settle down to wait.

John watches the still face of the river, in breadth no more than three leaps, and feels bottomless sadness. He mourns the passing of life, the death of his wife. He wonders all of a sudden what Cushy looks like now. The child is breaking the water's surface with stones. John hears the car.

He is expecting the Vauxhall, even as he knows that the car must now be a museum piece and that the black saloon of six months earlier is the car to expect; and so it appears, inching its way up the track on the far side of the river. John can see the dip and rise of its suspension as it creeps over the uneven ground. He has told the child nothing, just promised him a surprise, the boy has a hidden nature but is biddable. Now from the cover of the grass stems John sees the car halt and a man with a cloth cap and white hair beneath it get out.

Hart is at once recognisable. John stares as the man scans the landscape, walks around to the other door, which he opens, and takes out an overcoat. He has grown both fatter and shorter, it seems to John, and his face is a high colour that John doesn't remember, and his shoulders are stooped forward, but Hart he is without a question. The driver is now at the rear door, holding it open. Cattle in the field have been drawn to the car and are nosing in around it, their snorts of steam, their probing, curious heads. From the back of the car emerges a figure, around whose shoulders Hart, despite the summer's day, arranges the coat. Boss Pender steps out and Hart goes to deal with the cattle.

From where he lies with the child, Black can look into the river and see his father's diamond-sharp reflection, inverted. So reduced. Black has carried through all his years of exile the image of a big man, a full chest, someone whose hands were capable of choking out a man's life. This man wears no moustache, a lack which has the effect of making him furtive. His hair has thinned, he uses a stick to lean on. The Boss Pender John remembers had bushy hair

264

and stood erect; this is another man entirely. And yet this shrunken figure on the far bank whose pallor looks chilled despite the sun, whose eyes never rest, could not be anyone but the man John has come to see. Out of his hinterland and apprehensive he might be, but there is also in the carriage of his head and the way he stands there, a hint of the old impatience that expects punctuality and things to unfold to a schedule of his own making. John hears him say, "Hart!" without turning around, and sees Hart hurry over and look at a watch and give the old man the time, as if time is something else Boss still commands.

John, nestling the boy to him, has the urge to stay down in the grass, he knows that they cannot be seen and that if they remain hidden then his father will, in time, go away. But then, when he expects it least, when he is lost in absorption of the image on the water's shell, the child slips from under his arm and runs towards the river. John jumps up and runs and seizes him. Then he remains standing, the boy's shoulders beneath his hands, looking across at his father.

"Black?"

The voice is hoarse. John does not reply.

Boss Pender says, "The child was mine."

John at first does not understand.

"I did wrong. May God forgive me."

The whole passage of John's life takes form between the banks of the river. He sees himself as a boy like the one at his side, as a young man in love, as a fugitive, and now, as a grey-haired widower. He realises then that whatever his father once gave him, including life, that he, John, gave far more in return. He understands that the man whose eyes and his are now locked gave him life with one hand, but with the other hand took it and more away. John grasps for the first time the magnitude of the crime of which he was victim and in that new perception he sees the full extent of the evil that the old man represents. John's eyes swim from being fixed for so long, but in his father's face he can now see burning all the crimes for which Boss stands accountable. Huddled as if on a winter's day, death in his nostrils, fear in his eyes. Fear of judgment. This is how he will leave the world. John turns the child away from the river and they walk together back up the field to the village without turning around.

"Black!"

The child wants to stop and turn, but John will not allow it.

"Black!"

Father and son walk hand in hand up into the town. A bus to Londonderry will come at three. By eight that evening they will be home.

On Monday and Tuesday they prop the bales on their ends in fours to let the air finish them, on Friday John drives the same tractor with a front loader, getting the square bales into four or five collection points in the twenty-acre field. He has wondered all week about what effect the trip might have had on the child, what the sight of an unexplained old man standing on the far side of a river might mean. The boy has not asked, slept all the way to Gua on the bus, was preoccupied with a set of miniature farm animals that his grandfather Hunter had carved out for him over the previous winter.

The field is steepest at its right-hand corner, the top side nearest the ocean, its lip fenced with thorny wire to keep stock from the sheer drop. John picks up three bales, reverses down to where the dray will load them but as he does so, one drops off. He reverses on anyway, the heat from the sun beating into the flannel shirt on his back. He feels the need to explain to the child in some way the long journey to that river meeting. He remembers the year before last, during their dash in Andrew's trap to Coleraine, how he related the story of Boss and Glane to the child and although he doubts if his son even remembers, now he feels the need to correct the impression of heroism he knows he gave in recounting what his father once did for him. He knows because up to the Sunday before he still saw his father as a hero. Now at last he understands that the father he loved had killed, not for his son, but for himself. Everything is now clear. Cushy's disappearance. His father's terror that Sam Phibbs would find out the truth. John sometimes wondered about a child in Monument who, however inexplicably, was his flesh and blood. Now he realises that he had always been right, that the child had never been his.

He has finished the field and is gunning the tractor for the gate at the bottom when the errant bale up in the right-hand corner catches his eye. Halting, he does a sharp turn and storms back uphill. Ever since Sunday he has awoken in the morning seized by a strange elation: that part of his mind that has always, almost unknown to him, reserved for itself a dark preoccupation with the past, coupled with a concern, albeit unconscious, for his father's welfare, is now unfettered. An ancient sureness imbues him. *He did nothing wrong!* Lightness rides through him, a delicious feeling. He cannot remember when he has felt so unburdened. He cries out for the joy of it. He can go home! He can return to Monument. Cushy, after all, is still only his own age. As once he changed, so now he will change again.

Without stopping, he fishes the bale with one spike of the loader, chucks the gears into reverse and swings her round. He thinks of the boy. He laughs. He thinks of Cushy and how she will embrace the boy to her when she meets him. As once before, the future seems boundless, time has been defeated and John's heart makes a surge as the happiness that must for years have been trapped in there is released. Without warning, the ground dips beneath his big, rear wheel. John throws her into forward, hits the throttle with the heel of his hand. He wants to see the boy. The hill is all at once licking away from him. John swears. He brakes as he feels himself slide back into the barbed-wire fence. He feels the unstoppable momentum of the tractor's weight. The front loader is rising up. John makes to jump, but the bar of the loader strikes him over the ear, pushes him back down into the seat. And then, for a strange moment, he feels the wind whistle through his hair and sees, with sudden detachment, the cliff above him, where it has subsided under the weight, and in the final moments he becomes aware of the sea.

* * *

As Ollie sits by the bed and hears what Boss Pender is telling her to do, her dull dismay turns to outrage. All her life, or at least ever since she was old enough to assume responsibilities, it has been implicit that she will be the chosen one. Then, for his own reasons – because he disliked the man she has just married; because he said he wants his male heir of the next generation to succeed him – he has made her trustee for her lifetime and ordained that the ownership of the *Gazette* will pass to her son. As she has accepted all his decisions, so Ollie has accepted this wish. Now what he has just revealed belittles all her certainties. He is instructing her to import into Monument the son of a man who, she has always been aware, is exiled in Antrim and who represents evil.

The sleeping figure in the bed provokes in Ollie a curious mixture of emotions: love and fear, respect and disdain. Everything she is comes from him, yet now he threatens everything. He taught her ambition and cunning, how to use a situation to best advantage. She inherited his ruthlessness. Now she prepares to use it in order to thwart him.

*

Beagle & Co, Solicitors, in particular, Mr M. Beagle, have worked as the left hand of Boss Pender for fifty years. Mr M. Beagle is no longer state solicitor and the direction of the firm he has founded has become uncertain for want of leadership, but Beagle himself still puts in four or five hours a day in the spacious, first-floor office on Cuconaught Street, where he attends in the main to scrutinising the rental incomes of the many properties in Monument that have accumulated to him over the decades. Mr M., as he is known, a means in the early days of distinguishing him from his now deceased brother and partner, Mr O., is a small man who still wears a detachable collar to work, and a homburg hat in the street. He sits back, diminutive but somehow sinister, in a tall, wing-backed chair and cracks out a thin smile for Ollie Pender-Goode.

"You're a perfect picture, if I may say so, Ollie."

"You're very kind, Mr M."

"Your wedding was the highlight of the year."

"I thank God that my grandfather was spared for it."

"Ah, God help Boss. I know the situation, Ollie. I'm very sorry, but you know, when you get to my age you take each new day as it comes."

"There's a trust deed I've been told about," Ollie says.

"Indeed." Mr M.'s little wintry smile. He puts colouring cream in his hair, Ollie sees. "What about it?"

"My grandfather wants to change it."

"He hasn't told me."

"He will. May I see it, please?"

Beagle frowns. "I don't think I can show it to you without Boss's written instructions, Ollie."

"Mr M., the trust deed makes me trustee of the *Gazette* for life. My grandfather has a few weeks to live. When he dies I will be reviewing all the arrangements of the business, the position of all the paper's professional advisers."

"Ah, stop that kind of talk!" Beagle snaps, reaching to a drawer. "I've known you since the day you were baptised!" He takes out a legal document from an envelope and opens it on the desk. "I was going to show it to you anyway, Ollie."

Ollie takes less than a minute to peruse the document. "It's really very simple, Mr M.," she says.

Mr M.'s eyes flash. "Nothing is simple, Ollie, that much I have learned."

An hour later, as the day nurse removes a tea tray from the room, Ollie goes in alone and sits in shadow, a little apart from the bed. Boss is bolstered up, his hair combed, his hands, the only part of him that remain big, laid out in two knobby fists on the white sheet in front of him. As they sit there, the old man becomes slowly aware of Ollie's sobs.

"Ollie?"

Ollie weeps, her body shudders.

"Is it my time?"

She shakes her head.

"What's wrong with you, then?"

"Nothing. I'm sorry."

But still she weeps.

"What has happened?"

"Nothing."

"Something must have upset you."

"It doesn't matter."

"Tell me, dammit!"

She jumps. In death's ambit and yet he sits upright and his eyes blaze with all the old authority.

"I don't know what I have done . . ." Ollie says.

"You?"

"You always said my son would . . ."

"Your son? What son?"

"The son I will have!" Ollie cries, getting up. "What right have you to deny that child what was always promised? What right have you to give everything away to . . . to a stranger?"

Boss lies back, winded. "I want . . ." He can't find the words. "You will do as I asked you."

"On one condition," Ollie hears herself say.

His eyes grow round as he seeks her out anew in the dim room. "What . . . ?"

"I will go and bring home your grandchild on one condition," she says, knowing that she has to keep going. "I accept your right to die knowing that at least one male heir exists in Monument – but I will only agree to his coming if you at least change the provisions of the trust to include my son when he is born."

Her grandfather's mouth hangs open. Then she sees the fight go out of him.

"Very well."

"It must be changed in writing."

"And then you will bring home the boy?"

"When the trust deed is changed."

"You swear before God?"

"I swear." She goes to the door. "Mr M. is waiting downstairs."

The notarised amendment to the instrument by which Boss Pender has directed the affairs of the *Monument Gazette* to be carried on after his death consists of the addition of a single letter, the letter "s" added to the word "heir", making the sentence in question now read, ". . . I leave in entirety to my male heirs of the next generation". Mr M. Beagle seems relieved that his presence has been required for such a trivial matter, which he assumes has some-thing to do with Ollie's wishes for her family, whose existence still lie in the hands of God; or at least his relief endures as far as the hall door of No. 3 Pig and Litter when, following Boss Pender's execution of the amendment Ollie draws Mr M. aside into a room beside the hall door and informs him of her additional requirements.

Ollie goes north herself. She has Hart drive her up into the country of his birth, she leaves at six on a Wednesday morning not knowing if when she returns Boss Pender will still be alive. He has not taken food in two days, has already been anointed. Dr Armstrong shakes his head, squeezes Ollie's arm. Her husband-cannot understand how, at this trying time, she can go to Dublin on a business trip.

She has never been in Northern Ireland before. Outside Dundalk Hart produces the car's papers; a mile further on, uniformed men with suspicious eyes peer into the back of the Austin Princess. They are waved through, into the landscape of hills and tidy small-holdings. Ollie is caught between the thrust of her ambition and her strong sense of obligation to her past. In her tendency to see people as opportunities, she is her grandfather's true heir; in the same way as he was able to isolate his love for her from his wishes for the devolution of his business, so now can Ollie separate his wishes from her own. She will carry out what he has asked to the letter. She will bring the boy to Monument. That is the extent of her obligation. Boss will learn that his wish has been granted and will die contented.

The countryside widens out around Belfast where they stop for petrol. Ollie sleeps for the next hour and when she awakens she can smell the sea.

"Ma'am."

Hart has pulled in halfway along a hillside. The land on the left rises sharply and on the right falls away to a glittering sea. Stone walls thread their way through the landscape. Smoke is rising in a straight line from the chimney pot of a farmhouse. How Hart knew his way here, and which house to go to, Ollie has no idea, although Hart informed her that barely six months ago he drove Boss up here one day and that they had sat in this very spot, the old man staring at the farmhouse. Now they are rolling down the incline. A man gets out of the car that is already parked there. Mr M. Beagle gave Ollie this man's telephone number and she spoke to him two days before in his Derry office. Now he raises his grey, homburg hat and says, "Not a bad sort of a morning at all," and they go into the house together.

At half-past eleven that night, Boss Pender's big saloon car creeps back into sleeping Monument. Hart drives directly to Pig and Litter. The driver remains at the wheel of the car on Dudley's Hill as Ollie walks the child in through the narrow entry.

"He is asking where you are the whole time," the nurse tells her. "He's very close."

Ollie leaves the child out on the landing and approaches the bed. Boss's eyes are open, but he can no longer see. Even the work of a single day has been dramatic. Bone shines in his face. Ollie can smell his stagnation.

"Is . . . ?"

"It's Ollie, Boss. It's all right, everything is all right."

"Is . . . ?"

"He's in Monument, Boss. I kept my promise. Black's son is home."

"Bring . . . him . . . in . . ."

She goes to the door, brings the child a step inside the room. What must it have seemed like to Kaiser? The coal fire, the shadows, the old man like death itself on a white bier. The child shrinks back. But the old man wants to touch his flesh and blood, he wants to feel his own succession incarnate. So, although the child is terrified, Ollie forces him over to the bed, where, her hands on his shoulders to stop him retreating, Boss Pender reaches out and with one long, quivering finger, traces a line on the child's cheek. Kaiser yelps with fear. He sees, as he reaches for him, the coals of the fire reflected in the milky eyes, as if hell itself burned in the old man's head.

"Black . . ."

"Black's son, Boss."

"That's . . . great."

Fifteen minutes later the saloon car drives down Long Quay as far as Bagnall's Lane, where it turns right, then left into the car park of the Commercial Hotel. Ollie enters the hotel by the rear door and makes her way into the lobby where the public telephone is located. Soon another car arrives in the all but empty car park and the senior partner of Beagle & Co, Solicitors, emerges. Boss Pender's driver, Hart, carries over in both arms a laden rug and is placing it on the back seat of the former state solicitor's car when a Garda sergeant, Lully by name, who has been visiting his sister in Conduit walks past the car park and becomes curious about all the activity. Although he is off duty, he approaches and bids everyone good night. He inspects the car and notices on the dashboard documents needed to cross the border into Northern Ireland. There are fresh date stamps. The sergeant looks at the boy. He looks at Ollie. Suddenly the years fall away and he is back in a farmhouse near Deilt, making the notes that will form part of a murder file that has never been closed.

Mr M. Beagle is anxious to be on his way. Sergeant Lully watches the state solicitor's car drive out of the car park; then he continues on his way, a small glow of comfort in his chest that comes from knowing that all along he was right.

Later that night the assistant principal of the children's home in Demijohn Street formally receives into his care from Mr M. Beagle, solicitor, a sleeping child wrapped in a rug. The arrangements for the child's arrival are all made and his place secured by a generous bequest, made at Mr Beagle's discretion from the residual estate of the child's late grandmother, Mrs Grainger of Bohall House.

Three days more go by and Boss Pender dies. His funeral is the biggest ever seen in Monument. Eighteen priests concelebrate high Mass in the cathedral. Ollie personally rewrites the editorial of the special edition of the *Monument Gazette*. "He was", she says, "the shining example of my life and of this whole town that he loved so much. We will never see his like again."

Mr M. Beagle retired finally in 1969 and died five years later, in 1974, a month after he sold for £100,000 his interest in Beagle & Co, to a young solicitor named Kevin Santry, whose grandfather Paddy Bensey had made a fortune in the bookmaking business. Mr M. was not the type to dwell on the probity or otherwise of past decisions, rather he took the view that merit in some form or other resided on both sides of most arguments and forever to look backwards was a pursuit best left to the members of contemplative orders. He had therefore persuaded himself that the benefits accruing to a parentless child in an orphanage in Monument would easily surpass those of a similar situation in the North of Ireland, all the more so when you took into consideration the benign interest shown towards the child by the scion of perhaps the most powerful family in Monument. Mr M. had, there was no doubt, baulked at first when the – the word had been his own – assumption of a new identity for the child had been broached by Ollie. It was true, very true, that Beagle & Co administered the residue of the once-significant Grainger estate; and true it was also that the only surviving Grainger, Vanessa by name, had eloped to England with a groom from the yard, and that Vanessa Grainger had had a child by this unnamed man, and that the child, a boy, had died a few days after birth. This was all true. As was the sad fact of Vanessa's death in a riding accident in England which meant the extinction of a line intended to last much longer and initiated back in the 1930s by Selwyn Grainger, the heir to a sweated-labour fortune and once a client of Beagle & Co. But the solicitor demurred at Ollie's ultimate suggestion made in the hall of Pig and Litter. He stated a moral, not to mention a legal, objection.

"Moral?" Ollie had cried.

The solicitor affirmed his position.

"And what about the morality of murder?" Ollie asked him.

Mr M. blinked.

Ollie pressed, "What about, despite the existence of a signed confession, the willingness of a state solicitor, for reasons wholly concerned with his personal advancement, not to pursue someone on a capital charge? How do you think that would read in the *Gazette*, Mr M.?"

Mr M.'s eyes stood out like cue balls.

"You wouldn't dare," he whispered.

"Sue me," Ollie had said.

It was in the end, Mr M. reasoned, an accommodation that would hurt no-one. Every few months he sent small donations to a mission in Africa for the support there of faceless children. This was no different. And the child would be brought up a Catholic. He never thought of the matter again, except on those few occasions when he found himself in Demijohn Street of an afternoon when the children were out in the yard there, playing. Then he tried to remember the name he had given to the boy he had carried in that October night years ago. Grainger was always the first name that came to him because he clearly remembered the child's grandfather, Selwyn Grainger, a real gentleman with a bit of style about him who never queried an account. Then as the old solicitor left Demijohn Street and walked into MacCartie Square he would frown at his own memory. Not so much the question of who the child was – although he could no longer be sure of the sequence of events – but the name. Grainger, Grainger. Then, at the other side of MacCartie Square, if he was heading towards Pollack Street, Mr M. would always look up and see the name on the little dark lane which the sun never got to. Kaiser! he'd say. That's it, Kaiser! And pleased with himself that he could still remember when he wanted to, he would turn left into WiseMart, where he would buy his weekly paper, sit at a table in one of the new cafés and order a pot of tea and catch up with what was happening in that week's *Gazette*.

* * *

And I have made my decision. Kaiser will never know any of this. Since I began tonight, my sister has called so I am going to England. From there I will write to Kaiser, telling him that I am carrying his child. Nothing more. I feel better now that I have made my mind up. Everything will be fine.

Twenty-one

Overhead flew the web, in all its magic. At the end of the line it funnelled down like white sand in a giant hourglass into the folding machine. Although the printing took place in near silence for me, still my head hummed with it. That I was ending something, I was sure: that was all. No certainty existed beyond that of termination, the death of all the old assumptions. I trowelled ink into the ducts. The ink's smell, and that of the newsprint, and the very particular smell as they both united on the made newspaper as it emerged onto the belt brought me comfort. I needed to keep lifting papers from the belt's end and to make stacks of them. So many names swam up to my eyes: Jeff Dunphy, Lilly Coad, Tessa O'Grady, Hart. Black Pender, my own father dear, whose very essence I was somehow trying to capture in this web of words and whose reputation had so long awaited this moment. My entitlement here – my heritage – meant little to me compared with what had been done, first to my father, then to Jasmine. All to preserve – what? This shed full of machinery, a masthead. My father's final peace was a hopeful thing, a glad reality that I could understand and aspire towards for myself. I looked at my watch, then at the decks of papers and calculated that I had already produced in the region of eight thousand copies. About half my target. The printed bundles needed to be strapped around and put on a trolley for transferring out to the loading bay. I turned to look for one and saw Tim. He was standing by the Speedmaster. I could not recall how long it was since I had seen him, but despite his double-breasted Sunday suit, he had expanded abeam beyond my mental expectations, and had grown a beard of a curiously red colour. He stood there, his hands down by his side, his mouth ajar.

"Kaiser? It is you, isn't it, Kaiser?"

"Tim."

"You've grown a beard."

"So have you."

He stared at me.

"Aren't you meant to be out in Leire, Kaiser?"

"This is where I'm meant to be."

He was shouting in order to hear himself above the noise of the presses, scarlet words. "What are you – doing?"

"I'm running off a special edition."

He didn't want to take his eyes off me. "Can I – see it?"

"Certainly."

I handed over a copy at arm's length. He took it and stepped back. I saw him speed-scan the front page. He opened the paper at the centrefold and his head disappeared into it for a moment. When he reappeared, two large, dark lumps stood out on his forehead and his eyes were on rapid blink.

"You can't print this!" he shouted redly and I could smell drink off him.

"I just have."

"Fuck off!" he cried and took a step towards the end of the line towards the master switch, but I put myself in his way. He tried to push me, but I caught both his wrists and held him so that he couldn't go forward or back. "Fuck! You!"

"Don't try to touch anything, Tim."

"You're – you're crazy!" he said as I let him go. "You can't put out this shit."

From the corner of my eye I saw the papers corrugating up the belt. If I didn't remove them they'd back up and jam the folding machine. Tim was reaching for the telephone on one of the support girders. I hefted a double armful of papers onto the floor as Tim stabbed the telephone, then shook it. I cleared the belt and started a new pile on the floor.

"It doesn't work, Tim. I've disconnected the phones."

"You've – what?" He was casting around him. "Why are you doing this, Kaiser?" he called out, bewildered, the dead phone still in his hand.

"For Jasmine," I answered.

Tim's face bled to chalk. "For – her?"

"That's right."

"Kaiser, she's – she's been dead for eight years," he whispered.

Grief sank my blood and wrapped my heart in its fist.

"It doesn't matter, Kaiser, I understand." Now Tim was clever again. "I'm very sorry, you know I mean that." He was trying to edge his way around to the master switch. "I think we should go and have a cup of tea together and have a chat. I'd really like that. At least we could hear one another."

"Stay back. If you'd wanted tea and a chat, I've been quite easy to find."

"You were sick, Kaiser. You couldn't see anyone. Look." Tim's old Pender impatience was overriding his attempts at diplomacy. "I don't know how you set up this –" he gestured at the line "– this bullshit, but I can have you arrested and charged."

"For what?"

"For breaking and entering, for one thing."

I heaved another quick armful from belt to floor. "Would that stand up, d'you think, Tim?" I asked. "I'm your first cousin, I own half this place."

"You're – sick! You've got no proof."

"This is my proof, Tim. Read it. It's also proof of what that monster, Boss Pender, did to my father."

"Don't – don't talk like that about a great man." Tim was trembling. "Look at all he achieved."

"I'm looking at it", I said, "and all I see is a frightened, middle-aged man in a Sunday suit."

Tim rubbed his face with his two hands, a vigorous business as if to wake himself up.

"We've just been to a christening," he said, "Johnnie Love's new baby. This is some sort of a joke, is it? OK, OK. I'm sorry, I get it. Fair play to you, Kaiser. I'm impressed, really. But let's call it a day, now – all right? Would you join me for a drink someplace? Do you take a drink? I bet you could use one, eh? That Leire is an awful fucking place to end up in, I don't blame you for wanting to burst out and do something like this. But enough is enough. Now listen, my missus and two kids are outside. I'm just going to go out and tell them to go on home, that I've just met an old friend and that he and I are going down the town for a drink together, all right? I won't be a second."

"No."

He stopped, half-turned. I could see he remembered our last encounter.

"What do mean?"

"You're not leaving, Tim. You're going to help me load this edition."

"You're out of your mind." He made a run for it, down by the side of the Speedmaster, but I reached out and caught the collar of his jacket and yanked him back. Tim's feet shot forward and he fell over, hitting the side of his head on a strut of the machine. "You – filthy bastard!" He was on his knees, clutching his head. "I'll have you brought out of here in a fucking straitjacket if it's the last thing I do!" He dived for my knees, which in fairness to him I had not anticipated, and skittled me back into the stacks I had so carefully assembled. He had weight, if not power. One knee on my chest, he tried to reach up for the switch, but I cuffed him across the nose. He went back and fell headfirst onto the concrete floor, a fact that had me worried for a moment; but I was ill-served by such generous considerations for I saw the blur of silver in his hand as he came back up at me and I felt, in a manner both sick-inducing and detached, the connection with my forehead of what turned out to be a two-inch spanner. He struck me again, as I was on my hands and knees amid the scattered newspapers, reeling from the first blow. I went down, eyes level with his toe-caps, and he kicked me hard, near the throat.

"This is how it feels, Kaiser!" he panted and kicked me a second time, although I rolled away and took it on the shoulder. "Fucking little tart! I warned her! I had big problems, I told her, problems that fucking librarians don't understand any more than nutcases." Tim's shoe caught me in the ear. His mouth kept going out of focus. "So I'd got the banks to agree to allow me to pledge Glane against my property borrowings – understand that, Kaiser? I was pawning the future to secure the present. And what happened? This little whore with her sharp nose and her wet fanny wanted to go public with information that was none of her fucking business, shit which said that I didn't stand to inherit this fucking paper at all! That in fact half of it by rights should go to a deaf moron in the machine shed! D'you ever hear the fucking like, Kaiser? Did you?" His words were flying out in all shapes and colours. He was quite mad. "So what could I do – eh? I had to act – like I'm acting now – in self-de-fucking-fence!" He landed an almighty kick into my chest and stood over me, the spanner still gripped in his hand, heaving. Papers were plopping every way from the belt onto the floor.

"Did you kill her?" I whispered.

Tim crouched down, big round knee on my chest again, and dug the sharp teeth of the spanner up into my mouth. "What does it matter if I did or not, you pathetic bastard. Like I said, Kaiser, it was self-defence. Just like this is."

I felt the spanner drive up through the roof of my mouth. The pain shot me upright and I spewed out a mouthful of blood over his suit.

"Aghh!"

Tim rocked back in reflex, then grabbed for my throat, but I kept rising and met the bridge of his nose with my forehead, felt the cartilage crunch. Tim screamed. I stood back from him and he stood up, hunched, as if attending to his face, but then without warning he came at me again, swiping wildly with the spanner, missing completely but knocking the white spirit's bottle from the edge of the machine to the floor, where it shattered beside the stacks. Tim lunged for the switch, but I caught his arm a foot short of it and he locked me in a hug with both arms, grunting, by the feel of him, and closed his teeth on my right ear. There was little pain, but I was alarmed even at close quarters by the motions of his head, those of a dog worrying a rat, and although the faculty threatened was the one I least depended on, I was nevertheless keen to retain appearances. We were now grappling over the foot-plate between Pacers three and four. The eloquent rollers whirred. Tim forced me back and down. His weight again. I lost vision for a spell as the plate behind me came up and smacked the back of my head. With one hand I reached out to the floor on the other side of the line and felt the edge of the ink tub. Gouging out a handful, I slapped it into his face. Tim reared up off me, spitting and screaming. He staggered backwards, hands trying to clear his vision, hit the Speedmaster and sat down. As I stepped off the footplate on to the floor of the shed, I saw fresh movement near the door of the dispatch bay.

A woman wearing a very wide-brimmed dark blue hat was walking towards the end of the line. She was followed by two small children, a boy and a girl, no more than six or seven years of age apiece. The woman was smiling broadly despite the fact that she was smoking a cigarette. She was most desirable in a clean and moneyed way, her dress with its pattern of small blue and white flowers clung to her neat body, her legs shone in their sheer cladding and as she walked she swung her hips. The children were dressed up too: the boy in a shirt and tie and blazer, the girl carrying her hat, her shoulder-length fair hair shining, her pink-coloured dress almost to the floor. My feelings were twofold: regret for the impending loss of innocence, and grief for my own childlessness. Little time remained, however, for further reflection, because the woman, a study in slow motion, was removing her cigarette and staring, eyes standing out from their nests of mascara, at her husband, who was now struggling to his feet, gasping, his face pitch, his shirt-front blood drenched. She opened her mouth. A whole spar of noise shot into the air. Even as I moved forward to catch the cigarette, she dropped it by the stacks. Between us rose an orange wall. I stepped back, my first thoughts for the line. On the pillar there had always been a fire extinguisher. Then my breath left me as Tim took me from behind, driving me through the flames and onto the conveyor belt. The smell of burnt hair. The eyes of the small boy were huge but receding as his mother, still screaming, dragged him out from the shed. Tim had me by the throat now and was beating my head on the steel edge of the belt frame. Behind and above him I could see that the edition had taken, its just-laid ink flammable, and then, as I watched through wafting smoke, I saw flames shoot from the web itself, and for a wonderful moment – wonderful for reasons of physical beauty as well as of deep, curious comfort – the whole web was alight, flames spinning the overhead length of it like an inrushing tide on fire, great spumes of questing red licking the air above the line, sparks shooting for the roof.

Tim's fingers were dug into my neck and there was a moment of real fear, since the angle of my body precluded a vigorous response. Even though I was much the fitter, I could not summon the necessary leverage to fling off all 200-plus pounds of Tim, and we had long moved beyond dialogue. And yet, despite the dimming down of my vision, and the pain – mainly now in my back from the way I was wedged – and my general concerns about continuation and fulfilment, a strange undercurrent of happiness coursed through the deeper waters of my understanding. It was hard to define and unreasonable in the circumstances to try and analyse, yet it sprang, I believe, from the certainties to do with truth. It was as if this shed and all these machines were celebrating a much-overdue letting. I could feel their voices like a chorus. They reached, like the sparks and smoke, for the roof. Then I saw the web break and a livid balloon float up and explode. The pressure on my neck let off. Tim was going backwards, arms spread-eagled, mouth open. Tim was on fire.

This was so different from the many other violent occasions of my life, from which I had emerged without recall. No detail escaped me that last Sunday, rather my mind, as if the recall compartment had been suddenly opened and was voracious for particulars, swallowed everything it could. The roof was falling in burning slabs, themselves making new explosions of fire and shooting cannons of sparks back up into the naked night. And still ran the presses, despite lacking paper, as if a statement was being made in this final act. Tim rolled on the floor, the white scream pouring from him so bright I had to turn my eyes away as I edged in to try and save him. I wanted to. Not from any sense of taking pleasure in his disgrace, but so that people would know from his own words what had really happened to Jasmine. I saw his eyes and they begged. All the extremities of him, head hair and jacket, even his hands, shimmered fire. I needed something in which to wrap him. I stepped back and felt the downward rushing air. I dived across the belt. As I rolled I saw a heavy roof section ablaze in the space occupied a moment ago by Tim.

Heat had now expanded to make surfaces untouchable. The soles of my boots were melting and trying to bond me to the floor. Breath too, or those I could still take, burned a track down my throat and made me scream. Another spar from the roof, a gigantic torch, crashed down between where I stood and the dispatch bay. Smoke like airborne ink poured from the doors to the office and, as I watched, a whole series of little bright balls popped alight in the office building and made it for a brief but nonetheless riveting moment like an Advent calendar. The only other way out was by the fire door, through which some hours ago I had most appropriately entered, but that was at the extreme far end of the shed and every strut and angle on the way to it now carried a frill of fire. Funny, but the fact that my edition was lost did not dismay me as much as I thought it might have. It was as if its contents had been enlarged through the now non-existent roof into the night sky over Monument. I stripped off my shirt, wrapped it around my head and began to run.

I never had a doubt that I would make it, but that is the thought of many a man in the penultimate moment of his life. I had this vision of my legs that, no matter what, they would have to keep pumping like the presses had, although the presses were, I was aware, now still. I kept colliding with machinery, for my head needed to be tight to my chest if the smoke was not to get me. I ran. I thought of how my father would want me to emerge from this, whatever the price, something he had never managed. My pants burned and I beat at them. The geography laid down in my mind carried me forward, scalp kindling, face raw, smoke in my chest, the hairs gone from the backs of my hands and forearms. I met the door face on and it gave. I will never forget the balm of the air.

Falling, I rolled. I could see sirens zigzagging in night-jagging opalescence. I rolled and rolled. Half-asleep, half-dreaming, I lay in a glade, coat about my shoulders, ear to the woody earth. I heard in the distance the passage of a male badger as it trotted across a carpet of frozen beech leaves. Jasmine's hand reached over and brought me back into the warm-cupped embrace of her thighs. On my neck her breath, her breasts at my back. Now the badger was returned beneath the earth where he coiled, belly full, blood swirling to the dropping metabolism of his heart. O for the warm understanding of the seasons.

ENDNOTE

Day was failing over Monument when I came through it a few hours ago. Now zephyrs of livid purple are curling overhead, tight, tense whorls in an otherwise empty blueness. I'm back in my room. I sometimes wish my window would open more. I sometimes wish I could stand out on the ledge and fly into the dark, velvet spaces.

But I know Monument is down there, sunken in its valley, unseen by day, all its streets and squares and alleyways in which I grew up, all its people whose faces I recognise. Not only them, but also the very many who have died along with those who have been born since I came up here to Glane. Thousands of people, all familiar, because for everyone, you see, there is at least one day in their lives, and often two, when their names appear in the *Gazette*.

The Pender-Goode estate was forced in the end to sell Glane in order to clear Tim's bank debts. Had Tim been alive it would surely have driven him to distraction had he learned that the consortium that bought Glane promptly received the go-ahead to build the mental hospital here. Glane is very suitable, when you think about it. It's at a safe distance from Monument, it's built on a naturally secure site, a large plateau where once cattle grazed, accessed only up a narrow mountain driveway. It's isolated and self-contained. I have always liked it up here.

I did not recognise many people in Monument when we drove through it earlier to collect the old man. When Ollie died and Tim's widow left the town with her children, that was the last of the Pender line. Pig and Litter has been sold by the court, which now handles Boss Pender's trust. The money has been invested. Mrs Rice alone comes up here to see me. I look forward to her visits. She comes up a few times a year and always at Christmas, when she brings me a steamed pudding, and a gift of clothes – one year it is a pullover, another thick socks or gloves. She sold the flower shop years ago and now spends her time doing voluntary work for the St Vincent de Paul. It appears she always knew quite a bit about me; but so it seems did other people. We have become quite friendly, in fact, Mrs Rice and I. Last Christmas when she was up here she asked me to call her Heather. She talks about growing up in Bohall House in the countryside outside Monument, where her mother worked as governess, about the Grainger family and the horses and about lovely Vee, who ran away and never came back.

June 10th

Dear, dear Kaiser,

I came here to England last week because I wanted to sort my head out, to put distance between myself and Monument. Isn't that strange? I always imagined that my mother would be the person I would turn to at a time like this, yet when the time came I decided she wouldn't understand. I'm sad about that. You spend your whole life trying to persuade yourself about something you don't really believe.

The time has come to reach some big decisions, Kaiser. My reasons for them are set out in this letter. After this, I want you and me to go forward, unafraid, our heads high and our eyes only on the future.

You are, as are we all, made up of so many stories. Villains and heroes and broken hearts inhabit all our stories, but they are our stories and they make us the people we are, whether we like them or not. There is nothing any of us can do about the past. Only the future holds any meaning.

I looked at myself in the mirror this morning and tried to see a single sign of my pregnancy. Will you marry me, Kaiser? Will you marry me and take me away from Monument where I can have your baby?

There has never been anything between myself and Tim, believe me. The only reason I agreed to go out with him was because he had become suspicious about what I was doing and I wanted to throw him off the scent. I think I succeeded. He is a dangerous man, Kaiser. He scares me. He's got all sorts of financial problems and he will do anything to remove any threat to his position . . .

And now to my second decision. I do love you and only you, Kaiser – as I hope you have known long before now . . . Let's get away from Monument. Let's take our baby and start our life someplace new. It's for the best, I know it is. You will always be who you are, no matter where we live, just as I will be who I am. A name makes no difference. All that matters is our baby. All that matters is that it grows up knowing that its father is a great and loving man.

I was very down when I began writing this, Kaiser. But then, as I began to assemble my thoughts in this letter to you, I felt a great freedom. Nothing can hurt me now – because I have you and I have your baby. I'm laughing and crying as I write these words. Life is so good, Kaiser! So wonderful!

It was Mrs Rice and the old man who arranged my outing today. I gather it took quite a bit of organising. She arrived at dawn and we loaded into the Glane van, herself, a hospital orderly, a driver and myself. In Monument we picked up old Sergeant Lully. He's still upright and in good fettle, although he must be knocking on eighty – the old constabulary training has stood to him, I suppose. He has been one of the few people who has always spoken up for me over the years. We drove north.

"I always had my suspicions about the murder," he said as we neared Dundalk, "but I could never get Beagle to listen." Sergeant Lully shook his head. "It broke my heart when your father ran for it. I knew he never killed anyone. And then, all those years later, on a night when the whole town was waiting for Boss Pender to die and I came across Beagle and Ollie smuggling you into town, I realised at that moment who you must have been and that all along I had been right."

We drove until we reached Gua. The graves are in the Church of Ireland cemetery, right on the edge of the sea.

"This is only right," Sergeant Lully said and Mrs Rice nodded in agreement.

It was a warm feeling to see their names on the headstone, already green with age. Harriet and John. These are my people. They loved me. Today I stood with them as light rain drifted in from the North Atlantic and doused me. I want to be buried up there, when my time comes. Not in Monument. That is where I want to finish up.

In the meantime, I've been brought back south. Monument's evening lights begin to swim up into the hills, where they hang in the sky, level with my eyes. I'll go down and see what to do about my paper, one day, in time. From the copy I'm given every week I can see that it's running fine and has been for quite a few years. Not that I will want to change anything when I get down there, but I'd like to inspect the new presses and buildings, to smell the ink and the newsprint, to be there when the new line is at work. That's the most exciting aspect of the *Gazette* for me, the actual moment of its birth. Why this is I cannot say. Perhaps it's because of my blood. At lunchtime on the day I return I'll walk down Candle Lane and up Dudley's Hill into Pig and Litter. Not that I want to go into the house, on the contrary. I'll just sit in the garden, my back to the warm wall and drink in the smells of cut grass and flowers and peeling paint, and with my eyes closed I'll feel the sun on my face and the beat of the town beneath me.